Edited by Sara Lawson

Cover art by Damián V.

Jacket design and typography by MiblArt

Interior art by Sara Morello, Kateryna Vitkovska

SECRETS OF THE FAE

THE STARLIT PRINCE

C. F. E. BLACK

Sign up for my VIP reader newsletter and get exclusive access to free stories, giveaways, first looks at covers, and sneak peeks of new projects.

Vip.cfeblack.com/join

For those who have ever felt unredeemable

There was once a merchant who lived in a city in Spain. Now it happened that the merchant had invested his entire fortune in a ship which sailed the seas. All went well until one day he received news that the ship was lost. The loss of the ship meant that he was a ruined man.

From "The Lily and the Bear," *Tales of Enchantment from Spain*

TALIA

S tifling a yawn, I stared blankly at the snout of a wolf mask, thinking more about the sweat pooling inside my ballgown than the man's words. He had been waxing poetic about his vineyards in western Avencia for the better part of ten minutes, undeterred by my silence.

"But my grapes are not as sweet, of course, as present company," he said.

I nearly choked on my sip of sangria but recovered to offer a smile, wishing my bird mask covered more than half my face, so I would not have to worry about schooling my expressions. The man, unfortunately, took my smile as encouragement and angled his body even closer.

This usually meant they were about to ask me to dance, or worse, ask to call on me in the morning, where they'd inevitably see my father's straw roof and promptly turn around, vanishing to attend to what they would later claim, via a hasty apology letter, was some *urgent noble business*.

"Excuse me, Señorita….what-was-it?"

"Balcázar," I supplied through a clenched smile.

"Ah yes, Balcasan."

I rolled my eyes but didn't correct him.

"I would greatly appreciate it if you could put in a good word with your friend over there? I was hoping to dance with her before the evening expired, but she seems almost unapproachable." He tapped his chest with his free hand. "And I must say, she has had my eye since I arrived."

My polite smile fell as if I had been slapped. I didn't have to turn around to know his eyes hung on Zara Valencia, prettiest girl in the room.

I should have known better. He was not the first man to make such a request this evening, nor any other evening I'd spent in Zara's ballroom.

"I'll do my best." I gave him a dismissive curtsey before spinning on my heels and hurrying away.

Practically stomping through the ballroom, I looked over to where Zara was fanning herself flirtatiously as she giggled at something a broad-shouldered man had said. Even masked, she drew every man's eye. She'd had her seamstress make me a dress to match hers—with a shorter hem and less space for curves, of course—which had seemed like a fun idea, but now made me feel like one of the cheap pieces of glass cut to look like rubies dotting my mask. She leaned around the man and waved her fan at me, but when I only shrugged in return, she excused herself and hurried toward me.

Halfway across the crowded space, my friend was waylaid by a nobleman in a garish orange suit and fox mask. Her shoulders sank and her own bird mask lingered on me as I skirted the crowd for the open terrace doors at the back of the ballroom.

The night was warm but refreshing compared to the

caged air inside. Fewer conversations to avoid. Fewer disappointments to endure. I took a deep breath.

Already the moon was descending once more toward the horizon, but the dancing wouldn't end until dawn peeked over the endless rows of olive trees stretching across Zara's family's estate. The day before the official start of Festival de los Cuentos meant no sleep for anyone, save the youngest and oldest.

Frustrated, I tossed my red macaw mask aside, but it snagged on my long hair, yanking out several dark strands and nearly dislodging the lily wedged against my tight bun. The mask hit the gravel a little too hard and shattered the false jewels, which looked eerily like drops of blood on the path. A shudder swept down my frame. After a last glance at the loud ballroom, I turned toward the massive stable in the distance, my heart jumping into my throat. In mere hours, the first of the summer's most important races would begin, including the race that would determine my family's fate.

Palacio del Sol, named for his golden dun coat, was my father's best stallion to date, favored to win five to one. My costume tonight, my lack of sleep this past week, and my thundering pulse were all tied to this horse.

I gripped the hem of my ballgown, meant to mimic the myth of the scarlet macaw, wife of the sun, and followed the branching path toward the stable. My steps grew quieter as I left behind the gravel for hard packed earth.

A light flickering over the stable entrance illuminated the guard on duty who was currently slack-necked and snoring loudly. I shook my head as I walked straight past him into the wide aisle of the immaculate barn.

The smell of hay and horses washed over me as I moved into the shadowy aisle between stalls. Every one of these horses signified someone's hopes and dreams. So many bets were placed for the Midsummer's Races that fortunes were lost and made, and the fixed planes of society's strata became fluid for a single day.

Only the champion of this race would be entered into the *Carera de los Reales*, the royal race, held by the king himself at the palace in Coronada at the end of summer. The champions from the three largest races in Avencia competed in the royal race. Winning lifted one into the highest ranks of society, and this year, we had a real chance.

"Talia, there you are! I thought you'd be here," Zara teased.

I whipped around, startled but not surprised to see my friend standing in the barn's entrance.

"I told you to wear red so you'd be noticed by men, Tal, not the horses," Zara scolded as she waved her folded fan at me. Her dark, unruly curls were smoothed back in a slick knot at the nape of her neck, but after hours of dancing, the thick tresses were starting to rebel.

"You could have put me in a dress made entirely of jewels and their eyes still would have been on you. *You* could find a husband in a graveyard," I retorted, waving a hand at our matching red dresses. For one week of the year, all the women in town dressed like they belonged on a flamenco stage, with form-fitting dresses in bright colors, stacks of ruffles at every hem.

After a quick snort, Zara cringed in disgust. "One of the men who danced with me tonight was on his way to one. He was sixty-five."

"That sounds dreadful."

Shrugging, Zara peeked in at a horse. "Who's the contender?"

"Cielo. Over there. But his fastest time never beat Sol's."

"Everything will be different by sundown, will it not?" She grabbed my hands. "The dons will be lining up for your hand!"

A short laugh escaped my lips. "Yes, money will finally garner their attention."

"I didn't mean it like that."

"I do not disagree with you. I merely dislike that it's true." I pulled out of my friend's grip and turned to Sol's stall. "At least Papa will be able to buy the land outright from Ortiz. No more dreadful landlord hovering over our every move."

Zara cringed at the mention of Ortiz, sharing my feelings about the potbellied man who'd been asking for my hand in marriage every summer since I turned fifteen.

"Surely, you'll move," she said with a pout. "But do tell your father to buy a grand estate somewhere outside of Leor? You can't leave me."

"Just because we stand to win doesn't mean we will leave Leor," I assured. "My father loves it here. He says southern Avencia is the world's best place to train horses. Not that he's trained them anywhere else." I traced my hand lightly along the wood between stalls as I moved farther down. "And the race isn't won *yet*."

Zara huffed. "It's as good as."

As I passed my father's other horse, Corona, I nodded politely. He was fast in his own right, but no champion.

"Push him," I told the white horse, leaning over the half door of his stall. "Push him to his best time yet." The horse flicked an ear sideways. "I'm serious. No lounging at the back of the pack this time. You've got a job to do."

I moved on to the next stall, which was where Sol would be sleeping before his big day. The stable was dim, the light from the moon casting only the faintest shadows through the windows, but before I even reached the stall, my skin prickled.

My breath caught when my eyes adjusted.

Sol was gone.

"What is it?" Zara asked, placing a hand on my arm.

Unable to speak, I unlatched the stall door and yanked it open, scanning the floor more times than was necessary. He wasn't there.

Panic seized my chest and I scrambled back out into the aisle, knocking into Zara.

"Where is he?" Zara whispered. "Wait, look." She pointed to where Sol's saddle and bridle were missing.

"Someone stole him!" I shouted.

As I ran back toward the sleeping guard, he roused from sleep with a start and hopped up.

"He's gone! Someone stole my father's horse."

The large man blinked, then my words registered and he gripped his rapier with one hand and raced into the barn.

"He's *gone*, you idiot. Running into the barn won't do any good." I lifted both arms and rolled my eyes.

The sound of gravel pricked at my ears. Tensing, I scanned the dark road leading away from the barn. A tiny sliver of moon wasn't enough to light the night, but I spotted a pale shape against the gravel at the foot of the small hill.

"Zara! That's him—that's Sol. It must be!"

When the guard reappeared, I was already racing back into the barn. "There's been a theft," I called back. "Send word to my father."

The guard's quick footsteps diminished as he sped away.

"What are you doing?" asked Zara from behind me.

"Going after him!"

Ignoring her burst of laughter, I ripped open Corona's

stall door, reaching for the bridle on the wall. "Sorry, boy, but we're going to have to take a little midnight ride."

"I'm coming with you," Zara announced from the stall's doorway.

I placed a saddle blanket on Corona's tall back and narrowed my eyes at her. "You can't ride as fast as I can. And if I don't go..." My throat caught and the rest of the words died on my tongue.

She yanked a bridle off the peg nearest to her. "I'm not telling you not to go. Just that you're not going alone. Besides, it's dangerous to ride at night this time of year."

"Those are only stories," I snapped.

As I led Corona out of the stables, another thought hit me, causing me to choke on my next breath. If Sol disappeared for good, my family would have to pay out all the bets placed on him. Even if we sold every item in our home, and the house itself, that wouldn't be enough.

"I have to find him before my father wakes," I whispered, trying to lift my foot into the stirrup. My tight dress wasn't helping.

Zara scurried to mount the horse she'd saddled—another valuable racehorse I didn't recognize. At least her family could afford to pay the owner for the horse. "You know where he's going, don't you?"

"Puerta," I muttered.

The border town of Puerta de los Reyes, almost an hour's ride from Leor, teemed with merchants and vendors of every illegal good imaginable. The weeks before and during the Festival were the busiest of the year. Tradesmen from across the seas, tribal shamans from the east, and wealthy gangsters congregated in the market of Puerta to sell or trade their wares. Women of

Leor were strictly forbidden from ever venturing near its gates.

I whirled around at a tearing sound to find Zara ripping the side of her dress to allow her legs space to move. "You would," I said with a smirk.

"My hunting knives came in handy for once."

Zara flashed her bare leg at me, waggling her brows. These festival dresses didn't allow for the normal undergarments worn the rest of the year. Then she flipped the blade and held it out to me. With a resigned sigh, I took the blade, bent, and sliced the hem of my dress in a similar fashion. When I finished, I accepted a thigh holster from Zara and strapped the dagger to my leg. She too strapped a dagger to her leg.

Seconds later, I climbed into the saddle. "All right. Let's go," I announced, kicking my heels into Corona.

2

TALIA

*"And you, little girl, what do you want me to bring you?"
the merchant asked. "Bring me a lily."*

*Search as he would, he could find no lily to carry to
his daughter.*

My legs burned from holding a tight racing stance for so
long. I knew from experience that I could hold it only a little
longer. Zara, on the other hand, was already lagging behind,
not as accustomed to fast rides. With a quick glance, I spotted
her a little distance back, bouncing in the saddle, hair a wild
mess.

Up ahead, the only other person riding at breakneck
speed was my target. He was closing in on the city gates.

Clogging the road were late night revelers from Leor
ambling toward the seedy border town to conduct business
they'd regret come morning. With dawn still hours away,
Puerta swelled like the bay at high tide.

Dust drifted sideways on the ocean breeze. The thief was

9

riding the fastest horse in southern Avencia, and if he made it to Puerta before we did, he'd melt into the crowd like butter into hot rice.

With a glance back at Zara, I waved my arm forward in silent communication before tapping my heels against my horse's ribs, praying and cursing with alternate breaths as I sailed directly toward the one place I'd sworn never to go.

I gritted my teeth, crunching on bits of sand between my molars. "*Andele*! Come o—"

My word was cut off by the chilling sound of a distant horn. My posture faltered in the saddle as I scanned the dark horizon.

I sailed past a woman pointing back the way I'd come. Behind me on the road, screams pierced the night.

The horn sounded again, closer. People on the road ducked and glanced around. Several horses whinnied or reared. Corona, obedient as Papa had trained him to be, kept racing forward, but I sensed his unease in the sound of his breathing.

Still, I had no time to worry about any of this. Looking toward the gate, I caught the glimpse of Sol's golden hide flying under the archway that led into the city.

Stars and suns.

Then everyone around me was running, panicked, toward the city gate.

"It's the Wild Hunt!" someone shouted.

Shocked, I could not help myself from turning and searching the darkness.

On the horizon, illuminated by the gray line of the sea, rode a pair of figures. Distant as they were, their mounts had to be enormous. And they weren't horses. Their long, loping strides suggested something canine, but my hasty glance didn't give me enough time to decipher A strangling fear gripped my throat as I clicked my tongue at Corona and eased him out to the side of the road.

Zara was back there.

I was caught in a slow, frenzied tangle of pedestrians, wagons, and riders. The Wild Hunt was a myth they told children to keep us from wandering too far from home. But the two massive creatures barreling toward the road were most certainly real and entirely too large and too fast to be natural.

"Zara!"

I couldn't hear if she called back. My heart thundered so loud I barely heard the hoofbeats. My gaze snapped back and forth from city gate to my friend. With a shrill yell, I slowed Corona, whirled him around, and charged back toward Zara.

Her horse was lagging, but when Corona lined up with him, he snorted and leaned into the race like he'd been trained to do. Good boy. The loping figures were close enough now that I could see one was actually an oversize cat.

Corona reacted and put on more speed, like he knew better than the rest of us what was charging across the sandy flats. All the animals on the road had lunged into a flat out run, leaving all the poor folk on foot in a cloud of dust.

It was a race in every sense of the word now.

The Wild Hunt never entered cities. At least that's how the stories went. The gate of Puerta quickly reversed from a symbol of certain ruin to a haven of salvation.

Sweat poured down my chest and back as fear carved through my thoughts.

The beasts were close enough now that I could see pointed ears on one and spots on another. A wolf and a great cat.

At least I was on a fast horse. Zara was keeping pace. The ones on foot...I hated to think of their fate.

The wide gate was already bottlenecked with panicked pedestrians. I yanked on the reins to keep from crashing into a small buggy. Zara pulled up beside me, her hair half fallen. Dust whirled everywhere, obscuring my view of the Hunters. "Move!" I shouted. Other than a nasty look from a man beside me, nothing much happened.

I glanced over my shoulder. A wind gusted through, clearing some of the dust. The Hunters were closing in. According to the stories, they stole young virgins from the land of mortals—but I'd always thought this was a mere scare tactic.

Zara cursed and shouted in a manner that would have shocked her earlier suitors, but the crowd was too slow, oozing through the gate like molasses.

A scream drew my gaze backward to catch sight of a Hunter snatching a woman from the road. Just then, the crowd surged forward and I passed under the city gate. Her screams echoed until we spilled through the city's thick walls.

Zara pulled her shawl over her head, and I followed suit, aware that a pair of respectable women coming to Puerta would cause a stir. My heartrate still raced and the fear in the crowd was still palpable.

That woman on the road had been *taken* by those awful creatures.

I met Zara's gaze, and an unspoken gratitude flowed between us.

Hoping to catch a glimpse of Sol, I scanned the roadside, cramped with makeshift structures composed of boards and canvas, but there was no golden horse. Ignoring the feeling of hopelessness that threatened to choke me, I peered at the branching roads ahead.

A few men openly stared at us.

"Tal," Zara whispered, "I sincerely apologize for deciding we'd both wear red tonight."

A nervous laugh burst from my lips. I rested my free hand on the blade at my thigh, grateful for its presence.

"Let's find Sol," I announced.

3

TALIA

Finally, in his wanderings, he came to a house surrounded by an immense garden. Almost the very first flower he set his eyes upon was a lily—a beautiful white lily. – The Lily and the Bear

The horses drank heartily from a trough before we walked them down the narrow, twisting roads of the market. Vendors shouted at us as we passed, and the milling pedestrians barely stepped out of the way for the horses. The stalls and kiosks were as alive at this hour as if this were peak time for business, and no one inside these walls seemed the least bit concerned that a pair of mythological creatures had just swiped a young woman from the road.

The tents and shanty structures of Puerta stretched out in a sea of little brown points and sagging lines that faded into the night. I wove Corona around a pair of arguing men standing in the road, dodged a wagonload of flour sacks, and ignored every whistle that came my way. Sol was here. Some-

14

where. Faces turned from steaming pots and smoking pipes to eye these hurried newcomers. People here did not rush. They languished. A pair of young boys ran up, hands begging before their mouths could.

Zara flipped them each a coin before I'd even moved my hands. Heart hammering, I kept my eyes alert for any sign of my father's horse.

The smell of human sweat and muddy canvas washed over us as we picked our way deeper into the city. Every horse that crossed my path made my heart catapult into my throat.

"I can make you forget your troubles, lass," shouted a woman in a threadbare shawl.

I recoiled slightly, smelling the potent herbs without ever seeing them. "I doubt that's possible," I grumbled, pushing past the aggressive vendor.

As we walked, voices called out, selling everything the baser desires might want. One man jeered at us, claiming we could be rich if we just stepped into his tent for a little while. Though I felt safer on Corona, my leg was entirely too exposed this way, with strangers walking no more than a handsbreadth from my skin.

"Let's walk," I suggested.

I tugged Corona quickly down one lane, then another, Zara hollering for me to slow down. Easy for her to say. Her life wasn't about to go up in flames.

I shivered, despite the sweat trickling down my back, and gripped the reins tightly in my hand. "We need to find the horse sellers," I said over my shoulder. "Or the buyers. However that all works."

Zara walked up beside me. "Are you familiar with how the black market operates?"

"No. But I assume the thief will try to sell Sol."

We spotted a man leading two horses down the next lane and decided to follow him, hoping he might lead to a place where horses were bought or traded.

Zara hovered close behind. "Shouldn't we ask someone where to find buyers in this place? I do not wish to be here much longer."

"Looking for a buyer?" said a scruffy man with tattoos on his neck poking out behind a sweat-stained ascot.

"Yes," I replied warily.

"What are you selling?" The man tilted his scraggly head forward.

"A horse."

"Well, actually we're looking—"

I cut off Zara's words with a murderous look.

The way he studied our dresses made me squirm, but I lifted my shoulders and scowled at him.

"Romero is that way." He lifted a lazy finger. "And you need an appointment." The man tipped dangerously forward. "You might want to consider what else you might be selling, señoritas." He flashed a holey grin that sent disgusted shivers down my arms.

Eager to get away, I pulled Zara along and we slipped down a winding alleyway in the direction the man had pointed.

"What if Sol has been sold? Do we steal him back?" Zara asked, no longer trying to keep her fears to herself.

"We'll figure that out when the time comes."

Maybe we could send armed men after the buyer if we could get word back to town fast enough. Or I could simply scour the entire countryside until I found that horse.

We asked a woman starting a cookfire in the dim of a

single candle where to find Romero. She grunted and pointed. Then she stood and brushed her hands down her apron, waving us back.

"Why you want him?" she asked, her eyes lined with wrinkles from squinting in the bright sun.

"We think he has something of mine," I admitted.

"That man has nothing you want. Go home. Leave this place."

I glanced at Zara. "A horse of great value was stolen from me tonight. I must get it back."

"Or what?"

Startled by the woman's prying question, I blinked several times before words surfaced. "My family will be ruined."

The woman stared so hard I wanted to back up, but Zara was still standing mostly behind me.

"Decide how much ruin you's willing to accept, and go on home, before you find out what true ruin is. Magic ain't worth the price it demands."

"Thank you," Zara said politely, yanking me along the sandy path. "See, we should go. Now."

"If we go home empty-handed, my family will be a laughingstock at the races." I pressed my hands to my face and inhaled sharply. "We already owe Ortiz too much. Almost all the profits we stand to make are his already. Without Sol..." I let the sentence die.

Up ahead, silhouetted by flaming torches, three large men stood outside a tent, hands clasped at their waists, frowns carved on their dark faces. Heart pounding, I approached the closest man.

"We need to speak to Romero."

The man's chest jerked in a small, silent laugh. "Business?" The question was part-growl.

Lifting my chin, I said confidently, "Buying."

The gruff man let out a small hiss through his pierced nose. "You'll have to wait."

"How long?" I asked.

The man only huffed and lifted his chin. "Horses wait over there."

I steeled my expression and returned his huff. "Are they guarded?"

He sneered. "By me."

A man emerged from Romero's tent, received his weapons back from the guards, and departed with a smug smile on his bearded face.

Pacing in the small space beside the tent, I tapped my palms together, whispering to Zara. "I could say he got sick. Maybe then we wouldn't have to pay out all the debts."

"You're a terrible liar, Tal."

I pursed my lips. "What if I just told everyone that Sol was stolen, and then they would feel bad and…" I slapped my forehead. "No, they won't. They'll want their money back."

"We don't know yet what's happened to him. Calm down."

"If the Wild Hunt is true, maybe there's some magical way I can get Sol back."

Zara's eyes narrowed. "Magic is not something to joke about."

I crossed my arms but didn't meet her gaze. "Well, it's not even real, so it doesn't matter."

Zara's huff told me I'd offended her. She'd always been more apt to believe the stories told at Festival, even the outlandish ones about magical folk and dragons and immortals. As I waited, my mind flipped through some of the stories I'd heard at last year's Festival. One about a man who could disappear like shadows. One about a blue lion who roamed the earth at night. The popular one about the sun god's wife, who could turn into a macaw. None of those stories offered me any hope just now. No solutions. No Sol.

The smell of cumin and paprika and garlic wafted through the thin alleyway as someone prepared a pre-dawn breakfast. The pang of hunger in my stomach only meant the race was getting closer.

By the time my feet ached from standing in one place and my stomach gurgled in embarrassing fashion, I threw up my hands and walked toward the burly guard once more.

"How much longer? People expect me home." It was true.

The guard snorted in a particularly disgusting way.

Despair creeping in, a small whimper escaped my lips as someone exited the tent. With the heavy canvas pulled aside, I strained my eyes for a glimpse inside. The tent was certainly large enough for a horse to walk through. Light shone inside from a large chandelier and a patterned red rug ran into the depths of the tent.

Whoever owned this tent had money, that much was certain.

The man who'd exited stared unashamedly at Zara as he slid a blade back into a sheath at his waist.

Zara scowled at him and grabbed my arm. "Come on."

She yanked me into the tent before either guard could grab us.

"Oy! Come back here!"

We dashed into the bright space, realizing the entire front room of this tent was empty, save the rug and the elaborate chandelier. A guard stormed in after us.

Just as large hands brushed my arm, I yanked out of his reach and pushed Zara forward through a second set of canvas doors. I stumbled over the edge of a plush rug and knocked into a thin table set with a tall vase full of lilies. With a shout, I grabbed the table, but the vase toppled and smashed on the rug.

I looked up, aghast, hands moving slowly away from the intricately carved table. Three chandeliers lit the spacious tent. A tall chair with twisting wood armrests sat before a wide desk in the center of the far wall.

A man sat there, tall riding boots propped on the ornate desk, dark brows lifted in mild surprise. His jet-black hair peeled away from a tanned face with a particularly square jaw that stole my attention for the briefest moment.

The guard stepped in and gripped my upper arm so tightly that I yelped. With a single lift of the seated man's finger, the guard released me and stepped back through the canvas.

The man at the other end of the room titled his head and wove his fingers behind his head. "May I help you?"

I stared at the man in his shining dark suit, the very picture of wealth, and far handsomer than I'd imagined the dealers of Puerta. There was something odd about his appearance, something I couldn't place.

My mouth opened, but movement to my right startled me.

A peacock bobbed his head, unconcerned with our presence, and a bright red macaw walked back and forth on a perch near the man. My jaw opened wider.

I'd been dressed as that bird earlier this very evening, though my torn attire now bore little resemblance to my original costume.

"Here to help the fly problem? Or just destroy my lilies?"

My mouth snapped shut and my brow furrowed as I glanced at the spilled flowers. Just then, Zara yelped and grabbed my arm. A leopard strolled casually along the far wall of the tent then flopped onto the rug, apparently at ease.

Thinking of my father when he attended horse auctions, I straightened my spine, steeled my nerves, and cleared my dry throat. "Señor Romero, I'm here for a stallion I believe was brought here tonight. Dun. Sixteen hands."

The man softly snorted, sending a wave of irritation down my entire frame. I stepped past Zara and hardened my expression. As I moved, my leg slipped out of my altered dress. The man's gaze flickered downward so briefly it might have been only a blink. My hand slipped to the torn fabric, attempting to close the slit.

"He was stolen from my family," I continued. "He is to run in the races today, and we cannot lose him. We cannot—" I realized my blunder as soon as the man's lips curled with a wicked smile.

There was something in that smile, aside from the fact it made his face possibly the most attractive one I'd ever seen, that lifted the hairs on my arms. Never show desperation to a man with something you want.

Oops.

He chuckled. "I have already sold the horse you speak of."

My posture deflated as the air whooshed out of my lungs. Behind me, Zara gently took my hand. I stared blankly at the leopard, grateful my friend was holding on to me.

"He was truly a beautiful creature, well-bred and the picture of health," said the man as he examined his fingernails. "A feat, considering he was handled by mortals."

Picking up a paper from his desk, he stood and brushed the hair out of his face, exposing his ears.

I drew in a sharp breath. I could have sworn his ears were *pointed*. But his hair fell quickly back in place.

My tired mind was playing tricks on me. The faerie stories were just *stories*. Every year at Festival, the tales shifted a little, grew more dramatic, to keep the people happy. That was all they were. Entertainment.

Those two beasts outside the city walls were not entertaining at all.

"Remember that story of the horse breeder?" I whispered to Zara.

Her hand in mind squeezed.

Two years ago, we'd heard one story of an immortal fae who bred the world's fastest horses. In some versions, he was depicted as a morose and fiendish ancient creature who hated society and whose only solace lay in his prized horses. In others, he was a cruel master who drove all but his horses mad. One version said he kept a barn full of all the animals he'd cursed.

The man's eyebrows lifted slowly as he watched me, as if he could read the turmoil taking place in my head. My fingers traced the outline of my dagger under my dress.

"You won't need your weapon," he said casually. He tilted his head and eyed me with an amused half-grin. "I see that you entered before those useless guards could search you." He sat down on the edge of his desk, crossing his tall, leather riding boots. "So how desperate are you?"

My balance faltered, but Zara steadied me. Fae were the villains in most stories, save the ones where they acted like gods among mortals, and even in those stories, the fae were narcissistic.

But I couldn't leave here empty-handed.

Gathering my courage, I asked, "Do you have any fast horses for sale?"

He laughed outright, tossing his head back. "I have many fast horses."

"Fast enough to win at Midsummer?"

"Not only that, but fast enough to win the king's race as well."

I lurched forward, pulling out of Zara's grasp. "My father will pay you from the winnings."

"That isn't how this works. You pay, and then you receive the animal."

He lifted a finger to stroke the macaw's red breast. It bobbed its head and said in its squeaking voice, *Dawn is coming. Dawn is coming.*

Romero snapped his fingers in annoyance at the bird, but the animal seemed unconcerned and continued walking back and forth on its perch, muttering about the approach of dawn.

"Silence," hissed the man, and the bird ceased its chattering.

"I need Sol back," I admitted, finding no other avenue. "Bets have been placed on him."

He rubbed his chin. "I breed only the best horses, better than even your stallion. My lines go back to champions from a thousand years ago. You cannot possibly afford one of my horses."

"You sold *my* horse," I snarled. "If anything, I should receive the payment you took for him."

He stepped forward, close enough now that if I lunged, I could land a punch on that smug mouth.

"I bought the animal that was brought to me, then sold him for a profit. It's called business." Then swiping up the piece of paper off his desk, he added, "Your horse had his papers."

This stole the breath from my lungs.

"Who could do that?" I whispered, wondering how on earth Sol's papers had slipped into a criminal's hands without anyone's notice. They were kept in a locked box in our home. Then I gasped. "What did the man look like? The one who bought the horse?"

"Why should I reveal his identity to you?"

I sputtered out an angry laugh. "So I can catch him!"

He studied me with an acute precision that made me uncomfortable. "Just how badly do you need this animal?"

There was no compassion on this man's face. In fact, as I returned his hard stare, I thought I saw a flash of amber in his dark irises. I took a step back toward the door, nearly knocking into Zara. "Tell me who sold you the horse."

"I do not reveal the identity of my clients."

"Wretched man," I hissed, spinning way. At that moment, the final hold of my hairstyle came loose, and my long hair flopped against my back. The flower that had managed to hang on through the ride dropped quietly to the ground.

"What did you say?"

I stopped and turned to face him again. "I said you're a wretched man," I proclaimed through gritted teeth.

His lips curled into a strange sort of smile, but when he opened them to speak, the canvas behind him flapped open, and another man stepped in, hastily shoving down an over-size hood on a floor-length cloak. His blond hair was shoulder-length and disheveled, but as the hood pulled away from his face, a distinctly pointed ear was visible for one brief moment.

When I shot a glance at Zara, she'd seen it too, for her eyes were wide as dinner plates.

An early beard cupped this man's chin and his ice blue

eyes, paler than his skin, fixed on the broken vase. Romero half-turned to face this man, and something passed between them, a quick unspoken conversation that prickled my skin. The two men flicked their eyes back toward us at the same time.

"Oh, excuse me." The blond man offered me a small bow before facing Romero again. Under his cloak was a loose white shirt, no ascot. "They are not far from the gates," he muttered in a rushed voice, his tone sounding oddly like a warning. "We have a little over two hours."

I frowned, wondering what they were talking about. But then Zara was tugging at my hand, urging us to leave.

Dawn is coming, squawked the bird.

As we shuffled toward the flap we entered through, the blond man whispered, "They will not find you." When Romero didn't respond, he added, "Rafael?"

The fabric rustled when Zara pushed the tent opening aside, and the two men turned simultaneously toward us. The blond one's brows lifted in surprise, but Romero's face flashed with what was nearly a shadow of anger, quickly replaced by a tight smile.

"We must be going," I said, a wave of sweat now pouring down my back.

"Wait," said Romero, his word more for his friend than for me, though I froze nonetheless. "How many more days left in the fallow month?"

"Twenty-four."

For a moment, both men stared at us, an almost hungry expression rising on their faces. My stomach dropped halfway to the floor. Then, the blond man added in a low voice, "If you do this, do it right this time. I cannot watch you...Just don't fail."

A poisoned silence hung in the air, and my feet wouldn't cooperate to flee this place.

Turning toward Romero, the second man said, "Be ready to pay the price."

"I've paid my price. A thousand times over," snarled the dark-haired one, taking a step toward me.

"Tal!" Zara yanked at my hand, sensing the danger.

Both men shifted forward at the same time, their intention obvious. My veins alit with fear as I turned and ran.

4

RAFAEL

Startled, I stared at the place the two mortals had disappeared. I should catch her.

Hector turned toward me, his eyes wide. "Rafael?"

I shook my head and paced away from him, a feral growl tearing from my throat. Hector had the decency to lift both hands and say nothing. Almost as soon as she'd smashed that vase, that whirlwind of a woman had sparked a flame inside of me that I'd thought long dead.

Dawn is coming squawked the bird.

Turning away, I kicked the macaw's perch across the tent. The bird scolded me, flapping its wings and drifting angrily around the canopied space until it finally perched on the back of my chair.

"Go after her," Hector muttered.

Breathing heavily, I shook my head. "You said yourself the Hunters are out tonight. If they're here, the Crows won't be far behind. Fabian has all his hounds out."

"He's afraid."

I narrowed my eyes, picturing my twin's face in my mind. "Afraid I'll do exactly what I'm thinking about doing."

Letting that woman get away meant giving up this chance at finally achieving freedom. Possibly my last chance.

"But she didn't take a flower," I reminded him. "Fabian was very specific." Hatred seethed in my veins as I stared down at the shattered vase of lilies. I never went to the mortal lands without these blooms. Though, in a month, there would be no point in growing them at all. They too could die, like everything else.

Squatting on his ankles, Hector picked up a crushed lily. "She destroyed the entire vase. I think that counts." He rose, tossing a flower at me which I snatched from the air with careful fingers. "It is now or never. We have less than a month until your curse becomes—"

"Permanent. Don't think I forgot."

Hector kicked at a fallen lily. "Don't let him win. Don't let Fabian have the satisfaction when he takes that crown."

My wicked twin and his enchantress, when they'd crafted my curse so long ago, had woven in a temporary cord of hope, the most miserable part of it all. For nearly three hundred years, that fingernail of hope had carved my worthless heart into filigree shreds. But as soon as Fabian took the crown that had belonged to our father, my curse could no longer be broken.

I could sense Hector's own rage mounting. Turning to him, I saw reflected in his blue eyes the same wretched hope. I lunged for the tent doors.

That woman was either going to kill me or save me.

The crowded market street smelled to the high heavens. Mortals had a certain stench of death and decay to them, of sweat and putrefaction. Too many of them had rot in their bodies they knew nothing about, and too many of them hadn't bathed in far too long.

My cursed nose had its advantages, though, as I could also smell the small vestiges of my enchanted lilies on that woman's clothes. Following her trail, I wove through the merchant's stalls to cut her off.

People milled around the stalls, even at this hour. I disliked jostling through a sea of mortals in my final hours of freedom.

Two women fleeing on horseback through crowded streets were easy to track. They were clearly lost, darting around kiosks and turning blindly down narrower and narrower market lanes. I sidestepped between two merchant stalls to head them off, as they were about to be forced to make a right turn up ahead. They were at the city wall. As she came trotting down the lane, her friend right behind her, I stepped gently around a booth selling various blooms, grateful for the sweet scent they diffused.

With a flick of my wrist, I encouraged a cart full of glass jars to lose a wheel. It was all the magic I had in me at this hour, but it served its purpose. The cart toppled with a great crash, glass splintering everywhere. The woman's horse rose to its hind legs, but she held on. I smiled to myself. I could admire a good rider.

Her friend, on the other hand, bumped to the ground as her horse bucked. The horses were clearly exhausted and while the white one was well-trained enough to tolerate its rider, the red one was not having any more of this wild ride.

"Talia!" The curly-haired woman shouted from the ground.

Talia hopped off her horse and scooped up her friend,

glancing nervously about. Her eyes snagged on something that made her nearly drop her friend.

I paused in the center of the shadowy lane, following her gaze.

"It's Ortiz," whispered Talia, pointing.

Tracing her gesture, I spotted the balding head and curving mustache of the man who had recently sold me the perky stallion. He was marching directly toward the two women, a firm scowl pinching his face, though he didn't seem to be looking at anyone in particular.

"It was foolish to come here," Talia said. "To think I could fix this."

Her friend shook her head, nearly knocking her shawl off. "It would have been foolish not to try."

Talia stiffened, whipped her head around, and scanned the street, before turning back to her friend. She didn't see me. I probably shouldn't have enjoyed this, considering it would end in her early death, but I couldn't help myself. I stepped closer to her.

"If Ortiz sees us," Talia continued, "he'll be able to ruin our reputations."

As I watched her, my resolve faltered. She was a lovely mortal. The delicate curve of her cheek, the thin line of her lips, the smooth skin of her neck. No, I couldn't focus on those things. Sacrificial lambs were meant to be spotless, after all.

I tilted my head to stare down at her. This woman had risked her own life for a horse, and this made her entirely more interesting than any other mortal female I'd ever met.

"Señorita Balcázar, what under the heavens above are you doing here?" said the man who had sold me the horse.

Talia, gripping her friend's hands, jerked so violently that she nearly bumped against me. Her head turned back and forth quickly, presumably scanning for a way out, but a cart full of stacked rugs ambled by, pushed by Hector, who gave me a small nod. The women were trapped.

"And Señorita Valencia," the horse seller added.

As he approached, his eyes immediately traveled to Talia's leg, remaining fixed even as she tried to close the hem of her dress with her hand.

Heat flared inside me as I watched him ogle her. This man wanted her.

The tiny twang of guilt was easy enough to dismiss. A mortal's life was brief and wrought with pain. Perhaps she would end up in the warm embrace of the First and Last, which would mean her death was no more than a doorway to paradise.

Yes, I was only helping her along to eternal bliss.

Murder sounded much worse.

"You stole my father's horse, didn't you, Ortiz?" she spat at the mustachioed man.

She was a feisty one, unafraid. My lips curled into a satisfied grin.

His eyes narrowed. "Señorita Balcázar, for you to be seen here is a disgrace." Ortiz's accusation was so loud that several faces turned toward them. His mustache quivered over a partial smile, relishing this moment. Then he turned his beady gaze to Zara. "You too, señorita."

"It was you. You sold him!" Talia hissed.

From the shadows I smiled, watching her fists tighten, turning the same anger she had directed on me onto this worm of a man. But I stopped myself, refocusing on the task at hand.

"Come with me." Ortiz grabbed for Talia.

As she yanked away, she barreled into my chest.

"Pardon," she muttered, not looking at my face but jumping sideways to skirt around me. She waved her friend along.

"Your father will have no power to refuse me now," whispered Ortiz as he stormed forward down the bustling market street.

As Talia whirled back toward Ortiz, I stepped backward and sideways, moving with her. Her biggest threat was her smallest concern. Her ignorance would serve me well.

The large man reached out a knuckle and traced down Talia's cheek. She flinched away so violently that she once again knocked into me.

I steadied her. "Strike a bargain with me," I whispered as her cheek was still below my mouth. When she finally glanced up at my face, recognition blanched her features. "And I will take care of *him*."

"Are you…?"

"Fae, yes." She needed to know this much, or any bargain we struck wouldn't be fully binding.

She blinked and began to pull away, but I tightened my grip, halting her.

"I can save your family," I muttered. My plan would only work if she came willingly.

"What?"

Ortiz jerked her arm around, and she pressed her back to me. Inexplicably, I wanted to pull her behind me and fight this mortal man for her, but that was not my aim here.

"My lady?" The other man's voice quavered. "What are you doing?"

Over her shoulder, she whispered, "I'll do it. Just save me from that man."

5

TALIA

The merchant told his daughters all that had happened. He drew his youngest daughter into his embrace. "Dear little daughter, I cannot take you to the bear." "Do not fear," responded the brave little maid. "If I do not go, we all shall perish. I will gladly go to the bear." – The Lily and the Bear

The stranger made a quick *hmm* noise that resonated through my back, at once comforting and terrifying. In that little noise, there was a deep satisfaction, an unmooring of something large that I didn't understand.

What I did know, without a doubt, was that the man behind me was more powerful than Ortiz, and not only because he was fae—I had no idea fae were real, and I certainly didn't know what *real* fae were capable of. There was, however, a strength about him that sent ripples of fear down my arms, but once that strength was directed at my enemy, I couldn't help but thank the stars above.

The fae's strong hands moved me carefully aside, and Romero stepped toward Ortiz.

"And who are you?" barked my landlord.

Casually, Romero ran a hand through his black hair, revealing his pointy ears.

Recognition melted Ortiz's scowl into loose shock. He took a step back, but not fast enough.

The fae's arm shot out and grabbed Ortiz's chin, yanking it upward. The landlord stumbled forward, mouth squeezed open, eyes bulging.

"She's coming with me," he growled.

He released Ortiz with a small shove and turned to me, eyes flashing with an otherworldly amber glow. Zara gasped, but I kept my eyes on the fae. His shoulders relaxed and he tilted his chin up enough to stare down his nose at Ortiz. Keeping his eyes on the trembling landlord, Romero plucked a single, white lily from the lapel of his suit and he held it out to me.

"Quickly, now," he said, arm swinging out, inviting me to walk ahead of him.

In somewhat of a daze, I took the flower and marched down the road.

"What just happened?" Zara whispered, hurrying to walk beside me.

From behind us, Ortiz called out, "You will not be laughing when I take every last thing of value from you. In the end, Talia Balcázar, you *will* marry me. "

A darkness closed over my mind then, and I hadn't realized I'd slowed my steps until a firm hand pressed against the small of my back.

Had I really just made a bargain with a fae?

Zara clung tightly to my trembling arm as we made our way back through the city.

Outside his opulent tent, the tall fae stepped around me and held me still with one hand on my shoulder. I realized then that I was shaking.

"Our bargain..." I began, unable to finish the sentence.

"I will give your father a horse that will win the race. I promise it will not lose, but we must make haste."

My jaw fell open.

"You agreed to a bargain," he added in a low voice.

This wasn't kindness. He wanted something from me in return, but what did I have that a fae could possibly want?

Zara tugged at my arm, but I ignored her. "I...what must I do?"

"But Tal, he's *fae*," Zara whispered.

If the stories were true, then a fae's deal was binding. In a moment of panic, I'd already agreed to meet his terms, before I even knew what they were. I swallowed and nodded, steeling myself to face whatever horrid bargain I'd just agreed to.

He glanced around, as if searching the street for enemies. But what would a fae fear in the streets of a mortal village?

When he looked down at me again, his eyes glowed amber, a sinister reminder of his magic. "To uphold this bargain, you must marry me."

6

TALIA

M inutes later, his words still echoed in my mind as I patted Corona's neck with trembling fingers, wondering how on earth I ended up in this situation.

Eager to be in the saddle and leaving Puerta, I peeked around the horse to glare at the fae saddling his own mount, a magnificent dapple-gray mare. This man claimed he could save my family, and a fae, at least according to legend, couldn't lie. If marrying him meant saving *them*, then it would be worth it.

I'd been terrified of one day having to marry Ortiz. This couldn't be worse than that. At least this man was devastatingly handsome.

But marriage to a mythological creature wasn't what I'd had in mind.

Outside a ramshackle stable adjacent to Romero's tent, the night was at its darkest. Only an hour remained until dawn, and only five until the race was set to begin. Five hours to fix everything that had gone wrong.

Behind me, Zara hung close, uncharacteristically silent. Nearby, the blond fae, who'd been introduced as Hector, was adjusting the reins atop his own bay mare. A third unsaddled horse wearing only a halter and stamped his foot in the soft earth. He was a fine horse, tall and muscular, but I'd seen plenty of beautiful, confident horses lose races they were expected to win.

Romero stepped around Corona. He now donned a large cloak, identical to the one Hector wore.

"We must hurry," he said, voice low. "Are you a fast rider?"

I wanted to laugh, but only a small wisp of air rushed from my lungs. "I train champions with my father," I said, voice flat. I couldn't bring myself to look directly at this man.

He let out a small grunt of amusement. Then, without warning, he reached for my waist and hefted me up. Instinctively, my leg swung out over the saddle, but inside I reeled at his touch. He'd lifted me like a child.

"I can mount a horse," I grumbled.

As I settled on Corona's back, his hand tucked my left foot neatly into its stirrup.

Startled, I stared at the top of his hooded head.

His hand held my bare ankle below the leg that was so boldly exposed by my recent alteration. My cheeks flamed and I tried to pull the fabric around my calf, but it was little use.

His hood obscured his eyes, but I could feel his gaze burning into my knee. The slit had seemed so necessary when I'd been in such a rush to catch up to Sol. Now, I wished more than anything that I could sew the dress back together and pretend none of this had ever happened.

"At least tell me your first name," I muttered. If I was going to marry the man, I should at least know his full name.

His hand slipped off my ankle. "Rafael." Without another word, he spun away to mount his own horse.

Zara let out a small shrieked as the other fae, Hector, assisted her into her own saddle.

Soon all five horses were tearing out across the seaside plains, back toward Leor. As we charged down the road, I got the distinct feeling the two fae riding beside me were fleeing from something as they glanced frequently over their shoulder.

By the time we slowed outside of Leor, I was exhausted from two hard rides in the middle of the night. Corona was in no fit state to race again in a few hours. The eastern sky was already pale gray.

Rafael turned his hooded face to Zara. "Return home. Tell no one what has taken place."

When she glanced at me, I nodded reassuringly. But inside me, there was no assurance that any of this would turn out well.

Rafael growled, "Now."

She shot me a sympathetic smile before trotting down the road toward her family's estate.

I led the way around the outskirts of the city, toward the first slopes of the plains that lifted toward the distant mountains.

"Faster," urged Rafael.

"Let them rest," I snapped, patting Corona's neck.

He kicked into a canter, shouting at me to lead the way. I had no choice but to match his pace.

Dawn's first blue hues brightened the sky as I rode directly into the paved courtyard outside my front door. My family's home sat near to the road, where dust from passing carriages coated their meager garden with reddish brown hues. If the guard had done what I'd asked, my father might not even be at home, but out searching for Sol. And if the guard hadn't sent word to my father, he'd likely be pacing the kitchen, jittery with race-day nerves.

I hopped quickly from the saddle, before Papa could emerge and see my leg hanging out for all the world to see.

Rafael dismounted, shooting a glance at the road behind them, then at the eastern horizon.

"What do you think is out there?" I asked. The ominous way both fae snapped their hooded faces toward me silenced any further questions.

"We are out of time," Hector said, hopping down.

Rafael let out a small grunt. "Where is the lily I gave you?"

"I—no. I think it fell off on the ride."

"You *what?*"

Corona's solid frame prevented me from backing up when he lunged for me. "It was just a flower."

His shadowed eyes flashed gold again. "I promised you I could save your family from ruin, and you go and toss my blessing aside."

I poked a finger at his chest, not caring at that moment that he was immortal, imbued with magic, and much, much bigger than me. "You didn't *tell* me your little flower was the key to your *blessing.*"

He grabbed my finger and held it a moment. My shock quickly hardened into fear. Would he snap my bones for talking to him thus? Hector, who'd pushed his hood back, eyed Rafael with the hint of a warning on his pinched brow.

"We must go," said Rafael, stepping back. "We cannot linger."

I stumbled forward, almost colliding with him. "You promised."

"And I intend to keep my promise." He grabbed the spare horse's reins. "Take this horse. Enter him in the race."

I scoffed. "After that ride, he'll finish last."

"Do not presume to know more about *my* horses than I do."

The emphasis on the word *my* reminded me that he was fae, and that his animals were likely bespelled.

"My father hates magic. He'll not enter that horse." My words choked in my throat.

"Enter what horse?"

The moment my father exited our front door, his gaze slipped between me and the strangers, then widened as he noted the change in my dress.

"Talia, are you all right?" He rushed to my side.

"I'm fine, Papa." I angled away from him to try to hide the slit from his view. "Ortiz stole Sol, and he sold him, and this man saved me from…"

"Whoa, whoa." Papa held out one hand, palm up, the way he did when calming his stallions. "Start over."

I explained in more controlled sentences, what had taken place after he'd left the Valencia's ball. As I spoke, my father's face fell into a deeper and deeper frown.

"You mean to tell me don Samuel *stole* and *sold* my best racehorse? To this man?"

I nodded. "And then *he* turned around and sold him before I arrived."

Papa scooped me into a hug and patted my now disheveled hair. "I can't believe you went after him."

"I couldn't let Sol get away. He's been your best horse. He was going to change everything." An unexpected sob burst from my mouth.

Papa's hum of agreement calmed my nerves, but only just.

He held me with two hands and studied my face. "You should *never* have put my reputation above your own. What does it matter if—"

Rafael cleared his throat, cutting off Papa's words. "We must leave." His gaze remained fixed on the eastern sky, as if avoiding looking at us. "But I did promise your daughter a horse that would win today's race. Afterwards, you may do with him as you wish."

As my father began to protest such a claim, Rafael eased his hood back, exposing his pointed ears. Papa coughed nervously and pulled me behind him.

Unphased, Rafael continued, "But there is one condition."

Papa stiffened and I pressed my cheek against his shoulder, as if I could hide from what came next.

"We made a bargain. A champion for her hand in marriage."

For several seconds, my father did not speak. His entire body remained as rigid as a pine. Finally, he turned slowly to face me. "Tell me you did not verbally agree to this."

I bit my lip.

His calloused hands gripped mine. "Talia! *Mi princesa*, tell me it isn't true." He gathered me into a tight embrace as he shook with silent sobs.

"Take the horse," Rafael said, his tone brisk. His dark eyes flickered with an amber glow, like candles frustrated by a fierce wind. He was in a hurry, that much was true, but he almost seemed eager to leave us all behind, despite his bargain to marry me.

Then, as if aware of my train of thought, he added, "But to guarantee his victory, we must be wed. That was the bargain."

I pulled away from Papa. "How can you guarantee the horse will win, if we wed or not?"

"He runs as fast as I tell him to," was Rafael's simple answer. "Either I tell him to win, or I tell him to lose."

My father breathed out a huff. He poured years of training into his horses, along with hours of study into bloodlines, and expert intuition in speculation when making deals for breeding rights and brood mares. To have this man claim his method for training and breeding champions revolved around *telling the horse to win* was a slap in the face.

With a sigh, I whispered, "I already made the bargain, Papa."

He wiped a tear from his cheek, his expression angrier than I had ever seen it. "You despicable creature," he seethed. "I wouldn't take all the money in the world if it meant giving up *mi princesa*. But, as it stands, she's already given you her word. What will happen if she doesn't follow though?"

"She will die," the fae stated bluntly, leaving me breathless. He was shifting his weight, visibly nervous now, his eyes constantly flicking to the growing light over the easternmost roof.

"I will go willingly.," I said mostly to Papa. "If I stay, we will all be ruined. Ortiz will not stop until he gets what he wants."

To show my resolve, I stepped toward the fae. To my surprise, he crushed his eyes closed momentarily before nodding firmly. Across the small courtyard, Hector smiled and patted his horse's neck.

"Oh, Talia," breathed Papa. "Will I ever see you again?"

I ran back for another hug, startling a crow from his perch on the roof. My mother now stood in the doorway of our home, two hands pressed to her mouth. She raced out and embraced me too.

Looking at her desperate expression, I blinked back tears.

This was my choice, and I would carry it without remorse. With a deep inhale, I stepped away from my parents.

"Tell Zara I will miss her."

Rafael took my hand, startling me out of my sadness. His hand was calloused like Papa's, and it somehow felt achingly similar, though warmer and larger. To stave off more tears, I squeezed his hand hard.

Rafael coughed. "We must wed now."

"Here?" I asked. "In my courtyard?"

He nodded. "If a marriage is part of a bargain," he said, "vows may be exchanged anywhere. As long as there is a fae witness, the marriage will be acknowledged as binding."

"Acknowledged? By whom?"

Rafael didn't answer but turned to grasp my other hand, forcing me to face him fully. His expression seemed pained. Was it really that bad to marry me?

Still in a mild state of shock at all that had transpired, I barely registered that he'd already begun speaking his vows. He spoke quickly, as if his words meant as little as an auction- eer's calls.

"I will be your husband, bound to you by promise, bound to you in truth, entirely your own, for all the days you live. I will take on your victories and your losses, your blessings and your curses, and all that is mine will be yours, as I will take of yours and make it also mine. To you, Talia Balcázar, I bind myself, fully and forever."

I swallowed, momentarily unable to breathe under the weight of his glowing golden eyes. A fae—a creature I'd not known was real until hours ago—had just pledged himself to me.

Yet, the fae vows pointedly lacked the word love.

He leaned toward me—*O, sun, was he about to kiss me?* With

a faint smirk, he whispered, "I will say it again, and you can repeat it back to me." His breath was warm on my cheek.

"Wait," Papa said, stepping closer. Tears stained his face. "If she is to wed a fae, you will allow her to include her own people's vows."

"She must state our vows, or the marriage isn't binding."

Papa frowned and said, "Fine. But before she does, you will recite our vows. It is *my* requirement, if you wish to have my daughter."

There was nothing my father could do that could free me from the bargain. Even still, I closed my eyes at the sweetness of his request.

To my surprise, Rafael rolled his eyes slightly, and said, "Just be quick."

Papa scoffed, but he pulled from memory the vows I'd heard at every wedding I'd ever attended.

Rafael's voice strained with every word he repeated, as did his grip on my hands. "I take you, Talia Balcázar, as my bride, forever mine to cherish, to love, to provide for, to…"

"Protect," Papa repeated, agitation clipping his tone.

The fae's eyes flashed amber, brighter than I'd seen them. His fingers slipped from mine, and he averted his gaze, brow pinched.

I glanced at Papa, who returned my perplexed stare. But before he could speak, Rafael hissed out the word.

"Protect." The syllables spat from his lips like a curse, and with that word, something changed in him. The unsettling magical glow in his eyes blinked out. While I didn't understand fae magic or culture or why one's eyes might light up or go dim, I sensed that something significant might have happened. My stomach to dropped, for in that darkening, I feared that the light in his eyes would never shine again.

7

RAFAEL

Curse the suns of all the worlds.

The woman staring up at me, her face so pleasant in its simplicity—no elaborate glamours obscuring her form—was now mine to *protect*. Of all the blazing words in the human vocabulary, they'd chosen that one to be in their marriage vows.

Mortals were selfish and frivolous, anchored only by their petty religions and deep-seated hatred of death—so, of course, the mortal man's vows would revolve around protecting his wife as they marched toward the grave.

Hector's gaze burned into me, but I couldn't face him. In truth, I couldn't face myself, or this woman, or her two loving parents, so I stared blankly at the dusty whitewashed wall over Talia's shoulder.

She reached for my hands again, to continue this wretched wedding. I knew nothing about this woman but that she was not as afraid of me as she should be.

If only she knew what she was doing. What I had done.

In a daze, I repeated the final words of her human vows.

"To you, I promise my best efforts and my perpetual fidelity, my honest apologies and my greatest weaknesses."

The words were dull knives, destroying me.

I met Hector's gaze, and his expression chastised me like I was a child caught stealing.

Moments ago, watching her father press a comforting hand to his daughter's shoulder, embrace her with such care, and cry over her sudden departure, had evoked a jealousy so deep inside of me that I had never felt such rage. Or shame.

Then, it was her turn to recite the vows. I spoke them carefully, slowly, for her to repeat each phrase. Her voice never wavered, never faltered. She was everything I needed— determined, unafraid, brave to a fault—and yet with each word she spoke, I hated myself more and more.

"I will take on your victories and your losses, your blessings and your curses…"

I wanted to press a hand to her mouth and stop the words.

Her exquisite voice finished, "I will take of yours and make it also mine."

When she'd finished her vows, I stared at her, memorizing the curve of her eyebrows, the angle of her nose, the color of her lips. Mortals weren't lovely the way fae women were, but she was beautiful because what I saw of her was all there was to see, no mask, no glamour, no lies. There could be no atonement for what I'd just done.

In all my decades, my centuries, of life, I'd never once seen a fae father embrace his daughter the way this human had hugged Talia. Never once had I seen a mother cry over the marriage of her begotten. Fae married and gave birth for one reason: to attain more power.

In all the fae courts, in all the realms of magical creatures I had visited or would ever visit, there would never be for me what she possessed in that single embrace. The ache of it rekindled three hundred years of pain and in an instant set it all to blazing afresh.

From across the small courtyard, Hector's words nailed my fate to me. "You are now man and wife," he said, a gruff edge to his words.

I'd made a bargain, and she'd agreed to it. Hector had witnessed it and was bound by our world's laws to hold me to it. There was no way out of this now. To protect her, I had to hide myself from her.

8

TALIA

Rafael's hand slipped out of mine—more like yanked out.

A weight flipped over in my chest. All the days and hours spent dreaming of matrimony had crumbled like rotten wood, leaving me feeling much emptier inside than I'd imagined marriage would. Marriage was a union, a joining, a bringing together, and yet I felt severed from what I loved most. My eyes lingered on my parents, then swept over the familiar façade of my childhood home. The windows I'd climbed in and out of countless times, both to the laughter of passersby and the scoldings of my mother. The straw roof we'd had to repair after particularly heavy rainy seasons. The uneven stones in the courtyard that had been the cause of several skinned knees.

My mother wept silently beside Papa, and my chest threatened to cave in.

All I could manage to say to them was, "I love you."

"We must be leaving," my new husband urged.

"Why the hurry?"

He ignored me and walked over to his horse, mounting in one quick motion. When he'd turned his horse around to face the road, he reached a hand down to me. I didn't move.

"Time is our greatest enemy now," he said ominously.

"Fine." When I reached for his hand, he gripped my forearm.

"Jump," he said.

I did, and then I was sailing over the back of his saddle, landing behind him. He glanced over his shoulder before clicking his tongue at his horse. The lurch nearly sent me tumbling to the ground, but I flung my arms forward, wrapping them around the stranger's middle.

Not stranger. I'd just married the man.

A shiver coursed down my entire frame. His soft chuckle rumbled against my cheek, making me blush. Relaxing my grip, I leaned away, pinching my knees like I'd been trained to do to stay atop a horse.

As we charged out of the courtyard and away from my family, my new husband's scent enveloped me. His cloak smelled of damp earth and warm stones, and there was the faint aroma of citrus oil, but beneath it all was the familiar, calming scent of horse and leather, infusing my mild state of panic with a sliver of comfort that eventually worked to ease my tightened shoulders as we thundered down the brightening road.

In the predawn light the crowds were flocking into Leor for the first official day of Festival. Masks and costumes adorned many of the faces, but by tonight, nearly everyone in the streets would be in full festival attire. My heart sank thinking of how I would miss going with Zara to see the storytellers perform.

I hadn't even had time to pack a single item. My sole

possessions were my now ruined dress and dancing shoes, my coin purse, and Zara's borrowed blade. A knot formed in my chest, and every stage we passed seemed to drag my momentary happiness closer to the dirt.

With the growing crowd, Rafael had to slow his horse to a walk, but he emitted constant grunts of disapproval as he wove among the slow pedestrians.

To keep from focusing on what I was missing, I closed my eyes and leaned my cheek against Rafael's wide back.

Instantly, the muscles in his back tightened. A mild sting pricked my heart. I couldn't relax, but I could at least try to hide, and closing my eyes made it easier to believe I was invisible.

The sound of a board clattering to the cobblestones nearby spooked the horse, who lifted onto her hind legs. Rafael snapped a hand around my thigh and pressed it to him, keeping me from sliding backward. Embarrassment tinted with gratitude flamed up my neck at his touch.

Hector rode up close beside us. He eyed how tightly I clung to Rafael, then said, "Time is up."

With another glance at the now pale sky, Rafael nodded, his hand slipping off my leg.Over his shoulder, he said to me, "You will travel the rest of the way with Hector."

Confused, I startled a little as Rafael slid from the saddle. When he turned his hooded face up to me, the light revealed his handsome features, but his brow was knotted with either worry or anger, and I hated that I couldn't tell which.

"Where are you going?" I asked, suddenly frightened to travel alone with a fae who hadn't vowed to protect me.

"Hector will take good care of you," Rafael assured, sparing a glance at the blond fae. "I will meet you tonight at camp."

"Camp?"

"We will return to my home, but I can only travel at night." To my expectant expression, he offered no clarification. Instead, he lifted the reins, waiting for me to slide forward into the saddle. When I did, he added, "Be ready to ride after nightfall."

With that, he turned and darted away between the two nearest buildings, running like his life depended on it.

9

RAFAEL

The change ripped through my muscles as soon as I left my brother and my new wife behind.

Agony threatened to pull me to the ground, but I clenched my jaw as the bones elongated and kept running. Each limb tightened, then stretched, joints crunching and grinding. Though it took only two breaths for the change to be complete, those seconds were small eternities, carving out their dominion over me like tiny armies. My massive claws raked against the cobblestones, drawing the attention of an aproned shopkeeper in the alleyway. He screamed and hopped back through his open shop door.

I loped after him, rage rising, as it always did.

His face, that grimace of fear. That fragile mortal, already half-dead, could still *walk* on his two legs, while I was confined to crawl the earth on paws while the sun shined.

With a growl, teeth bared, I lifted a paw and obliterated the door that fool thought could keep him safe from me.

Screams rang out. Wood splintered. A little girl stood in

52

the center of the bake shop, frozen in terror, her hand clutching one of the fake lilies the poor wore in their hair.

On my hind legs, I stared down at her through the wrecked door. The girl's face reminded me of Talia's and I hesitated.

A man grabbed the girl and bolted out the front of the shop, breaking my momentary trance. My vision blurred and the animal inside me raged. I tore into the shop, shattering pastry displays and upending tables. I clawed the bowls and cups off the shelves. Shards of pottery and glass stabbed my paws, and I growled even louder, fueling my fury with pain.

Seconds was all it took to destroy the shop. Crashing back out, I lumbered away from the bakery, its lingering scents torturing my heightened senses. A reminder of what I truly was.

10

TALIA

Even after Rafael was out of sight, I kept staring at the place he'd disappeared. I almost forgot I was holding a horse's reins until the mare moved beneath me.

"Where is he going?"

Hector answered in a low voice, "Rafael will answer your questions, when he is ready." He mirrored my narrow glance, as if challenging me to ask another question. "At least you and I no longer have to hurry. But we should keep moving."

Soon, the sun broke over the nearest building and the day grew hot before we'd even left Leor. As we walked the horses through the thickest part of the crowd, I smelled the fried dough of my favorite pastries and heard the first shouted words of the nearest storyteller.

"Come hear the story of the night lion," he called, voice trained to carry over the din of jolly festival goers.

I turned longing eyes to the man on stage, wanting to stay and listen. The storytellers always started with familiar tales, beloved tales, and worked their way up to the darker, scarier

54

ones after nightfall, when the children had mostly all gone to bed.

"You enjoy the stories?" asked Hector.

Nodding, I urged Rafael's horse forward.

Something about the blond man seemed to stiffen, as if offended by my answer. He hesitated before replying, "I'm certain they've misled you about the fae."

"I'm certain they have," I admitted, shooting a cursory glance at where Hector's pointed ears were hidden carefully behind his long hair, "considering I didn't know you really existed until last night."

He huffed in amusement and then continued on in silence. We walked against the flow of people. Many of the faces I now passed would witness the race.. At least if Rafael's horse *did* win, as promised, Papa could still pay out all the angry people who would come knocking on his door. After that, there should still be enough money left over to purchase my parents' house and land outright, leaving Papa free of Ortiz once and for all. And if Rafael's horse was capable of winning at midsummer, perhaps the stallion could also win the King's Race as I had secretly hoped Sol would.

This comforting hope carried me until Leor had vanished in the distance. Once the city fell from view, a weight of dread settled over my shoulders. The horse swayed underneath me, and the sun beat down harshly on my dark hair and the black fabric of my shawl, which I used to drape over my shoulders to cover my ballgown as best I could.

Soon the leather began to rub tender spots on my legs. I kept fidgeting, trying to place the seams of the leather in different places to stave off blisters, but was unsuccessful.

"Where are we going?" I finally asked, tired of the silence.

As far as I knew, there were no nearby towns in this direction.

"Rivenmark."

My heart somersaulted. "The fae lands?"

Hector nodded but never looked my way.

"Where are they?"

He chuckled slightly at this. "Everywhere. And nowhere."

"What's that supposed to mean?"

His blue eyes flicked toward me briefly. "Mortals see so very little. There are entrances all around. That hill over there. The river back that way. The cliffs to the east."

"And why don't we use that hill over there?" We were walking away from it.

His knuckles tightened under his riding gloves, making the leather squeak. "Mortals can only enter through certain gates." After a moment, he announced, We're here."

"At the gate?"

Stretches of flat earth surrounded us on all sides, and the gray line of the sea stood far off to the left. If I looked hard enough, I could just barely make out Puerta's white stone walls.

"No. At camp."

As we rounded a copse of trees, a large tent came into view, one of the grand, octagonal kind that looked more like something from one of the illuminated texts in Zara's library. It even had a small gold flag on top, though the flag was too limp to see any identifying sigil on it.

Hector hopped to the ground. "We will leave again at nightfall, so rest while you can. The journey home will take all night."

"Why do you travel at night?"

"Why do you ask so many questions?"

I rolled my eyes. "Please tell me there is more than one tent."

Hector laughed as he led his bay mare into the clearing.

Gracefully, I slid to the ground, but my feet cemented in place, as if they'd grown roots, and I clung to Rafael's horse.

From the clearing, Hector called out, "I don't bite. And besides, Rafael would murder me if anything was to happen to you."

Tossing a glance back at the road, as if expecting to see my so-called husband, I let out a loud sigh. A fae had wed me and left me in the space of a half hour. Not the best start to a marriage, but at least I wasn't bound to Ortiz, which was the alternative. Would Rafael's hasty departure prove the harbinger of an unhappy, distant married life?

Lifting my chin, I determined not to resign myself to eternal discontent. Plenty of people had been betrothed by their parents and still found love. This marriage, at least, had been my decision. Sort of.

"Tell me he's not a bad man," I said to Rafael's horse, patting her sweating neck.

I nudged Rafael's horse through the trees and into the open area where Hector was already unfastening his saddle-bags. From here, I could see that there were, in fact, two tents, the second situated behind the first.

"Your quarters, Señorita—I mean, Señora."

I balked at him, the first person to use my married title.

"There's a creek over there for the horses," he added, nodding his head to the right. "I will take them. You stay here and settle in."

"I can take them."

Hector took a quick half-step my direction, then eased a hand through his long hair. "No, that won't be necessary. My brother is picky about how his horse is cared for. It's been a long day. Go and rest."

A flicker of fear danced inside me, but maybe I'd misread his actions. "Rafael is your brother?"

Hector ducked his head down to check his horse's hooves. "Yes. Half-brother."

I glanced back at the nearby creek. "Is there something dangerous out there?"

Stories of mysterious beasts flooded my mind. I'd already learned the Wild Hunt was real. What if every beast of legend truly walked, somewhere out there?

But instead of giving a reassuring answer, Hector simply said, "Yes," and stalked over to grab the reins from me. He led the two horses away, leaving me standing in the bright sunshine, hands on my hips.

The hot breeze ruffled my ruined dress, and a stab of disappointment flooded my veins. I hadn't brought a scrap of home with me, unless I counted Zara's blade. I pulled the dagger out of its sheath and studied its dull hilt.

I guess I accidentally stole this.

Zara wouldn't care. I clutched the dagger to my chest and turned toward the tent Hector had indicated was for me.

When I threw open the tent flap, I paused. A light glowed within, revealing the most elaborate tent I'd ever seen. In the center was a tall bed, glowing pristinely white under a glittering chandelier and surrounded by a delicate netting to keep out the mosquitos. A carved wooden chest sat to one side of the bed, and an ornate dresser complete with mirror stood to the other.

If this was how the fae camped, I wondered what Rafael's home would look like. A spark of excitement danced through my chest. This wasn't exactly an estate, but if it foreshadowed what was to come, I couldn't find any complaints.

At the foot of the bed, an open trunk bursting with heaps of colorful fabric waited.

The ruffles and the silks indicated that they were women's clothes. I pulled one out, frowning at it.

Suddenly I flung it back, slamming the lid down and turning away. There was no way I would wear some other woman's discarded clothes.

I stormed out of the tent, not knowing where I was going until I stood once more on the road, staring back at the distant walls of Puerta de los Reyes.

"Going somewhere?"

Hector slipped from between the trees but kept to the shadows, his hands behind his back.

"The clothes? The ones in the tent," I demanded. "Whose are they?"

"You do know we have magic, yes? Your stories at least told you that much?"

A wave of uncertainty brought more sweat to my flushed skin. Magic. It was despised by some and sought by others. My father had always spat at the idea of magic, hating that some people thought they could cheat out of life's discomforts or alter their own misfortunes. And now his future hung on a horse magicked to be faster than the rest. I closed my eyes and looked up, praying silently to the sun that my father would enter the horse and take the winnings.

At my long silence, Hector cleared his throat.

"I understand what you must be thinking, and I can assure

you that the trunk full of clothes only appeared in that tent the moment your vows were complete."

My eyes flicked up to him.

Hector smiled, but the warmth of it didn't reach his eyes. "Rafael Romero has been waiting for you for a very long time."

I stared at him for several moments. Running wasn't really an option. I'd have to steal one of the horses to get away, which felt wrong, considering Rafael had already given Papa one of his horses. And if these fae really had magic, what good would come from trying to escape? Besides, I'd said my vows.

I was bound.

My resolve cracked, and I walked quietly back to the tent, slipped inside.

From outside the tent, Hector called, "You should find everything you need, but if you lack anything, just let me know."

"Oh, just my husband," I muttered grumpily to myself. Not that I was looking forward to our happily ever after.

When I sat down in the cushioned chair, my leg stuck out grotesquely from the rip in the skirt. I cringed, hating that so many people had seen me in such a state, including the stranger I'd recently married. He wasn't supposed to see that until...well, later.

The thought made it hard to swallow for several seconds.

But he'd vanished, and I was here, sweating in this fabulous tent and smelling somewhat like an unfortunate fish stuck in a shrinking tidepool.

I hopped up. The fine fabrics in the trunk drew my eye.

Magic clothing. How preposterous.

But when I knelt to feel the shining silks and soft linens, I chuckled softly. Magic or not, these were exquisite items. Zara always said fine clothes were meant to be enjoyed, not hung in an armoire somewhere—or, as it were, stuffed in a trunk.

I pulled out one blue dress. The fabric was lighter than any I'd felt. It swished and moved, unlike the stiff fabrics of many of my dresses. The ties at the back loosened easily, and there was no hard ribbing in the bodice at all.

I laid the dress over the bed and then pulled out a deep magenta one. It had ruffles along the bottom hem. A ball-gown. Draping that one over the bed, I scooped up a third.

In this manner, I examined every single item in the trunk, from breathtaking ballgowns to silken nightgowns that made me blush and linen riding blouses. Each item brought a new smile to my face, a fresh burst of excitement at the idea that these were all for me. But none more than a pair of riding breeches that look as though they would fit me perfectly.

My smile broadened, then faltered. How could he have known I wore breeches when training horses with Papa?

At the bottom of the trunk was a pair of tall boots. I lifted my foot to compare, and found the shoe was my size. Unexpected sadness rippled through me. Ever since I'd been big enough to ride a horse, Papa had supplied me with tall riding boots similar to the ones he wore. He'd always said I needed the proper attire if I was going to train champions with him.

For a ghost of a man who knew little other than my name, Rafael Romero strangely understood me. A wave of goosepimples prickled my arms as I glanced behind me at the tent entrance.

It was too personal. Too...frightening.

I stumbled away from the piles of clothing and slapped a hand to my forehead.

Stars above. I'd married a *fae*. Now I was bound to this man's *magic* as much as his body or his name or his wealth. The wealth I could handle. Even the name I could grow accustomed to. And I understood fully what it was to be joined together with my husband, though the reality of that particular piece of the puzzle was not something I wanted to dwell on.

It was the magic, however, that I couldn't stomach. If, as their vows declared, all that was his was now mine, what did that mean of his magic? For surely I couldn't make things appear out of thin air.

Just to be sure, I closed my eyes and pictured Zara standing in the tent with me.

No one appeared.

The heat inside the tent was quickly growing to a stifling temperature, and though the customary afternoon siesta was still a couple of hours away, I was already yawning incessantly.

Quickly, I glanced around at the opulence within the tent, looking for something small, heavy and movable. I settled for an octagonal table, carved with intricate leaf patterns.

I picked up the table and yelped in surprise as the top immediately lifted off. After nestling it back on, I moved the whole thing and settled it right in front of the tent door. That should at least alert me to any intruders while I slept.

I set the washbasin and pitcher beside the bed and bathed behind the mosquito netting, as if it were a changing screen. After wiping away all the dirt and sweat, I discovered on the dresser a bottle of sweet-smelling oil. It had a lovely citrus scent. I rubbed a little on my arm and it warmed against my skin. Soon, my whole body felt brand new and smelled like a fresh orange.

In minutes, however, sweat again dampened my skin and I frowned. In the pile of clothes now lying across the bed, I dug out a nightgown of the highest quality. It dripped from my fingers like oil and felt cool as water on my skin.

I changed and climbed into bed, sighing with relief as I settled in among the fluffy pillows that, strangely enough, remained cool against my skin. If this was magic, maybe it wasn't so bad.

Soon, my exhaustion won out and I sailed into a dreamless sleep.

11

RAFAEL

The long shadows of sunset followed me to the campsite, where my new bride hopefully slept. She needed rest before tonight's ride. Meat sizzling over the campfire tantalized my heightened sense of smell.

Hector sat by a cookstove, adding a pinch of something. "Rafael," he said without looking up.

I ambled into the campsite on all fours and walked toward my tent.

Hector glanced up, briefly observing a gash on my shoulder, and frowned. "You can still make this work," he said, voice low.

The gash was painful—the steel blade had just enough iron to weaken me without killing me—but there was nothing to be done about it until after the change. With my snout, I pushed aside the tent flap and peered in at Talia, asleep on my bed and utterly peaceful.

My nose, so much more powerful in this form, recoiled from the overpowering citrus scent wafting out of the tent.

She'd used my oils. It was a smell I associated with freedom, with respite from my curse.

I withdrew my head and snorted. Like a flower plucked from its stem, she would wither in the blink of an eye, yet to crush her would be to destroy something lovely.

Hector watched me, his expression brimming with reprimand. This wretched long tongue of mine was useless for speech, and Hector knew it. He was going to lecture me before I was capable of a rebuttal.

"The vows were a smart move on her father's part, but they didn't change anything."

This time, my snort was part growl. Those additional vows had changed *everything*.

Hector shook his finger at me. His companionship was more than I could ask for, a lifeline these past decades, but when he abused his privileges of speech like this, I couldn't help but seethe at him.

"You promised to protect her. You still can." He ignored my intensifying breaths and continued, "You never specified *what* you would protect her from. There is the Wild Hunt, your brother, who will no doubt send someone to sniff out what you've done, the *other* residents on your estate. Plenty of dangerous things she'll need protection from." He lifted both hands like this solved everything.

I stood and stormed toward him, my large nose only a few inches below his chest.

Hector backed up. "Okay, I see that you don't agree. I'm simply trying to help you." His shoulders sank.

My stomach rumbled at the scent of saffron as Hector stirred our dinner. For a moment, I watched the tent where Talia slept. Had I heard a rustle of fabric from within?

"She is only mortal." Hector approached me, sensing my turmoil.

The dull knife of regret I carried inside me at all times twisted. I hated mortals. For they were utterly powerless and yet had the capacity to walk about on two legs every day. To sup with friends. To drink *coffee* as the sun came up.

With a growl, I swiped my massive paw across the earth, spraying the campsite with dirt. Long claw marks stood out on the ground in the last of the sun's rays.

"Rafael, this is your freedom we're talking about." He squatted right in front of me. "You can't toss out this dream because the wording of some vow was tricky. You're smarter than that." He smiled and tapped the side of his head.

Dismissing him, I walked back to the simmering pot over the campfire. He was right in one aspect. The vow was broad enough that it didn't shackle my original intent. My claws sank into the soft earth a moment before I collapsed to my furry belly.

But I couldn't kill her. Last night, I'd vowed to protect her, and as I'd spoken those words, I'd wanted to uphold them. I'd wanted to protect her from the aches I felt every day from living in two different bodies. From the anger I knew when people cringed away from me. From the agony of the change. From the screams of lovers who learned the truth.

To pour my curse upon her, to let her soft, warm skin rip apart into coarse bear hide would free me from my long-suffered curse. For the one cure my twisted brother had worked in was true love—something he assumed would be impossible for me.

A simple exchange, I'd thought. One last attempt to free myself, for all my attempts before had failed. But I'd seen in Talia Balcázar a woman not afraid, and I'd snatched at that trait like a fish to a fly. Perchance, I'd thought, she would not be afraid of me.

Now I felt as if my black heart had rotted straight through, like a dead log left too long on the forest floor. Talia may be mortal, but she did not deserve this. I buried my snout under my paws—paws that would become permanent if I failed to break this curse.

At that moment, the sun slipped beneath the horizon, and my entire body bucked with the start of the change.

12

TALIA

A strange sound outside the tent startled me awake. Something large was snuffling on the other side of the canvas.

Staying perfectly still, I stared up at the folds of the mosquito net with wide eyes, every hair on my arms bristling while my heart stomped as though it was a flamenco dancer.

It was still daytime, but the light was thinner, angling in from near the horizon, silhouetting the large creature against the canvas.

Sweat broke out all over my body as I watched the massive shape amble by. All I could detect were shoulders and a long back. The animal's head was down, as if on the prowl, and the light was too low and mottled from the trees to determine exactly what creature this was.

And based on my encounter with the Wild Hunt and my hasty marriage to a fabled fae, my mind spiraled quickly into the worst possible options.

I laid perfectly still, taking shallow breaths and gripping the sheets in tight fists, until the animal moved away from the tent. A low voice sounded nearby—it might have been Hector's, but I couldn't tell.

The sound of a crackling fire and of sizzling oil comforted me. The lovely smell of saffron and herbs wafted through the canvas.

My stomach rumbled. The last time I had eaten was dinner at Zara's ball, a full day ago.

I glanced to both sides of the tent, searching and listening for any hint of the large creature. My fear was quickly overtaken by my hunger, and I rolled out of the bed, my feet sinking to the plush rug.

Hector's voice carried through the canvas. "She is only mortal."

Rafael must have returned while I slept.

A low growl raised every hair on my arms and neck. I froze. The animal was still out there. I stood completely still, hands clutched to my chest, heart beating madly, until the thin orange light filtering through the tent faded into darkness.

"Dinner is ready," Hector called out. I wasn't sure how long I'd been standing there.

I glanced at the lovely blue dress laid across a chair, my fingers brushing the soft fabric once again, then sighed and reached for the breeches.

When I stepped out of the tent, my stomach growled eagerly.

Before me stood a long table with eight highbacked chairs. Two tall, silver candelabras glistened under flickering light.

Lounging in the head seat, feet propped on the table, was my mislaid husband. His chin lolled against his chest, and his eyes were closed. He wore another crisp suit, this one pale as sand, that contrasted with his dark skin.

For a moment, I stared at him. His dark hair was damp, as if he'd recently bathed, and while most of it was slicked back, a few strands had fallen loose and hung limply against his cheeks. The shadow of a beard hugged his chin.

I hadn't realized I'd moved closer until I bumped the chair nearest to him with my toe.

His eyes fluttered open and locked with mine.

I turned away, searching the clearing for the army of servants that would have been needed to assemble all this. But there was no one else except Hector, who was bent over a cookstove.

Hector glanced up from his work, a quick smile flashed as he stood.

"Have a seat, Señora Romero." He lifted a hand toward the chair beside Rafael. Across this one place setting was laid a white lily.

I pointedly avoided looking at my husband as I approached the table, but his gaze was heavy on me.

"Where did you go?" I asked, voice clipped.

He slowly dropped one foot then the other to the ground and stood. After a curt bow, he dropped back into his chair, kicked the side of the nearest chair so that it angled outward toward me, then sprawled into another wide-legged, relaxed slouch, like my presence here was as trivial as the birds'.

I pursed my lips and stepped down to the next chair. When I took a seat, I daintily realigning the chair beside me. Rafael *hmphed.*

"Who else is coming?" I asked, reaching for the already filled wine glass from the adjacent place setting.

"It's just you and me," he said with a small smirk.

I glanced at Hector, both brows rising. "And him, I presume?"

Hector chuckled and brought two steaming plates toward the table. "This is your first meal as a married couple. I will not interfere." His tone sharpened as he aimed his last words at Rafael, almost like a warning to a child to behave.

Before I could think of a response, Hector bowed and slipped away through the darkening trees. The last gold tones of the sunset were glowing on the western horizon, and a strong breeze batted the thin candle flames.

Though my mouth watered, I kept my hands in my lap and stared fixedly at the dancing light of the candle. Finally I drew a deep breath and glanced at Rafael, unable to subdue the flush that blazed up my neck.

He read my gaze plainly, and for a moment, his flat expression was quickly replaced with a flash of what might have been forced politeness. "Hello, Talia," he said, voice devoid of warmth.

I nodded demurely, hating that this was how my marriage was starting out.

To sever the awkwardness, I picked up my fork. The fish, decorated with a sprig of thyme and wedge of lemon, smelled heavenly. A question erupted from my throat.

"Why did you marry me?"

His fingers stiffened around the stem of his wine glass. After an agonizing moment of silence, he placed his glass down and began eating.

The longer we ate in silence, the deeper I sank into myself.

Before my courage entirely ran out, I added, "Will this be the kind of marriage where we do not speak unless we talk of things that interest you?" At dances, I'd heard young women complain of marriages like this.

His eyes snapped up. He set his fork down and leaned back, studying me.

"Will you speak at all?" I asked, not hiding the anger in my voice. At least anger was better than the ache growing in my throat.

"What shall we speak of?"

"I...er..." I squirmed as he blinked at me. "Your horses."

One side of his lips twitched up, and a rush of heat flooded my cheeks. To hide my blush, I shoved a bite of food into my mouth.

"What do you want to know?"

The openness of that question was unexpected. Perhaps he would allow me to speak, to ask questions. Shoving down the excitement in my chest, I thought about everything I wanted to know. Did he use magic to train his horses? That might sound rude. What races had his horses won? That also might sound rude.

In the distance, the sound of a tree cracking startled me. The wind wasn't blowing *that* hard, but perhaps a dead tree had finally fallen. He whirled around briefly, only to refocus on me just as quickly.

He took a careful bite, his expression clearly awaiting my response. Questions raced in my mind, and with a jolt, I realized the midsummer race was now hours in the past.

"Who won?" I spluttered. "At midsummer? Did your horse win?"

Rafael slowly took a sip of wine, torturing me. "Indeed. I watched the race."

"You were there?" Jealousy bit at my tone.

"No one saw me. And I assure you, it was better that you were not."

My heart sank. I picked up my own wine glass, hoping he didn't notice my obvious deflation at his dismissive words.

"But my horse did win, yes."

I pressed my eyes shut, picturing my parents embracing. My heart ached that I wasn't there to celebrate with them. But they wouldn't even be celebrating if I hadn't come here, with him.

"Your father is now a very wealthy man."

A sigh escaped my lips. It was worth it. Ensuring my parents' futures for a loveless marriage was a price I was willing to pay. That's what I'd agreed to in that snap decision in the marketplace.

The food, while divine, disturbed my uneasy stomach, and the creeping regret was mitigated by the knowledge that I'd saved my parents. And Ortiz could rot in the sun for what he'd tried to do to my family.

Neither of us reopened the subject of his horses, so as we ate, we exchanged only silent glances. His expression revealed very little. This immortal was entirely in control of what he showed to others, and he had determined, it seemed, to show me nothing at all of his true self. Each time our eyes met, I had the unsettling idea that he could read every thought inside my head.

"Listen," Rafael hissed, his finger shooting into the air, though I hadn't said anything in several minutes. He scanned the clearing, his body tense.

My heart hammered in my chest, but all I could hear was the breeze rustling the branches of the nearby trees. Memories of the large creature outside the tent filled my mind.

"Return to the tent," he commanded in a low voice. "Now."

The breeze picked up, pushing the single white lily off the table. The faintest hint of a growl carried on the wind.

13

TALIA

Though the ground was entirely flat, my feet still found things to trip over in my haste to flee to the tent. The second time I tripped, I went all the way to my knees, my hand scraping against the small pebbles in the dirt.

An arm scooped under my shoulder and lifted.

Rafael urged me forward, all the while staring at something behind us. "Get inside," he warned, body tensed for a fight. In his right hand was a jeweled dagger hilt.

I scurried into the tent, but as I slid between the canvas, I cast a glance back at Rafael as a massive wolf emerged with a rider on its back. Its rider lifted a blade over his head and let out a growling battle cry. I screamed.

Rafael hurled his dagger. The fae rider cursed and gripped his shoulder, his sword clattering to the ground.

My eyes widened in admiration. Rafael, now weaponless, stood eerily straight and still for a man facing a monster. He then lifted his hand.

I clutched the canvas over half my face, and watched with

held breath as Rafael lifted a hand toward the wolf. It was the same movement I'd seen my father use countless times with unbroken horses.

The wolf slowed, closed his frothing mouth, and sat down.

The rider screamed in rage as he lost his balance and fell to the ground.

In seconds, Rafael stood above the cloaked rider, holding a tiny blade I did not see him procure. He squatted down and pinned the man's cloak into the ground with the tip of this small knife.

The wolf, meanwhile, sat with his tongue lolling to one side of his mouth, breathing fast and looking more like an oversized than the fierce creature it was just moments ago.

The man on the ground writhed and cursed. "So you can tame them all now?" He thrased out, but Rafael stepped casually out of the way. "Just not the beast within, eh?"

Rafael kicked the man in the ribs.

Hector ran onto the scene, thin sword in his hand. He raced to the fallen rider, stepping between them. He held the blade to the rider's throat.

Rafael looked at the wolf, spoke another soft command I couldn't quite hear, and then it bolted from the clearing into the night.

Then, to my horror, Hector stepped aside, allowed Rafael to rip his knife from the earth, and the two men stepped away from the rider. The rider scrambled up, but both Rafael and Hector trained their blades on him.

"Go," Hector commanded.

The man in the black and yellow robes dissolved in a shimmering column of smoke. I yelped and cupped my hand to my mouth. Rafael turned and walked toward me. He gently tugged the canvas from my clenched fist and let himself into the tent, edging around me close enough that I could feel his heat.

I followed until I stood staring at him inside the tent. Alone.

"The Hunter tracked your scent." His eyes darted toward the unmade bed. "You should have kept the flower."

Walking over to a vase holding a bouquet of the white lilies, like the one he had offered me in Puerta. He pulled one out and smelled it. "They mask our scent from the Hunt."

I frowned. "If you'd mentioned that, I would have kept it."

Ignoring my comment, he added, "Fortunately, he came alone. If he'd had another Hunter with him, our only course would have been to run."

"But you tamed that wolf so easily." I took an involuntary step toward him.

He stuck the flower back in the vase and turned narrow eyes on me. "What appears easy to you came at a great price."

The edge to his voice stopped me in my tracks. I'd thought of him as safe, but this man was dangerous too. Only, for some reason, he'd chosen to protect me. I was unaware he'd moved toward me—or maybe I'd stepped closer too?—until he spoke, startling me from my near trance.

"We must leave. He will return. When he does, he will not be alone."

RAFAEL

We rode away from the camp not ten minutes later, Talia clinging to my waist like a scared cat.

"What about all your things?" she asked over my shoulder.

"They will be where we need them before we arrive."

She harumphed. A sound that brought a smile to my face.

I choked on my next breath. The emptiness inside me, vast as it was, found a little more of my soul to rip. The sensation of her small arms around me was entirely too wonderful, too necessary. I let myself relish the feeling for several breaths, as if we might possibly find happiness, before coming to my senses and releasing her hand with a grunt.

She loosened her grip, clutching the cantle of the saddle instead of my waist. The gesture was pronounced—she didn't want to hold on to me—and a little more of my sanity slipped quietly into the breeze as we cantered away from the campsite.

I whispered to Lily, pulling the only magic now left to me after calming that wolf, and she accelerated into a gallop.

The road was empty, our progress unhindered as we thundered across Avencia's southern plains toward the border of my homelands. Hector rode beside us.

Every few breaths, I muttered again to Lily, and to Hector's horse too, the words that would carry us over these flats faster than their natural gait. The horses drank in my quiet commands and pushed harder.

"Sorry, girl," I muttered after one such command. At least she couldn't feel any pain or discomfort as long as my magic carried her. It was after that her exhaustion would catch up.

As we reached the mare's top speed, Talia again had to grip my waist. At first, her touch was tentative, then as we banked into a wide turn along the riverbank, her arms latched tightly around me.

Fear was a potent smell only animals could detect, but I'd trained my nose to identify it even in this form. Her own fear was subsiding as she rested against my back. I closed my eyes briefly in shame.

This was exactly what I'd wanted when I'd fixed on her as my healer.

And yet...

If my hope of healing came to pass, this fragile dove clinging to me for life would surely die. And somehow, the feeling of her small body against mine pricked me with regret. I ground my teeth and ignored the feeling, instead simply drinking deep the intoxicating knowledge that she felt safe with me.

We soon left the large road behind, tearing out across a field toward where the river tucked into a small ravine. For now, the horses were outpacing the Hunters, but not far behind us, their trails of dust lifted into the dark night.

It cost to enter through these gates, a price I had grown

accustomed to paying, but I feared for the woman behind me. Mortals rarely crossed into our lands, and even rarer still through the hanging gates—the entrances reserved for those exiled by their courts. Their maps didn't know where these entrances were and their minds couldn't handle pain the way ours could.

With the Hunters on our tail, we had no choice.

Only at the top of the ravine did I slow our pace. Hector was beside us in seconds. The horses breathed hard, but not as hard as they would when the magic left them. Talia lifted her chin and peered around me.

"Where are we?" she asked. Her muscles finally had a moment to relax.

If only she knew what was about to happen, she wouldn't relax at all.

"At the entrance to the fae lands."

She let out a surprised sound.

Hector caught my eye and lifted his brows. I offered him a faint nod, confirming his unspoken question. *Yes, I will protect her.*

His sadness rolled off him like waves at the seashore, and swirling in its depths was seething anger. He'd traveled this world by my side for over two centuries. My pain had caused him vast suffering also, and he wanted to see me healed more than any other living being. He turned toward the river.

"The way through is...not easy," I said over my shoulder. I didn't realize I'd pressed my hand to hers again until she wriggled it free.

"What do you mean?"

Hector cleared his throat.

"It's hard to explain, but you must do as I say. Don't open your eyes, whatever you do, until I tell you we're through."

When her arms once more looped around me, I coughed and, to divert my mind from how fast her heart beat against me, I clicked my tongue in my cheek and urged Lily forward.

Hector followed. With a final reminder to keep her eyes closed, we charged toward the ravine. A slight wavering in the air rushed up and then around us, and then the ground vanished beneath us.

Talia screamed and pressed the wind from my lungs.

"Eyes closed!" I shouted. "It's about to get worse."

Lily whinnied and raced on, over nothing but swirling mists that curled around her hooves, toward an imposing gate with grass and roots hanging down from its two massive stone pillars.

Talia clawed at me, her chin grinding against my spine.

Before us, hanging from twin ropes suspended from the gate and gently spinning, were her mother and father, lifeless and blue.

Her body tipped sideways, limp with shock.

Reaching backward, I stopped her fall. "Stay with me. It isn't real."

Her whimper told me she didn't believe me. I shook my head and held her tightly to me, as best I could this way. One of her arms looped around mine and clung like a squirrel to a branch.

My twin's face stared at me from the other side of the hanging gate, a glistening crown on his head. I'd learned to ignore his specter, but this was the first time I'd seen him in the crown he was to inherit at the end of the month. Beside him, to my shock, stood Talia, dressed in an exquisite yellow gown. Covered in blood. My nightmares called out to me, but I shut my mind to their voices.

Talia shook so hard I envisioned her falling to the depths,

a place no mortal could return from. I might have been shaking too, but I quickly collected myself. If she saw my nightmares, she would see *herself*. Dead.

I whispered to Lily to slow to a walk. Talia didn't resist as I unhooked her hand from my shoulder and pulled it forward, twisting in the saddle to loop my other arm around her chest and drag her into my lap.

"Close your eyes," I whispered over her head.

She jostled against me and the horse's neck, but I held her tightly so that she did not fall. The world around us shone with bright stars and a waxing moon. Trees hovered over the abyss below, their clumps of roots dangling down toward the world below. The lights in their branches appeared as more stars. From one such floating tree, I saw Zara's body fall. The man from Puerta's market, Ortiz was his name, leaped over Zara's fallen body and raced toward us, a sneer on his shining face.

"I see your nightmares too," I said, unsure why I was stroking her arm with my thumb. "But that is all they are. Try to forget them."

She looked up at the place where Fabian's crowned visage stood beside her bloodied form. "Who is that?"

"Eyes!" I grumbled, lifting a hand to block her view. Had she seen the nightmare version of herself? I wasn't sure what that would do to a mortal's mind, or what she might think of me if she figured out it was *my* nightmares she was seeing along with her own.

With a small whimper, she pressed her back to my chest and turned her face away—her head fit perfectly under my chin. For a moment, I didn't breathe. My arms around her squeezed.

Hector reined his horse in beside Lily, their hooves

making no sound as they walked on air. He lifted his brows and glanced down at Talia.

With a huff, I stared blankly through the gate as we walked under it. Fabian's face dissolved into shadow as I passed him. Talia's dead face continued to trace my movement, the nightmare form of her vanishing slower than the other images.

Not long after crossing under the gate, the real Talia's breaths evened out and her body relaxed, her head lolling against my collarbone. The gate vanished, and we were once again walking on solid ground. A quiet mist swirled at the horse's hooves, and mushrooms the size of oaks lined the road.

"Shadow lords are out tonight," Hector said, nodding up at the sky.

Twin dragon figures flew high above, silhouetted against the moon's light.

My skin prickled, and I tucked my arms more firmly around Talia. "Perhaps they're here to torment some other cursed soul."

Hector glanced behind us. "One can hope." When he looked again at us, he asked, "Can you outrun them with her like that?"

"The Hunt or the Shadow lords?"

"Either."

I inhaled sharply to reply, but her citrus scent momentarily stole my thoughts.

Hector shook his head. "Remember why you married her."

My head tilted down, and her wind-blown hair tickled my lips.

"Rafael, time is nearly up." Hector jerked his chin at the moon above, which was almost full. "If there were another way, we'd have done it long ago," he continued, leaning forward slightly in the saddle. "You must do this. In a thousand years, what will her life be to you?"

I swallowed. "If in a thousand years, I'm a free man, her life will have meant everything to me."

TALIA

When I awoke, I was lying in a massive bed with posts made of the trunks of living aspen trees. A canopy of green leaves mottled the sunlight now pouring down through a domed glass ceiling. I pushed back the blanket, startled to find it was woven entirely out of rose petals. The petals were browning at the edges.

A bee buzzed lazily along the blanket until it saw me watching. It zipped away, drawing my eye toward the walls. I sat up, rubbing my eyes. One entire wall appeared to be made of a bee hive. I cringed and clutched the blanket to my face. Jars of honey sat on every surface. But the honey in the jar nearest me on the bedside table had crystalized. Upon inspection, every jar I could see had cloudy, forgotten honey in it. The beehive itself appeared nearly abandoned, save for one small corner still crawling with insects.

I crawled carefully out of the bed, keeping my eyes on the bees. Not until I'd walked to the edge of the bed did I note the breeze on my face. The enormous floor-to-ceiling windows facing the bed were not windows at all. No glass covered the spaces that overlooked a wild garden.

Greenery, untrimmed and half-eaten by caterpillars, stretched in all directions. Flowers of every color exploded from bushes and vines, left to their whims to take over what they pleased. The result was both madness and beauty.

Rolling hills of green suggested vineyards beyond. They looked so much like the vineyards surrounding Leor that my heart stung a little. Thinking of home brought back memories of the nightmares.

Visions of my parents, hung like criminals, danced before my eyes. I slapped my hands over my face, desperate to rid myself of these memories.

Another image filled my mind. I thought I'd seen myself, covered in blood, wearing a ballgown.

Rafael had said the images were not real. Only nightmares. The way he'd held me, whispering away my fears, had made my heart stumble in my chest.

But when he'd thought I was asleep, he and Hector had said things that had chilled my very blood.

Remember why you married her.

If there were another way, we'd have done it long ago.

He'd married me for some ulterior motive, that much I'd gathered, considering marriage had been his bargain. I glanced around the room, trying to anchor myself to this strange new place. My riding jacket lay neatly over the back of a tall chair. My boots flopped sideways in front of a cold hearth large enough for me to walk through.

Her life will have meant everything.

At this memory, my breath caught as I continued my exploration of the room. Books lay scattered on a low table and stacked on the rug. A rabbit nibbled the corner of one book, its nose twitching as it stopped to look up at me.

When I lifted my brows at the little brown creature, it bounded away, through the open wall into the garden.

Racing after it, I crossed the room, barefoot, until I stood in the angled sunlight at the edge of a paved garden path that had long since been taken over by weeds.

Three small steps led out from the bedroom floor to the grassy space. The stories always painted the fae as architects of nature, but this man I'd married seemed to have lost his touch. I stepped into the full sun, scanning the grounds for signs of Rafael. Birds startled from a nearby tree. The tree reminded me cruelly of the part of my nightmare where Zara had fallen to her death.

Nothing would stop me from running straight out of this house. But I'd made a bargain, and I'd heard Rafael and Hector speaking of something called Shadow lords, which sounded more ominous than the Wild Hunt.

"Good afternoon."

I yelped and stumbled forward, only to step on a grass burr and yelp again.

A woman stared at me with a small, amused smile curling her lips. Her skin shimmered strangely, as if coated in luminescent powder. Blond hair looped around her head and spilled down her shoulders in symmetrical waves. As she walked toward me, her blue dress rippled like it was made of the lightest silk. The neckline was loose and carefree, almost like an undergarment, though it was studded with jewels.

"Hello," she said, a slight accent touching the word. She inclined her head in a polite manner. "He said he'd brought home a wife."

Me. That would be me.

My lips fumbled a few syllables and I tugged at my wrinkled shirt hem.

This female fae offered me a warm smile. "My name is Everence. I am Rafael's cousin."

"Where is he?" I blurted, then flinched at my rudeness.

Recovering my dignity, I dropped into a curtsy. "My apologies. It is a pleasure to meet you. I am Talia. I am somewhat muddled after our journey here." I dropped my gaze to my bare feet.

"He said you were so strong, though!"

I blinked and looked up at her. "Strong? He cradled me like a babe as I'd wept."

She stepped into the sunlight and extended an arm behind my back. "Come, let me show you the house. The cooks are preparing you a feast, and then I'll show you the stables."

A little while later, as Everence led me around a part of the garden veritably taken over by an unruly wisteria vine, I caught sight of Rafael's stables, and my lips parted. If Zara's family's stables were a manor house compared to my father's humble barn, the stables at Starfell were the royal palace.

Ahead sprawled a wide, immaculate structure. Two aisles, four rows of large stalls. The roof was comprised of tightly woven branches of living trees that supported the outer walls. There was no leaf out of place or unwanted weed here. Ringed paddocks stretched out beyond the barn, followed by verdant pasture. Horses grazed in the sun in the distance, and one magnificent black creature stomped around in the nearest paddock, his mane shining like spilled ink.

"Oh," I breathed, unable to contain my smile. Papa would love this place.

The fae woman stepped politely aside and watched me with keen eyes as I drank in these heavenly stables. Tucked between two distant pastures was another enormous structure that resembled a stable.

"Are there more horses over there?" There were already more stalls in this barn than I'd ever seen in one place.

Everence bit her thin lips hastily. "Not horses, no."

I both itched to know and couldn't bring myself to ask what was housed in that huge barn.

She took my arm and led me into the horse stable. It smelled like home, the sweet scent of oats and hay bringing a sad smile to my face.

"Starfell is...somewhat of a refuge," Everence said, her tone careful. "Rafael never closes his doors to ones in great need. But as such, the grounds are not a safe place for you to wander alone. At least not in that direction. The inhabitants of that barn know not to come near the horses, so you should be fine coming and going from here."

A shiver of unease raced down my spine, wondering what sort of thing that lived in a barn, could also know where it was allowed to roam.

"What does Rafael do during the days?" I asked.

Everence's smile dimmed briefly. "He must be the one to tell you, I'm afraid." At my disappointed expression, she caught my arm. "There are many fae who disapprove of humans as...spouses. You must never go looking for him, and you must never leave the grounds unaccompanied. Promise me."

Brows lifted, I coughed out an agreement. Do not wander

alone. Do not look for your absent husband. Do not leave the estate.

Running away juts got trickier.

"What *am* I to do here?" I croaked out.

The woman at my elbow turned her ice blue eyes at me. She looked much more like Hector than Rafael. Her cheekbones glittered slightly, and her overlong eyelashes billowed like ribbons in the breeze every time she blinked. It was lovely but slightly distracting.

"You have a great purpose here. But it is up to you to discover it on your own. Nothing in the house is off limits to you. It is vast and full of secrets to learn and books to read. The horses are yours as much as his, and there is a lake back that direction which provides one with ample places to relax or watch the pixies at play."

"Pixies?"

Everence laughed. "They are quite beautiful when they think no one is watching them." In a whisper, she added, "You must never let them see you. For if they do, they will turn into the worst pests you've ever known."

As we walked the length of the left hand side of the stable, I thought over her words. "Hector is one of the fae who hates humans, isn't he?"

She laughed. It sounded like a summer brook. "He has more compassion than is quite normal for many of the high fae." She touched her lips with her fingers. "Hector has stood by Rafael's side when no one else did. Not even me."

A shadow ghosted over her face and she turned toward the stalls.

She hadn't answered my question.

She pointed out the stall for Rafael's favorite riding horse, Lily, and for his most prized stallion, Espera. With a heavy sigh, she kissed the nameplate marking Espera's stall. His full name was *La Espera Fue Larga*, the wait was long.

I cocked my head at both his unusual name and the woman's strange action. It was clear these fae loved their horses, which meant we had at least one thing in common.

Lily was in her stall, asleep. I recognized her as the horse who'd carried me away from my family to this place. The last time I'd seen her, she was galloping over thin air, past the very real vision of my dead family. The memory took me, and I cringed, slamming back against the wall.

Everence spun, eyes wide. "Everything all right?"

"I saw visions of my parents," I said, not including the fact that I'd seen myself in that nightmare too.

"The nightmares are crafted to hurt deeply. Rafael told me what you saw." At my shocked expression, she added, "Oh, yes, your nightmares are his own now. As his are yours."

There was something deeply significant in that statement. The fae vows had said we would share all things. This, apparently, meant our deepest fears. But I had no idea what his were. Then my head nodded in understanding—there had been a dark-haired man watching us from beside the hanging gate. He'd worn a tall, golden crown that glowed faintly.

I nodded at her, recovering myself. "I apologize."

"No need. "I have something that will cheer you up."

Following her out into the sunlight once more, we approached the paddock where the black horse pranced. She beamed as she lifted a hand toward the horse.

"This is Espera. Fastest horse in the world."

My mouth dropped open in a very unladylike fashion. "But…"

Everence's laugh was contagious, and soon I was laughing

too, mostly to cover my astonishment at such a preposterous claim.

"He was born here at Starfell three and half years ago. Rafael trained him harder than he's ever trained a horse. Watching them race together is pure joy."

I shook my head. "Rafael *races*?"

She kept her eyes on Espera. "Here mostly. As part of training. We have a track in that direction. Espera lights the sand on fire when he races with Rafael."

An incredulous cough burst out, and I could do little to cover it up.

" Ask him to show you one day." Her eyes lit with a spark. "Better yet, ask to race him."

"Interesting name for a racehorse," I mused, watching the stallion stomp the earth.

The blond woman inhaled slowly before answering. "It would surprise you how fitting his name is, once you understand Rafael."

"If he ever stops disappearing," I muttered under my breath. But Everence heard me. She snapped hard eyes at me, the most severe expression I'd seen on her face so far. But then she went back to pointing out and naming the different horses.

We watched them for some time and spoke of races we'd witnessed. It felt so normal, and yet the talk of races pricked in me a longing for home. I'd missed the biggest race of my father's career, though, arguably, it hadn't been *the* race we'd all prepared for. Everence pointed out each animal by name, and I heard in her tender tone the admiration she held for the horses.

"Do you ride?" I asked, already thinking of ways to spend

my days at this enormous fae estate that I wasn't supposed to leave.

To my surprise, she shook her head. "Oh, not unless I'm traveling a long way. And only then, when I can have one of Rafael's horses. He doesn't part with them easily, you see." She grinned. "I prefer to admire them from afar. Beautiful creatures."

"Oh," was all I said as my shoulders sank.

Sensing my disappointment, she added, "I love them so because of what they've done for my cousin. When he came into horse training, he was in a very dark place. The animals restored his joy."

Part of me wanted to know what she meant, and part of me just wanted to escape from this place and never wonder about these fae again. Breaking my vow would mean death, but what if I just ran away? I *did* marry him. That part was done.

By the time we turned from the pasture to walk back through the barn, fireflies had begun to spark against the close of day. Several times, I had the distinct impression something was watching me from the trees bordering the pasture, but every time I scanned the shadowed woods, I saw nothing. Still, I couldn't shrug off the feeling of the Wild Hunt watching. Everence seemed perfectly at ease though, so I tried not to fear what lurked in the trees.

There was much to learn about Rivenmark, of its mysterious magics and courts and horses that could set the world ablaze. But above all that, my mind wandered ceaselessly back to Rafael. Why did he disappear in the day, and why—stars above—had he married me? That amber glow in his eyes, the one that I'd seen extinguish during our vows, was tied to his magic, I was certain. It had flared and then gone out like a snuffed candle when he'd married me. Perhaps I had unknowingly killed some part of him, and now he resented me for it.

"Everence," I said, turning back toward the stable. "Would it be all right if I took a ride just now? I'm not all that hungry, given the feast earlier."

She inclined her head. "Of course."

Following her back into the barn, a lightness entered my steps and a smile I couldn't shake lifted my spirits.

RAFAEL

My heart stumbled in my chest as Talia rode out of the barn on Alegria. The way she held herself in the saddle, the tight smile on her face, drew me forward, out of the cover of the trees. I traced her movement until she cantered out of sight.

A strange prick of emptiness stabbed at me when I lost sight of her.

Her body had felt so small in my arms. The memory of her sleeping face, peaceful though streaked with tears, plagued my mind as I lumbered on all fours in the thick woods along the edge of my estate. Here the sunlight was less burdensome to my eyes, the heat less oppressive to my furry hide.

Outside the cave I'd made livable with my brother's help, I sat on the shade-cooled earth and sniffed the air. No whiffs of Hunters on the breeze today. Only the scent of my horses, so much stronger to my animal nose.

I thought of the stallion that had passed through my hands in Puerta de los Reyes. A creature with great potential, if only he'd had time to learn to hear the magic that I could sing to him. But he was too old to learn such things, and thus of no use to me. He'd go on to win his new owner some fortune, certainly, but he would never match the horses from Starfell, my horses.

I always hated to part with any of my animals, especially to a mortal, which was why so few could afford them. Talia's father, who now possessed a Starfell stallion, had indeed paid dearly, though even he did not know how dearly.

A small sapling had sprouted up near the entrance to my cave. I swiped it from the ground with my paw, spraying the entrance with dirt.

Talia Balcázar had endured the passing into Rivenmark better than I'd ever imagined.

Facing nightmares had shredded many a mortal's sanity. It had done so to countless humans who'd crossed through the hanging gates. But Talia's screams still echoed in my head, and I wanted to rip everything from the world that would cause her to ever make that sound again.

Wandering into the cool darkness of my cave, I tried to see my bride as nothing more than one of the mortals I'd come to hate. Flecks of flesh tossed out by the First and Last as little mockeries of my existence. They bloomed and died as fast as flowers, but were not nearly as pretty or as sweet smelling. They bled and stank and never, even on their worst days, had to wander on clawed paws and sleep in caves. But they loved like no other creature I'd ever encountered.

The darkness of the cave had its immediate effect, lulling me to sleep. For a brief moment, I fought the natural instinct to sleep away the day, but soon my willpower gave out.

I awoke to the sound of my brother's voice.

"You cannot hide from her."

Hector strolled in, hands behind his back, illuminated by the fading light behind him. "She rode to the border of the estate."

I leapt to my feet.

"Calm down." Hector chuckled softly. "She's sitting by the lake. And before you ask, no one escaped to go after her. Yet."

I huffed out a loud breath through my long nose and walked to the cave entrance, sniffing the air and glancing at the cloudy western sky.

"She likely won't try to go any further tonight. It's nearly dark."

My eyes narrowed, and Hector lifted his hands.

"Save your words. If it would make you feel better, I can go and collect her."

A low growl rumbled in my throat. I ambled back into the cave, toward the tunnel that led farther into the earth. Hector crossed his arms.

"I thought she might try to run."

I turned to glare at my brother.

"But she didn't. You've found an honest mortal. I salute you. You could cast off this form forever."

His words taunted every fragment of my soul, and I hated myself for wanting to run toward that hope, even though it would cost too dear a price. That was the price my twin had crafted when he'd set my curse.

Make a mortal fall in love with you, and only then can your curse lift, he had said. *But mortals are prideful and fickle and driven by looks even more than our kind. Who would fall in love with your hideous hide?*

Turning away from Hector, my younger brother, the one

who'd stood by my side after what Fabian had done, I walked deeper into the tunnel. He followed dutifully, still stringing out his arguments.

"If this world doesn't kill her, Fabian will. We both know word will reach him of her presence sooner rather than later. It doesn't leave you much time."

My massive head drooped down with his every word.

When we entered the broad cavern at the end of the tunnel, he leaned against the rock wall. "You destroyed her the moment you married her, whether she takes the curse or not. Might as well give it one last solid effort."

His reasons were all the ones I'd repeated back to myself a hundred years ago when I last tried to win the heart of a mortal. I'd never thought I'd try again, but a century has a way of disintegrating one's promises to oneself.

Cradling her in my arms had felt better than anything I'd done in my miserable existence.

Watching me pace, Hector exhaled slowly. "*Think* about it, Rafael. One girl. One month. She'd barely suffer. And you'd live out your immortality in your rightful place, with your full magic."

My claws bit at the stone floor. He meant well, but his words gnawed me from the inside. When he stepped forward, he placed a tentative hand on my massive shoulder.

"If you cannot resolve to do this, let her decide," he muttered.

I lifted my head.

"Do not hide yourself from her. Be her husband. Let her see you as you are. And let her decide. If she falls, you are free. If she does not, then in a month's time, we can return her to her family and then she will be free—and we can pray

Fabian ignores her existence." He lifted his brows in a knowing way.

His reasoning pulled at me. I wanted him to be right. But every woman who'd ever learned the truth about me had fled. Every last one.

Here was one more chance, perhaps my last.

Sensing my capitulation, Hector repeated, "She is nothing more than the sacrifice you need. Nothing more, brother. Send her on to the First and Last. Perhaps he even sent her to you to set you free."

My bones ached, and the amber color of my magic filled my vision briefly, as if the ancient power in my veins yearned to be let loose. *She* could set it free.

With a furious roar, I dismissed my younger brother to await the change. Magic and willpower twisted and warred within me as I desperately wanted to unleash the power I'd been born to but never fully known. In seconds, the change knocked my body to the floor.

My chin hit the stone, then my temple. I twisted, curled my knees in, as I'd learned to do, and shut down the part of my mind that registered pain.

For a minute after, I lay there, breathing hard. The clothes I'd worn last night still smelled faintly of citrus, from having held Talia so long. I'd not had time to change before sunrise. The few and constantly changing servants at Starfell were strictly forbidden from these tunnels, yet their scent plagued the place. For creatures, both mortal and fae, who claimed to be afraid of me, their curiosity proved I wasn't entirely horrifying.

Hopping up, I hurried toward the waterfall at the edge of the cavern, stripped off my clothes, and stood under the water until every vestige of animal had been scoured from my skin.

Only then did I don my best riding suit and stride toward the barn. *It is for her protection*, I had nearly convinced myself by the time I crossed the garden. *For she doesn't know the dangers that lurk on my property.* Or what awaited her should she cross out of my estate grounds.

Quiet footsteps on moss-covered stones alerted me to someone following me.

"Ah, Everence."

My cousin flashed a neat smile and bobbed a curtsey. Not necessary, but she never omitted manners, even to a beast.

Her silvery hair glowed in the quickly darkening night. She'd picked up a few nettles on her skirts, and a butterfly had discovered her braids and refused to quit them, like they might possess some sweet nectar yet.

"How is she?" I coughed to clear the roughness from my voice.

Everence's pale blue eyes traveled almost longingly toward the stables. "She is as strong as you said."

The unspoken reprimand landed heavy on my chest. I glanced at a rogue rose bush, all thorns and few blooms. Everence had a soft spot for mortals. "This is my last chance..."

"You brought her here to save yourself," she interrupted.

My mouth turned down. "Fabian ascends the throne at the close of the month."

My cousin's eyes narrowed but she did not look at me. "She doesn't deserve to die."

"But I deserve to remain forever a bear, robbed of my magic, and eventually stripped of my capacity to think as a man?"

Her face fell slightly, and she shook her head.

"Hector says to let her decide," I added.

"Hector would tell you anything to stop your pain. He's a good brother, but that doesn't make him a good man." Her ice blue eyes finally landed on me, heavier than anvils. "She *wants* to know you. If you go to her now, you are endangering her."

I slid both hands down my face, as if I could wash myself of my sins. But when I looked up, my angry cousin still stared at me. A gruff sigh escaped me. "Hope is poison, Ev. I drank it, and I reacted, just as Fabian planned."

"Do not shift the blame onto him," she snapped. "You saw an opportunity, and you took it."

Storming forward, I could no longer contain my buried rage, my shame. "And what? Is one mortal life of more value than my own? You would see me suffer eternally, when there is a possible end to my pain?" I recited Hector's words.

Already, the sting of those words gnawed at my senses, like a poison eating away at the edges of my sanity. Three hundred years of weaseling out a justification for my actions did not, in the end, suffice. My cousin said nothing, only she did not pull her eyes away from mine, and in her searching gaze, I heard every word of rebuke that ever had been spoken or ever would, as they played softly in my mind, the voices of a thousand demons reminding me what I was.

Not only a monster in the flesh, but also a monster in the heart. Precisely as Fabian had designed when he'd set this black curse upon me. Not a monster in full, but a monster in part, so that as time passed, *I* would create the other half of the beast. Willfully, terribly.

I broke her stare and looked up at the stars that so vividly mocked my curse. I could no more speak to my wife again than I could face a pool full of my own sins.

My voice came out in a rasping whisper. "She is here now, and I vowed to protect her. You know the creatures who wander here at night."

Her blue eyes softened. "Humans are gifted with their weakness, you know. They find out much sooner than we do that their flesh is insufficient."

"Yes, they rot almost as soon as they fully mature."

She scowled at me. "That's not what I mean."

"I don't need another of your lectures on humankind."

"I believe you do." She propped a fist on one hip, apparently not finished railing me for the evening. "Their weakness, dear cousin, is what makes them constantly searching for something stronger on which to lean. Be careful of the protection you grant, or else you'll look down and find her resting comfortably against *you*."

With a grunt of assent, I stormed away, visions of Talia's small body cradled against mine—my nightmare, my dream, all rolled into one. The Crossing had shown me this nightmare, and I had pulled my wife into my lap all the same, my desire only to push back the horrors torturing her mind.

My vow to protect her was going to make me kill her.

Fae didn't stomp, as it was in our nature to tread lightly everywhere we went, but as I stormed into the wide aisle of the horse stable, the very trees around me trembled at my steps.

Lily still needed to rest after the hard ride last night, so I bypassed her stall for another of my favorite horses. As I passed Espera's stall, I kissed my hand and tapped his nameplate with my fingers.

He looked up at me with a shining black eye.

"Not tonight, my friend."

Espera snorted and kicked the stall door. Several other horses whinnied their disapproval.

"Oh, is that right?" I pointed a finger at him. "You think you deserve a night ride? I've been gone three days. Three days."

In my head, a strange thought occurred to me. *She would love to see him run.*

And why did that matter?

I grasped the stall door and leaned my forehead against the wooden slats.

Protect her. Destroy her. The two motives were intwined so closely, as were the methods I would use to execute either. Handling a dove to keep it safe was as likely to harm it as it was to help it. And while I knew it was wrong to want to push off my heavy burden on her tiny body, I also knew that if given an easy chance, the temptation might win out in the end.

A soft muzzle bumped my knuckles. My face jerked upward at the touch, and a splinter slid into my forehead.

"For that, I will ride you, you insolent creature." I smiled at him. "I'll ride you till your hooves melt."

He knickered in triumphant delight.

The night air sailed through my hair, drying it out, as we cantered down the darkened lane. On this part of the estate, the woods were thick and the roads rarely used. Fireflies danced among the trees. There were no pixies in sight, which meant Talia had come this way. The little wily creatures preferred to cavort in private, and humans were entirely too loud to sneak up on a pixie.

Espera tossed his head as I slowed to a walk, but he obeyed. Silence clung to the otherwise jubilant forest. Even the cicadas and the frogs had ceased their songs. Humans had a way of turning nature off, and I felt her presence before I spotted her, sitting on a rock, knees drawn up, beside a saddled white horse.

She didn't notice me, her dull human senses allowing me ample time to watch her before she heard or saw me. A stag moved in the woods, deep to the left. I could only see him for a second, and then he was gone, but his spooked departure startled Talia, and she stood on the rock, eager to catch a glimpse of whatever had made that small rustle.

Her slender frame blended with the shadows in her dark riding attire, but the lack of light was no trouble for my eyes. I dismounted and with a quiet command ordered Espera to walk softly as we drew near. I was almost upon her before her head whipped around.

So violent was her movement that she lost her balance.

I moved without thinking, stretching my arms out to catch her, but she'd already steadied herself without my help. For a moment, I stared up at her, troubled at the way she peered into my eyes and completely unable to look away.

Finally, reason returned to me and I dropped my arms. "Monsters walk these woods at night. You should be more careful," I warned.

As she climbed down from the rock, her eyes darted around the dark forest. When she reached the forest floor, she stood too near.

I coughed and stepped backward. "It isn't safe here. I am not...safe for you."

Her mouth parted, and for several seconds she hesitated, a look of anger and defiance brewing on her face that said she was preparing to battle my every effort to push her away. There was no fear in this one. I would change that.

"You saved my parents from poverty, and me from a life of

ruin, which would certainly not be *safe* for me." Her hand reached out and touched my chest.

Stars and sun, it was torture not to wrap my own around her warm fingers and press my lips to her palm. *Stay your hand. Stay your wretched heart,* I commanded myself.

Fists formed at my sides. She noticed and quickly removed her hand. In that withdrawal, a world died.

Good. It was a world I could never have.

Talia pulled her eyes downward. "Everence mentioned that dangerous creatures lived here. But she said they stayed in that direction."

"They obey my commands, but never before has a human wandered these woods at night, alone. In our world, human blood is valuable for many things."

"Valuable?" She croaked out the word.

The fear in her eyes was exactly what I'd aimed for, and yet I hated it. Turning away from that fearful look, I pressed on, stepping over moss-covered stones. "Your blood is resistant to iron and, considering the amount of iron it contains, can be used as a weapon against us."

Talia clamped her hands around her forearms, perhaps thinking of the red blood pumping just under her skin.

"But the real reason you should be afraid is that human blood is the requirement to end many a fae curse."

As her eyes again scanned the forest, she sidestepped toward me, missing entirely what I was saying to her. My cousin's warning echoed in my head.

"Everence should have told you not to leave the starlight behind."

She glanced up at the thick trees. "How does the starlight help?"

There was much she didn't know. "Light has power. Sun,

moon, stars. We have delegates to see to these powers, courts for each source of power, you see. And—"

"Oh, I've heard of those," she interrupted. The corners of her lips formed perfect points when she smiled.

"Very good." I nodded, certain that whatever stories she'd heard included many half-truths, at best. Fae couldn't lie, but we could plant misconceptions and brew prejudices, especially among gullible humans, as was the delight of many a bored immortal I'd met along the way. "Shadows have their own power, a stolen power, a greedy one. It is not wise to venture into the shadows when danger is so nigh."

I scanned the sky for any signs of Shadow lords but saw none.

This time, she took a step away from me and grasped her horse's saddle. This was a much safer move, and I nodded my approval.

"You should return."

"You are not?"

The disappointment in her voice stung me.

"Rafael," she said, her voice cautious and perhaps louder than she'd intended, for she cringed almost as soon as she'd blurted my name. "Why did you marry me?"

I ground my teeth as I stared down at her. A thousand answers passed through my head, unable to fall from my lips, for each of them was a lie.

After too much silence, her gaze hardened. "What am I to do here?"

Sun above, for such a tiny human, she had grit. I needed to control myself, for her determined eyes were clawing my composure and my willpower into shreds.

"You may assist in training the horses, of course."

Her face lit like a struck match and I had to turn aside to

hide my smile. I climbed in the saddle, and Espera spun in an impatient circle. "Tomorrow, you will meet Javier, the head trainer."

I held Talia's gaze longer than I should have, then kicked Espera into a gallop.

TALIA

"Catch him," I whispered over thundering hooves, smiling at the simple pleasure of racing again.

I leaned into the canter, which quickly became a gallop, as I left the woods with Rafael riding just ahead of me. I urged Alegria faster, smirking as we pushed past Rafael and his prized stallion.

He cocked a half grin at me and whispered to his horse. In two strides, they were ahead. I wasn't going to let him win that easily. Every horse had more speed, if you knew how to ask. I tried Rafael's method and simply spoke to her.

The horse responded, opening up into what was surely her fastest speed. There was a subtle difference in the way it felt sitting atop a horse running fast and a horse racing to win.

My shrill, delighted laugh stole Rafael's attention as we pulled up beside him once again.

His fierce eyes flashed with mischief—and I nearly swooned out of my saddle. By the time I recovered, he was a length ahead, and *stars above* his horse's hooves were throwing sparks.

My gaping jaw snapped shut and I bit my tongue. The pain dissolved as I watched tiny fires explode along the ground with each hoofbeat. The pair of them were soon so far ahead, all I could see were orange flashes, like fireworks dancing down the path.

He rode all the way to the house without stopping and disappeared from view. Disappointed that he'd left me alone, I slowed Alegria and walked her past the front of the house. I stared in wonder at the great edifice. *At my new* house. I hadn't yet seen the front from this distance, where I could take it all in at once.

The house sprawled rather than loomed, its pale gray walls reaching outward so far it was almost as if I was riding straight into its stony embrace. The front was half-covered in untrimmed ivy which drooped carelessly in some places and in others reached with greedy fingers toward unclaimed space. Each window was lit from within with a warm glow, save the lights of the entryway, which alone were dark and unwelcoming, as if the occupants were entirely at ease among themselves and wished for no one to intrude.

The following morning, my feet marched with a decided bounce, all the way to the stables. When I entered the shaded space, I breathed deeply.

Little bits of sunlight poked through the branches above, which waved slightly in a gentle breeze. Rafael seemed to have an aversion to ceilings, like he wanted to be able to see the sky at all times. I wondered what happened when it rained, or if there was some magic to keep this place dry.

Several horses slept in their stalls. Others glanced up at me. Espera was back in his stall, resting.

To Espera, I whispered, "He said he was dangerous. But you aren't afraid of him, are you?" Espera's black eye stared at me. "That was impressive last night."

At the end of the barn aisle, movement caught my eye. I spotted a familiar face and frowned.

Hector strolled lazily down the long aisle. "Good morning."

"Where is Rafael?"

"Unavailable."

I pinched my lips and turned back to stare angrily at Espera. "For how long?"

"You realize our experience with time is quite different from yours. To us, a month is nothing. A year, even, we barely note its passing."

Excellent. I changed the subject. "He told me I can assist in training the horses." I would not become one of the idle rich, sitting alone with a paintbrush in my unskilled hand or practicing the piano forte.

Hector clapped once, either because he thought my words hilarious or strikingly practical.

"Indeed." His tone was sharp but his expression bordered on approval. "You are rather confident for a woman of your breeding."

Was I a horse?

Hector smirked. "Let me introduce you to Javier."

My chin lifted as I followed Hector out of the stable into the back paddock, where a yearling cantered around on a lead line. In the center, holding the line and a lunge whip, was a dark-skinned man with a ponytail that reached his waist. He had a wide face, handsome and angular, and pointed fae ears. From the top of his ears to the bottom, delicate silver chains dangled.

He never once looked away from the horse circling him in elegant, quick strides. His body turned slowly around in the sandy space. His shoulders were wide and strong, but he was shorter even than me.

"Javi," Hector called out.

The man didn't look up.

"We have your new assistant."

The title pleased me immensely, a broad smile flashing across my face, even though his words suggested my role here wasn't as Rafael's wife but as this man's help.

Javier grunted and barked out in a raspy voice, "Come here."

Hector lifted a hand toward the man, and I jumped a little as I started forward. Already, I disliked this man's ordering me about, but I was more than pleased to have a role here that I actually wanted. Horses I understood.

I walked into the circle and stood right behind the man's shoulder, as was proper. I turned as he turned, acting as his shadow. Though I didn't know this man, I couldn't keep the smile from my face. This was familiar to me. He completed three circles before he held out the lunge line to me.

His expression was so hardened that I took the line without question and stepped into the place he'd been standing. Instinctively, I clicked my tongue in my cheek to urge the horse on. He never missed a beat, but continued cantering round and round. Javier crossed his arms and stood behind me a moment before backing up out of the circle entirely.

"Tell me how he moves," rasped Javier.

I wasn't certain what this man wanted, but I watched the horse a moment, studying his legs. My father had taught me to see potential in a racehorse by watching the length of his stride, the lift of his hooves, and the way he held his head.

The corners of my mouth turned up. "He stretches forward with each stride, like he aches to cover more ground than is physically possible. There is speed in him, but he hasn't learned how to tap into it yet, based on the way he's holding up his head and flicking his ears in annoyance. He knows it's there, and I think he doesn't like running in circles."

After I finished, no one spoke as the horse completed another loop. Then, a slow clap began behind me. As I spun, my eyes landed on the trainer as he applauded.

He walked forward, raising a hand to slow the animal. With a snap of his fingers, the horse stopped suddenly and snorted. Javier patted the horse's neck. "You speak with confidence. How you do know you are correct about Tinieblas, here?"

When it came to racehorses, speculation was everything. A fast dam didn't mean a fast foal, but it might, and a pedigree was important, but there were diamonds in the rough, too. What my father had made plain to me was that a horse would tell you what you needed to know. One had to make confident assertion in the world of racing if one was to have any luck at all.

"He told me," I said plainly.

Javier's quick eyes found mine, and they blazed with curiosity, with approval. Something about him seemed older, though there were no visible signs of aging on his perfect fae skin. He didn't have that air about him that most attractive young men I'd met carried with them everywhere they went, an air of wanting to be noticed. He held my gaze a moment, the faintest smile touching the corner of his lips.

"Mortals do not have the ability to speak to animals," he said, turning back to Tinieblas, aptly named for his jet-black coat.

"Fae do?" I blurted.

He snickered. "Some. Our powers vary greatly. Tinieblas here has told me many things, including that he did not speak to you at all."

I gaped at the horse. "You can talk?"

The horse tossed his head.

I might have been over excited to be training the world's fastest horses on my immortal husband's enormous estate, but I thought I heard a strange voice say *Only to those who listen.*

Blinking at the horse, I thought of my father. I'd seen Papa test the stable hands on their first day of work over the years. I tilted my head and stared at the dark yearling. "I understand him plainly enough."

Javier's shoulders lifted in a quiet chuckle. "You are right, mortal. But I am not certain you grasp the full extent of your own statement." His face dropped once more into hard lines and searching eyes. "For the one with whom you share all things has complete authority over these animals." Something about his word, paired with his sweeping gaze as it brushed over my shoulder in the direction of the *other* barn, suggested he meant more than the horses. "Compromise that, and we shall have a right nasty disaster on our hands."

With that comforting thought, he dismissed me to track down another black horse named Phantom way out in the back pasture. As I stepped through the tall grasses, I glanced at the other large barn in the distance, wondering what sort of creatures lived there, and how Rafael maintained his authority over these animals. Javier had been clear, the vows I'd taken really did grant me a share of all that was Rafael's. Even his magic. **so she inadvertently lets the monsters loose the night she hears the truth...

Three days passed without a single glimpse of Rafael. As the sun set, I strolled back from the stable, choosing a path through the garden I hadn't taken before. The stepping stones beneath my feet were cracked and worn, mottled with moss. A late afternoon rain, the first I'd seen of it in these lands, had left the grounds damp and cooler.

A large praying mantis, the size of a small dog, extended his legs toward me from beneath a thick hedge. I yelped and leaped aside.

Another voice yelped back.

A figure charged from below a vine-covered pergola just ahead and blasted past me, smacking my shoulder on the way by.

Eyes wide and breaths fast, I stared after what looked almost exactly like a tree fleeing.

A heavy sigh drew my attention back to the pergola.

Everence stepped out from beneath the shadowy space. As she moved, ice crystals spread to the plants nearest her. My brows shot up.

"She won't be back," said Everence with a disappointed frown.

"What was that?"

Her ice blue eyes flared with silver light, and I instinctively cringed away. "A dryad I had conscripted to work here."

When I didn't say anything for several seconds, Everence chuckled, her anger from a moment ago dissipating.

"A dryad is a tree fae. Occasionally I can convince them to work here, explaining that they will work alone and be well paid."

I blinked in confusion.

"They usually say yes when they see the state of the garden. But if they ever see—" Her words cut off abruptly. She shook her head. "They never stay long."

"I haven't seen any servants here, other than the ones who serve the meals."

Everence nodded. "Those are the alojas. They can shift into women for a few hours a day, and they are some of the most talented fae. Artists, chefs, architects. Even the high fae are not artists, despite all of our magic."

"None of you are artists?" Somehow, this was more shocking than a creature who was only part woman.

She lifted a hand and curled her palm in the air. A milky white sculpture of an owl appeared in thin air above her hand. "I needed no talent for this. Just an idea and a bit of magic. It isn't the same. And it is valueless." She handed it to me.

It was made of ice and it stung my skin. "It's beautiful, though."

Almost as soon as my fingers held it, the entire thing melted and my hands dripped with water.

"Not meant to last, though. The most powerful fae lack the magic of art. Mortals are the best artists. It's one reason fae sneak into your markets." She smiled at me.

I'd never thought of art as magic. "I'm no artist."

"I've seen you pulling the weeds. The path toward your

room is the loveliest part of this garden. And a garden is art as much as a painting."

"Can't you all work your magic on plants?" I'd heard plenty about fae and nature.

She waved a hand across a rose bush, covering it in thin frost. "Yes. But again, it isn't the same as putting in the time to make something lovely, the way you humans do. I'm constantly amazed at the way mortals pursue beauty through pain. It's fascinating." She turned toward me, eyes glowing faintly again, but the light was somehow softer this time. "You willingly accept a sore back and knees to pull weeds from the earth. A lifetime of painting ruins your eyes and years of writing with a quill hurts your hands. You punish your bodies to look stronger or thinner." She grasped my arm. "You care so deeply about what matters to you that you endure discomfort to pursue it. You even die for what you love. Humans amaze me."

Her hands were cold on my arm and a shiver raced down my spine.

"Not all fae think so," I said.

"No." She shook her head. "But few have spent as much time around your kind." She stared at me a long moment. "In this eternal summer, I long for the chill of winter, the magic of my mother's court. She was a duchess of the Shadow Court, sworn enemies of the Sun Court, but my father was the one who showed her how to make her magic useful for good. Theirs was an impossible love, and they moved into the mortal lands to escape my kind. I spent my childhood in the mortal lands, watching every soul I befriended and loved grow old and pass from this earth."

My eyes widened. Everence dropped my arm and walked

down the garden path. The stars were starting to peek through a clear purple sky as the light faded.

Over her shoulder, she said, "I grew tired of so much death, so I returned to this world. The Shadow Court is a terrible place, so I sought a home among my father's lands. He was brother to Rafael's father."

"Was?"

Everence's mouth hardened. "My father still lives in the mortal realm, but Rafael's twin brother murdered their father to take his power."

"Oh."

She continued, oblivious to the shock on my face. "When I learned of Rafael's fate, I came here. I do what I can to help him maintain the estate, but my magic is not as developed as most high fae, given I spent my first two centuries among mortals."

A cough burst from my lips. I kept forgetting how old these people were. Hector had said time passed differently for them, and he was right. My shoulders sank. "Does Rafael stay away for long periods of time?"

Everence turned toward me with a sad smile, full of pity. "He travels to buy or sell his horses and stays away sometimes only a matter of days, sometimes many months."

My shoulders fell, and I stared at the ground.

"However, tonight," she said, "you will likely find him in the library."

18

TALIA

The hallways of Starfell all looked so similar, devoid of decoration. I followed Everence's directions as best I could. I hadn't spent much time exploring the house, instead spending the past few days mostly outside, with the horses or wandering in the garden. When I found a stairwell with spindles carved to look like twining vines, I climbed.

The stairs creaked violently, as if rarely used, and there was dust on the banister. The second-floor landing was paneled with dark wood and the lights, fortunately, burned at all times in this enormous place, for I never met a hallway that was not lit by a dozen lights. Chandeliers, wall sconces, and candles set at intervals along thin tables brightened the bland hallways with a strange, empty cheeriness.

A pair of tall double doors looked like the ones Everence had described. They were ornate, inlaid with swirling ivory leaves and hammered gold vines. I stared at them a moment, admiring the workmanship. The handle opened easily, and I found myself standing on the second floor of a blazing, bright library.

So vast was this library that opened up beneath and above me that my jaw fell open as I took in the towering shelves, the balcony I stood on that wrapped around the entire space, the hearth on the ground floor the size of a small house, and, most surprising, the lack of any ceiling at all. The night air poured down around me. Stars spilled out over the inky sky like white sand on velvet. In the center of the room was a grove of aspens, straight as bed posts, and green with summer foliage, though a few branches were dead, devoid of any growth at all. Under them sat a pair of stone benches. Instead of a wooden floor, manicured green grass crisscrossed with stone paths carpeted the bottom level.

My gaping mouth lifted into a wide smile.

Zara would love this. Her father's library was one of her favorite places in her home. But there had to be thousands more books here. Soft chairs sat along the balcony, each with a burning candelabra beside them, as if waiting.

And yet, no one was here but me.

The place suddenly felt entirely eerie. It was odd for such a large room to be so well lit and yet be vacant. I walked along the balcony, avoiding the wide, sweeping stair that led to the ground floor. My hand along the balcony drew not a fleck of dust. The tomes were well kept, no cobwebs here. Someone was fastidious about this space.

My heart fluttered as my mind pictured Rafael emerging from the depths of one of these deep leather reading chairs. But he was nowhere in sight.

As I completed the loop around the balcony, dark gouges in the grass below drew my eye. Behind the grove of aspens, it looked like someone had ripped up the earth with a plow, but senselessly, without pattern or purpose.

I descended the stairs quickly, rushing to the grove of trees. On my knees, I touched the upturned earth. An animal had done this. The trees, too, had claw marks. Five slashes in neat little lines that sent shivers down my spine. These gashes were made by something savage.

"Who told you you could enter this place?"

I stood up so fast my head spun. Rafael descended the wide stair. He wore a slim black suit that shimmered faintly with iridescent threads, and his hair was slicked back and damp.

My heart tripped in my chest.

"Ev—Everence," I muttered, stepping backward.

Rafael looked aside. "Of course she did." His eyes flicked to the gouges in the ground, then quickly back to my face. "How is the training going?"

"Oh, fine!" The words spewed from my mouth. I bit my lips and hoped the blush flaring up my neck was beneath his notice.

The sides of his mouth curled up. "I'm pleased to hear it."

For a moment, neither of us spoke. A thousand comments stampeded through my head, but I tossed them all aside, trying to think of something better.

By the time the silence grew oppressive, he broke his stare and said, "I do not often allow anyone else in my library. However, as you are now part of this household, I suppose you are welcome to this space."

His words were cold, his posture businesslike, with hands clasped behind his back. I nodded. He swallowed.

Pointing to the claw marks, I asked, "What happened here?"

"Monsters live here," he replied casually.

"Oh." I paused. "But you'll keep me safe, won't you?"

He paused, then said, "That is my aim, yes."

He walked in an arc around me, glancing at me every other step. My pulse increased each time we made eye contact.

"I haven't seen any monsters yet."

He tilted his head back and laughed loudly. "I'm pleased to hear that too." Then he stopped walking and faced me. "Stars, Talia, what would you do, if you saw a monster?"

I couldn't answer, only stare. "Say it again."

"The curse?"

"My name."

His body lurched forward, then stopped. He was just outside the grove of aspens, the light from the library illuminating him on all sides. I stood beneath the shadow of the trees.

"What is holding you back? Is it because I am mortal?"

He closed his eyes. I stepped forward.

"No." When he opened his eyes, they widened briefly. "You should never have agreed to my bargain."

"When we crossed through that awful gate, I heard Hector say that you were running out of time. For what?"

His expression hardened. "You heard us."

"I heard you say that my life meant something to you. But you won't come near me." I stepped forward again.

"Talia." He lifted a hand and held my arm, preventing me from coming any closer. "You should go. At the end of the month, Hector will return you to your family. I would do it now, but as it stands, I cannot break my vow."

A gasp exploded from my lips. "What?"

"The reason I married you was foolish. I regret it now."

My shoulders fell and I clapped a hand over my still open mouth. Pain stabbed my chest as I choked out a sob. "You don't want me."

Rafael yelled an angry note and stormed toward me. Terrified, I stumbled backward until I bumped into a tree. To my shock, he wrapped both arms around me and pulled me to him. Confused, I swallowed my tears and let him hold me.

"If I could change things, I would," he muttered over my head. "I would rewrite the three hundred years of my existence to prevent you from feeling this way right now. You deserve nothing but happiness, and I stole that from you."

He pressed his lips to the top of my head, and with that gesture, I threw out all of his senseless words. I tilted my head back, forcing him to meet my eyes. His arms loosened their hold, but I didn't step away.

"You fear I am not happy here?"

A tremor shook him. "You must not be."

"Is that a command or a statement?" His lips were close enough to kiss. But he was going to be the one to do that, not me. My heart hammered so violently I knew he could feel it. When he didn't move, I whispered, "I chose this."

His hands moved from my arms to my face. His lips brushed against my cheek. "You have no idea what you chose."

He released my face and stepped back, one knuckle pressed to his mouth.

Chest heaving, I placed a hand to my cheek, as if I could keep his warmth there.

The library door burst open, and Hector rushed to the top of the stair. "Fabian must have heard. Someone from his court just arrived."

19

RAFAEL

I stormed through the dark entryway. Talia had fallen behind, unable to keep up. Tossing a glance over my shoulder for any signs of Talia, I threw my hand in the air and the lock exploded off the door handle and slid across the tile.

Hector cracked his knuckles. "Are you sure you want to let him in?"

I seethed as I stared at the floor. "No. But if I don't, he'll take her away."

"You speak like you still want her to fall in love with you," He replied in a low voice. "You cannot have it both ways, brother. Either she falls for you and dies when the first change tears apart her mortal body, or you make her hate you and thus offer her a chance to live out her paltry years."

My teeth ground together. "Talia Balcázar deserves better than what I chose for her. I can do nothing but attempt to protect her from the evils of our world until my curse is permanent and our bargain no longer valid."

Hector nodded. Behind me, footsteps announced Talia's arrival. My blood froze.

She scurried into the unlit entryway and stopped short. I stared into her eyes for a long moment, searching to see if she'd heard us. Her brows tilted up and her face was flushed from chasing me across the house.

"What's wrong?" she asked. "Who is here?"

I inhaled with relief. "My twin brother has sent someone to meet you. Don't worry, I won't let him hurt you."

With a nod to Hector, I lifted a hand and the doors swung open. As the cool air rushed out into the night ahead of us, I thought of all the ways I might destroy my brother, once I was confined to my bear form.

A grand carriage rolled up the long drive. Talia, descending the front steps behind me, let out a shocked laugh. Instead of four wheels, there were six, each as tall as a man on a horse, and its walls were not flat, but layered to look like unfurling flower petals. The entire thing emitted an ephemeral glow.

Hector shook his head. "That is the ugliest carriage I've ever seen."

Six horses, each winged, pulled the enormous coach.

From within the glowing golden flower emerged a man in a white suit. The trim of his sleeves and the long tails of his waistcoat glowed bright white. I frowned at the ridiculous display and took a small step in front of Talia.

"You arrived quickly," I said. No bows were exchanged.

The suited man looked around, ignoring me for a moment. "You got married," the man said, eyes snapping to Talia. "Without telling us."

"I am not obligated to tell my brother anything."

The man *tsked* and turned his attention on me. "He takes great interest in your wellbeing."

"You are not welcome here," Hector growled, his body tensing.

The man sniffed in mock offense. "You are not at liberty to turn me away. Besides, you should have been expecting me. The Hunters reported to us. Said you'd cajoled a mortal into a marriage bargain. Did it work?" The man's gaze traveled down to my feet. "Pity, I can't tell. But since she's still standing here, I guess not."

"What do you want?" I barked.

"I wish to meet your wife."

I cleared my throat and stepped aside. "My wife, Talia Romero Balcázar. Now you may return to the Sun Court."

She bobbed a wobbly curtsey.

"There's no need to show respect to this man," I told her.

He *tsked*. "You can't call her your wife if she doesn't even share your real name. Oh, she doesn't even know it, does she?"

I stepped closer to her again, allowing my shoulder to slide in front of hers. "She knows enough."

"Oh, but *does she*?"

Talia drew a sharp breath and knitted her fingers into my own. Stars, I wish she wouldn't do things like that.

"Return, Sinsorias. Tell my brother what you wish."

The man leaned forward, putting his glamoured face right in front of hers, not in a bow or a gesture of respect, but in an offensive, condescending way. I yanked Talia's hand back, jerking her away from my brother's courtier.

"Not yet, Romero. I will stay the night, or rather the day, as your strange schedule permits."

"I permit you nothing."

"You need not." The man straightened and sneered at me. "I have been ordered by the king to—"

"He's not king yet."

The man's sweeping brows rose. "To take your new wife back to the Sun Palace."

My hand shot out and grabbed the man by his glowing lapels. "You will *not* touch her." I spat through gritted teeth.

His eyes widened, but he managed to plaster a smile on his pale face. "Oh, your brother will not take no for an answer." Sinsorias cringed back, his hand flying to his lapel to draw something out from beneath his vest. A thin gold chain held a long charm at the end.

A bone whistle.

Hector cursed. I stared hard at the whistle in his hand, ignoring the sinking feeling in my chest. Talia's hand linked with mine once more, and this time, I squeezed back.

"I for one will not sleep out here," Sinsorias announced, tucking the wretched whistle back into his vest. "I request that my host and his bride join me for dinner. In your home, as it were." He waved his wrist about and marched up the steps behind us.

We walked up the wide stone steps, over unruly ivy to the twin front doors half-covered in cobwebs. At the top, I hung back, allowing Talia to enter first. As she glanced back at me, I tried to memorize her face and the way she looked at me like she wanted me to stay beside her.

Curse the sun and all his court. I stomped up the rest of the steps, keeping my chin high as I brushed past her. Hector's quirked brow said he knew exactly what was on my mind as I stormed through the forgotten entryway, through a hallway that led into a second, larger entrance hall, different only in that it was lit with blazing chandeliers.

Our footsteps echoed in the vaulted space.

Sinsorias peered up at the ceiling crisscrossed with beams. "And I thought you lived in a cave." He cackled to himself. "Where are all your servants, Romero?" He covered a false gasp. "Oh, that's right. No one wants to work for a—"

"Say another word, and I'll rip your throat out."

"With what, your claws?" He tilted his head.

"Get out of my house."

Talia glanced in wide-eyed confusion between us.

"Ah, see there," Sinsorias said, snapping in my direction. "Your wife disapproves of your lack of hospitality."

"She's not…" My tongue grew heavy and thick, forbidding the lie.

"Ah, ah, ah." Sinsorias wagged a finger at me. "Your marriage was binding, of course. Your lovely brother, I assume, was the witness? Well, then, our sovereign thanks you for your hand in this, as he never misses the report on all binding marriage vows. His crows are always watching."

Hector's knuckles cracked as he fisted his hands. "I can kill him for you, if you'd like."

I lifted a hand to stay him. "Not tonight."

Sinsorias smiled. "That's right. I have the power to call hell down upon your home." He patted the chain at his chest. "Like I was saying, you cannot deny to me that you ran off to the mortal world and brought us back a wife so you could—"

The roar that ripped from my throat drowned out the man's next words. Talia shrank away from me, and while it was best for her to hate me, the fear in her eyes stabbed me with pain.

20

RAFAEL

I pressed a hand to Talia's back and rushed her from the
entryway. That fool of a fae didn't know hell from a
dark closet.

If I still possessed the powers I was born with, I would
have lit the man on fire from the top of his well-groomed
head. The man my brother had sent was teetering on
madness, either by consumption of too much borrowed
power in his unprepared and untested body, or because of
fear—or both. And a fearful man brimming with unmastered
power was a dangerous thing to keep in one's house.

My footsteps thundered on the hardwood, and Talia had
to skitter along beside me to keep up. Hell was not a pack of
hounds nor the wicked fae who rode them. What the Wild
Hunt could unleash was merely death, and that was not
entirely a bad thing, considering the misery I'd been forced to
live in. No, death indeed could be a mercy.

But for Talia, it wouldn't be death. The Hunt, if called,
would only carry out what Sinsorias himself had been
commanded: to take her to my brother, who would no doubt

treat her in much the way he had his own twin: with suffering.

At all costs, I could not allow that slavering servant of my brother's to use that whistle. Perhaps if the month expired, and Talia no longer posed a threat to Fabian, he would let her pass back into the mortal world, unharmed. I would do everything in my power to delay our departure for the Sun Palace, but I had to keep Talia from showing any signs of growing affection for me.

Talia stepped away from my guiding hand. "Stop!" She fisted her hands at her hips. Her cheeks held a rosy flush and sweat dotted her hairline.

I wasn't used to the way mortals experienced exertion, and it somewhat fascinated me. We were only walking, after all. With my thumb, I smeared away a drop of sweat, tracing the line of her face perhaps a little too slowly.

Stars, what was that? I clasped my hands behind my back and frowned.

Her eyes widened like a spider had landed on her cheek. After a few loud breaths, she said, "What is going on here? Please tell me. I have a right to know."

She did. But I wasn't going to tell her. "You must stay away from that man."

Her exhale came out rather growl-like. "Then explain what that thing was that made all three of you turn ghost white."

Eying her, I made a snap decision. Maybe if she knew a little of what was at stake, it would keep her from saying or doing something foolish. "A whistle that summons the Wild Hunt."

She emitted a small, choked sound that sank deep into my chest. I stepped closer. "He has been leeching power to the

Hunters in exchange for using them to torment me when I step out of line according to his plans for me. But he will not have reason to use it." At her expectant gaze, I added, "I will not allow him to bring you any harm."

Her eyes softened. Stars, I'd blundered twice in a single minute. Everence was right. Human weakness pushed mortals instinctively toward that which would keep them safe. I wasn't accustomed to this and would need to tread more carefully. The high fae hated vulnerability, and hated even more the idea of needing *protection*. To us, it was an abomination to need anyone or anything. Need was a weakness.

And Talia's need blossomed in the redness of her cheeks, the perspiration on her brow, the quick breaths moving her chest. I had to intervene, to cut off this inevitable *leaning* which might place her affections in the wrong place—on that which would kill her.

She might be a frail mortal, helpless in the face of the Wild Hunt, but she was no grass reed to be pushed down by a strong gale.

I ground my teeth, trying to think of something to say to murder that hopeful look in her eyes, but I thought of nothing, so I turned and marched down the hallway once more. She followed. A dove chasing a fox.

I led Talia to the Bee Room. "You should change before dinner."

She walked halfway across the room before whirling on me. "There is much I wish to know," she said, fists clenched at her sides.

I nearly smiled, but this would only have offended her, so I kept my face rigid and said nothing.

"You bring me here, giving up one of your horses—which

I *know* you value—and then you proceed to ignore me. Except back there in the library—what was that?" Her arms waved like windblown willow branches. A mighty little storm.

Feeling my resolve faltering again, I turned aside. She deserved the truth, but she would loathe me forever if she knew the real reason I'd bargained with her to marry me. The horse—and her life—had seemed a small price to pay at the time.

"There are dangers here you do not understand," I said evasively. "I aim only to protect you from them."

The fight in her eyes softened, but only briefly. "Why bring me here, into danger, if you so admirably desire to protect me?" Her arms folded across her chest. "I know you can't lie, but I'm not sure I believe you."

Smart one, this little storm cloud.

"Talia, I—"

She marched forward, momentarily silencing my words. When she was an arm's length away, she paused. "Yes?" She cocked her head sideways and eyed me narrowly as I backed away, my hands raking through my hair.

I had to push her away. She was in dangerous territory and didn't know it.

Shuttering my expression, I said, "I made a mistake. You are not what I had hoped for."

Her face fell, and my useless heart blackened a little more. The worst part was that she knew I couldn't lie. She heard what her experience had taught her.

"I will send Ev to assist you. We dine at ten bells. And Talia," I said, urgency on my tongue, "You only need endure this to the end of the month." Picking up a hammer to nail the coffin shut, I added, "Then you can return home and find a man who can love you."

As I strode from the room, my chest ached sharply, in ways I hadn't allowed in a long time.

The formal dining room dwarfed the long table and tall chairs, the mountainous display of hydrangeas, hastily put together by my staff, and the tree-like candelabras throwing flickering candlelight over the crystal. I sat stiff-backed in the head chair, flicking my gaze between the twin sets of double doors at the back of the room.

I needed Talia to enter first, so that Sinsorias wouldn't be here to scrutinize my observation of her arrival. He would merely happen upon us already seated next to one another, quietly ignoring each other.

The left doors opened and Sinsorias strode in like he owned the place. His suit was now deep blue and woven with the annoying glowing threads my brother loved so much. Sinsorias's pale neck and chin took on a sickly pallor when lit from beneath. His eyes, which sat so far back in his skull, hung in deep shadows, untouched by the glow of his suit. He looked like a child holding a candle under his chin to tell ghost stories.

The bells chimed from the massive clock in the mostly empty grand ballroom.

Sinsorias stopped in front of the chair to my left, bowed curtly, and stood there, waiting for Talia's arrival like he was some splendid gentleman. I offered him a lazy lift of my brows, nothing more.

"Your manners have become rather animalistic, Romero."

He enjoyed using the name my brother had chosen for me when he'd cursed me and sent me out, never to return again. Pilgrim. Wanderer. Exile. I had lived with the name Romero so long that it no longer bothered me, but his use of it cut like a knife that slips quietly into your palm while peeling an apple.

To his comment, I smiled and growled low in my throat. Let him think me fully a beast, and report this back to my brother.

The other set of double doors clicked open. In walked Everence, a coy smile on her face, followed by Talia.

My chair screeched as I stood. My eyes lingered on the pale-yellow dress hugging Talia's frame. It highlighted her dark skin and provided a sunlit backdrop for her dark tresses, which flowed down almost to her waist and were set with small glowing stones and a white lily over one ear.

"Stars," I hissed out.

By the time I recovered, I was aware of Sinsorias' cold stare. Hardening my expression, I pinned my eyes on the far wall, but I sensed Talia watching me carefully as she took the seat to my right. As I sat once again, I caught Everence's gaze and flashed a nasty frown. Traitor.

She merely smiled politely in return.

"You remember my cousin, Everence Bristleberry?"

Sinsorias half-stood and nodded, his thighs knocking into the table as he did so. "Sinsorias Vere, honorable representative of the Court of the Sun Sovereign, my lady. It is a pleasure to see you again, as always."

I took a sip of wine to cover an amused chuckle. To her credit, Everence merely lifted her chin at the mention of my brother's official title.

Sinsorias stiffened slightly at her snub, but he did not call out her manners as barbaric. Instead, he turned his attention to my wife.

"You are Lady Romero? *Doña Romero,* as your people would say."

She cut hard eyes toward me. "Yes."

My blood ran hot. My words had worked.

Sitting up straighter in my chair, I watched her intently.

"This man discovered me in a vulnerable situation. He promised me things. I took his offer. And here we are, two strangers in the same house."

To avoid Everence's pointed gaze, I leaned back and took a sip of wine.

"He barely even looks at me," she continued, stabbing me with shame. "I have no utter idea why he brought me here. Not the faintest inkling." Resentment dripped from her words like hot candle wax.

Sinsorias, fortunately, studied Talia, missing the way my jaw worked as I tried to remain unaffected by her words. I needed her to hate me.

"I can tell you why he brought you here," cooed the courtling.

My fist landed heavy on the table, rattling every spoon and shaking every goblet. "You will do no such thing. Your role here is observation only, no meddling."

The man's lips curled into a sneer, but he inclined his head in acquiescence. "Very well, I shall enjoy observing you two on our journey to the Sun Palace."

I turned my face away slowly, unable to fully mask my anger. He was a snake, a viper I hadn't seen until I'd stepped right on him. I'd walked right into this trap, and I knew what he would say before he opened his slick little mouth.

"We will leave after my mare gives birth, not before," I grumbled through clenched teeth.

The man's brows lifted, but he nodded. "As it were. I shall

be most pleased to see you two spend the next week at each other's side."

I pushed back from the table, and the meal hadn't even been brought out yet. "You will not stay an entire week, and you are not at liberty to demand anything from me."

His eyes slid dangerously to Talia. "You do realize that I am under strict orders from your sovereign to remove her at my discretion."

My breaths came faster, and I gripped the edge of the table to keep from slapping the man across the face. Any offense too grave, any misstep too egregious, and he would snatch Talia away, with all the power of the sun sovereign behind him. There was no telling the temporary magic my brother had granted him to oversee this task.

The table splintered between my hands. Talia yelped and Everence caught her shoulders to keep her from toppling from her chair.

"You will *not* harm my wife."

Sinsorias tilted his head and cocked a brow. "I see."

I glanced first at Everence, whose expression was edged with a knowing disapproval. She was well acquainted with my temper. Talia stared at the flayed table, then her gaze slowly traveled up my arms to my face. My wife looked at me with unfiltered awe, and in my heart, entwined together like a greedy vine choking out a beautiful tree, was the thing I wanted most in the world and the vow to never let it come to pass.

For the briefest moment, I drank her admiration like sweet wine, poison though it was.

Then I stormed from the dining hall, announcing I would dine in my room.

21

TALIA

He fled from the table as if chased. My eyes lingered on Rafael's back until the doors closed behind him.

The fae courtier was watching me, and I remembered Rafael's words that he didn't want me, but my heart beat madly in my chest, and my lungs couldn't draw breaths deep enough to quell the shock still coursing through my body.

I could still hear the word *wife* like he was speaking it in my ear over and over again. It had snapped from his tongue, sharp as a curse, and yet had caught my heart in a vice grip and was not letting go.

Finally, I became aware of the man, Sinsorias, clearing his throat, for maybe the third time. I pulled my eyes away from the doors and glanced at Everence. Her lips seemed to be fighting a smile.

Rafael confused me. Ghost-like memories of his tenderness contrasted with his hurtful words. But one thing I knew for certain: Rafael hated the man sitting across from me. I shook my head slightly. "How rude," I said, feigning indifference as I reached for my wine. "Is this how fae treat their guests?" The wine was strong and dry and smelled divine.

Sinsorias spoke, but I didn't listen, couldn't stop the words still echoing in my head. Rafael's chair was emptier than the other vacant seats along the vast table. I kept glancing at it, saddened each time that it sat unoccupied. More than once, Everence had to nudge my shoe with her own to snap me back to the present.

"How was the journey through the gate?"

I blinked at the courtier, his glowing suit a flashy distraction from his sharp features and strange nose, which was too straight and too narrow to be real. There were the nightmares, but there was also the memory of Rafael holding me, of whispering away the visions as he assured me they were contrivances of my own mind. A flush swept up my neck, but I grimaced and forced myself to recall the awful visual of my parents hanging from nooses.

The memory worked, and I nearly wretched onto my plate.

My interrogator's loud, amused sniff was his only response for several minutes as Hector, who'd appeared pushing the dinner cart, carved a large tenderloin at the table and served us all buttery soft slices. Apparently, the woman I'd seen fleeing earlier was their one server.

I was hungry, but not particularly interested in eating. I wanted to find Rafael. To figure out what was really going on here.

Back in Leor, people worshipped the sun. The sun had burned me many times, which, according to the lore of my people, meant I'd offended him somewhere along the line. As soon as Sol had been born, and we'd named him, and our luck had seemed to change.

Or so I'd thought.

Sol now belonged to some renegade and I was married to an entirely confusing fae nobleman whom I barely knew and who might or might not despise me. He wanted me safe from this stranger, but then Rafael had walked out and left me in here with him.

When the meal was finally over, and I'd managed to say as few words as possible, Sinsorias stood along with us, and offered a polite bow. His venomous stare and ridiculous suit stripped the gesture of anything pleasant.

"You will join your husband now?" he asked, eyes alight with malicious anticipation.

"You might be fae, and I might be a poor human, but I have never in my life been asked a less appropriate question."

Everence tilted a small, approving nod at me. Sinsorias, on the other hand, eyed me flatly and only bobbed his chin as Everence and I turned to depart.

The hallways were long, mostly empty, and devoid of rugs or tapestries to dampen the clacking of my small heels on the wooden floors. I sounded like a flamenco dancer next to Everence's silent footsteps.

"You did well in there," Everence said, holding my arm as we rounded the third turn from the dining room.

So it was just a performance? Had Rafael's words all been for show?

She noticed my sagging shoulders and added, "Oh, it will all make sense one day, I assure you. Rafael is...well, he has dealt with much opposition over the years, most of which has come from that man's employer, Rafael's other brother, Fabian."

"The Sun Sovereign?"

Everence nodded.

"What?" I spluttered, unable to contain my shock. Had I married fae *royalty*? And if I had, what exactly did that mean?

Everence stopped and turned me toward her. "He has lost much of his power, thanks to his brother." Her eyes closed tightly, and her mouth pinched, as if she wanted to say more but held it back. When she looked at me again, her icy blue eyes blazed with intensity. "Do not give up on him, no matter what you learn or hear or...discover."

She turned and marched away so quickly I could only stare after her dumbly. When she'd vanished around a corner, I realized I was standing in the hallway that led to the beehive room. My room, I supposed.

Did I have to just stay confined to my rooms all night? I wasn't in the least bit tired. This was my house, after all, and I could walk where I wanted.

I was still hungry, considering how little I'd eaten in that interrogation chamber. Now that the bizarre fae courtier wasn't looming over my every move, I decided I could eat a little. Everence had shown me where the kitchens were earlier, so I made my way there.

The kitchens were empty, but someone had magicked the dishes to wash themselves. A light flicked to life as I entered the domed space. Black stains marred the ceiling, and a long wooden counter sat embedded in one wall. On that counter sat a basket of oranges and a half-loaf of bread wrapped in cloth. I took an orange and turned to head back out the narrow hallway leading to the main house.

A dark figure stood against the far wall, watching me with tiny eyes. The creature had long arms that resembled sticks and a face dotted with lichen. She wore an apron.

After the shock wore off, I nodded my head politely. "Sorry if I frightened you."

The creature's eyes, which were entirely black, widened. "You're the wife," it said with a small, raspy voice.

I coughed out a yes.

For a moment, I waited for the creature to speak again, but it became clear it had nothing more to say. "Good evening," I said, curtseying with the orange in my hand.

As I walked past her, the dryad said, "You haven't changed much."

I peered at the tree-like woman and shrugged. "I suppose not."

"If you don't change, I wonder who will get the house. I hope it's her."

"Who? Get what house? What do you mean change?"

The dryad turned and without a word slipped away into the darkened hall off the back of the kitchen.

22

RAFAEL

My bedroom door rattled as someone tried the knob, but I did not rise from my couch. My fingers twirled my favorite dagger.

"Brother, let me in."

With a wave of my free hand, the door swung open.

Hector blazed in, scowling, rustling the leaves of the ivy that grew up the walls. A few of the birds nesting in the nooks at the base of the domed ceiling ruffled their feathers in annoyance.

"You look like a horse just stepped on your foot."

He walked toward the open floor-to-ceiling windows and stared out at the flashing lightning in the distance. "Your man is following her."

The dagger stopped spinning. "What?"

"Sinsorias didn't go back to his carriage or any room in this house. My magic came up empty in every room. All I can figure is that he followed her."

I rushed to the windows, scanning the grounds below. "She's outside?"

Hector shook his head. "She feels safe here. Did you not warn her?"

"I specifically told her there were monsters."

"You should have told her specifically which ones."

My eyes narrowed at my brother. "You fetch her this time. I...fear I should not." The library had nearly gotten out of hand. "You don't think he will try to take her away, do you?"

Hector stared at my reflection in the glass. "You care for her."

My jaw flexed several times before I found the right words. "You cannot think me capable of destroying her."

"I think you fully capable. It was, after all, your idea."

The barb of those words cut straight to my dark soul. I spun and threw a punch where his face should have been, but he'd already moved, leaving only a ghost of a reflection where I'd punched.

"Missed again," he said with a smirk.

"When you fight without magic, we'll see who wins."

He lifted two hands. "While I see that you've changed your mind about her—still foolish, if you ask me—I can offer you no solutions. Running from Fabian will only ensure that every assassin employed by the Sun Court will never stop hunting you, as well as the Hunters themselves." He moved to stand beside me again, this time a little farther away. "Do not throw away what you've built here. Do not bring more ruin on yourself for her sake."

This past half-century, I had found a semblance of peace here. A way to endure. But it was a veil to be torn, a veneer destined to shatter.

I wanted to believe Hector, to agree that her life wasn't worth the effort to save. But I could no longer hold to that idea than I could keep water from running downstream. "Her parents love her more than any fae ever loved a child."

Hector settled a hand on my shoulder. "A mother wolf tends to her pups for a time, too."

This was different. Theirs was a love that would last past separation, past death itself.

"You will stay with her, or you will send Everence to accompany her. One or the other of you will remain by her side."

Hector's arm fell. "Fine." He stared down at the two barns illuminated by dim moonlight. "My advice, though I know you don't want it, is to let her fall in love with you. At least that way, you find happiness. This way, you keep your curse forever, become permanently animal in a matter of days, and eventually lose your mind."

I scoffed. That kind of *happiness* would forever be tainted by what I'd done to attain my freedom. Only days ago, it had seemed so right.

"She'll never fall for me now. I wounded her too deeply." There was a freedom in knowing she was safe, but I frowned as I watched my reflection. Letting her live meant becoming like the animals I kept caged in my other barn, cursed in their animal forms so long they no longer had sound minds.

Hector remained silent so long I punched his shoulder. He jumped and finally answered. "If I had any sense, I wouldn't say this to you, and perhaps I might keep my brother and see you finally healed." He turned to me. "She is still very much in danger of falling in love with you."

"I made her think I didn't want her."

"Did you see the way she held your hand when Sinsorias arrived? Were you oblivious to the way she was looking at you in the library?" He rolled his eyes. "When you left the dinner table, she was barely able to stay present in the conversation."

"She was angry at me."

"Don't be an idiot."

Thunder rumbled gently in the distance. I snapped my gaze back out to the gardens below. "I was certain she was safe. That I had cut off all possibility of... If Sinsorias saw what you saw, he will—"

"Take her to Fabian."

I grasped Hector's shoulder, pulse rising. "I will find her."

Hector gripped my arm and squeezed hard. "If you really want to keep her safe, you could always just let her see you."

I shoved his arm away and leaped out the window, landing catlike in the weeds, dagger still clutched in my fingers. My eyes closed against the unbidden memories brought out by Hector's words. Those early years, when the change was still fresh and I hadn't yet learned to shut down my mind and my heart against what I had become, had left me tormented and angry. I had proposed to many women, mortal and fae, in the hopes of finding one capable of loving me, but every time they'd seen me as a bear, they'd fled.

Every single one.

I raced through the garden, heading for the one place I assumed she would go.

The distant storm flashed madly in the sky. Low thunder echoed my footsteps. The barn was lit, which meant people were there. But when I charged into the bright light, I saw no one. The horses looked up. They were all awake.

"Where did he take her?"

The nearest horse said *Away.* Another said *He took her, yes.* Another voice in my head answered *Tall man, short girl. Gone. Yes.*

Lily was the best at communicating in complete thoughts. She'd been practicing with me the longest. I darted to her stall.

"Where did they go?"

Lily nudged my hand with her muzzle, hoping for a treat. *They argued, but she followed him. He said she needed to come with her.*

I slapped the wood. He must have ensorcelled her, which meant she must have eaten fruit. Dinner had been prepared with cayenne and garnished with St. John's Wart, both for her sake, but fruit would reverse their effects at warding off evil.

"Where, Lily, where did he take her?"

He said home.

Curse every star that ever shone its light on me. I sprinted from the barn, taking a route through the garden that led around the house. Thorns snagged my ankle and branches slapped my face.

If I was too late.

If my brother managed to get his hands on her.

I would tear out the very foundations of his castle and bury him in the rubble.

The massive carriage still sat in front of the house. No one had come to park it elsewhere. Even the winged horses were still in their harnesses.

That fool had hoped to leave quickly.

I heard voices before I saw them.

"All right, fine, you can pet them."

"Yay!"

Talia raced around the carriage with a giddy smile on her face. My heart sank. She was definitely spelled. When her eyes drifted toward me, she paused, then skipped down the row of horses.

"Talia." I cleared the unexpected knot in my throat. "Talia, come with me."

"Oh, but I'm going home now. He says you are dangerous. Isn't this carriage lovely? It'll be like riding inside a giant flower!"

She danced in a circle.

Sinsorias slipped around the carriage and froze momentarily before his hand jerked to the chain at his neck.

Before he could draw out that whistle, I hurled my dagger. It sank through the back of his hand and pinned his palm to his chest.

Howling in pain, he dropped to his knees, still grabbing for the chain with his free hand. I took two long steps forward and kicked his hand away. He spun as he fell to the ground. The movement ripped the dagger tip from his clothes and slung his injured hand wide. Blood rushed from the flesh of his palm.

"Move and I will end you."

He groaned, feeling the effects of the iron. Killing him now would only alert the crows. They smelled death across continents.

Talia watched with a vacant expression, hands loosely holding the skirt of her yellow gown. I pinned one knee to the courtier's chest and yanked on the thin chain. It sliced into his skin, leaving a thin red line. He tried to shove me off, but I slapped his hand down so hard that it hit his own chin. He moaned.

My hand closed around the bone whistle. With a firm yank, I broke the chain and stuffed the whistle in my jacket pocket. Then I yanked my dagger from his hand and pressed the tip under his chin.

"Try threatening me now, slave."

His eyes sharpened. Through gritted teeth, he growled, "Your brother expects to meet her at his coronation. If she is not there, he will never stop hunting her, even after your miserable flesh is past hope of saving. The joy of knowing it brings you pain will be enough to satisfy him." He flashed his eyes at Talia. "Marrying her was her death sentence, no matter if it is by your hand or his."

My hand holding the dagger shook with rage. Sinsorias hissed as the blade nicked his soft skin and fresh blood trickled out. I jumped backward, before my anger won out. Twice now, I'd almost killed for her. Killing a member of the Wild Hunt meant facing the wrath of the fully assembled Hunt. Killing my brother's courtier meant facing his wrath. Face to face with him, I would lose, and I couldn't protect her. Not when his magic was far stronger than my own.

I shook the blood from the dagger, then wiped it on the edge of my jacket and stuffed it back in its sheath at my waist. Talia's eyes widened as I stepped toward her.

"You're dangerous," she said, parroting what she'd been told. Or maybe it was the blood on my jacket hem and the man squirming in the grass behind me that elicited her comment.

"And you're ensorcelled. I'm taking you with me."

23

TALIA

Rafael hefted me over his shoulder.

I giggled as I bumped awkwardly against his back. The night was so lovely. He smelled like cloves and oranges and I couldn't exactly remember why he'd just stabbed that man. I thought the flower carriage was going to take me home. I wanted so badly to go home.

He crunched through a tangle of thin, thorny branches, then bumped up the front steps of his house. The house was a mansion and it was also my house. I *was* home. The man with the flower carriage had brought me home. Or maybe I'd never left. I couldn't remember how I'd gotten outside in the first place.

Rafael set me down inside the shadowy archway, his hands sliding up my ribcage. Giggles burst from my mouth.

He kicked the door open and slung me over his shoulder again.

"Wee!"

He snorted in annoyance.

"He said you were dangerous, but this is fun." I grew tired of holding my head up and let myself jangle uncomfortably against his back. I was growing lightheaded.

We walked down a long, checkered hallway, up two steps and through a paneled drawing room, down two steps and back onto checkered tile until we crossed a familiar hallway that led to my quarters. As my eyes drifted closed, I focused more intently on his intoxicating smells. I smelled fear on him.

My head snapped up. Wait, how could I smell fear? What did fear even smell like?

He stopped at a lovely door painted with purple flowers. The trim was carved to look like vines, but they had been painted to appear covered in frost. Holding my legs with one arm, he knocked with the other.

"Put me down," I grumbled. His insistence on carrying me like a sack of potatoes was giving me a headache.

"Hmph."

"I can stand."

He tilted forward and placed me on the floor, one arm still holding most of my weight. He appeared entirely disinterested in the way my body was pressed to his side. I couldn't exactly *ignore* this fact, even though my hand throbbed and I had no idea why I wanted to laugh at everything.

Everence opened the door and sucked in a quiet breath. "What did you do to her?"

Rafael grunted again. "He spelled her. They were already at his carriage."

Everence stepped aside to allow Rafael to guide me into a darkened sitting room. The only light came from a fire crackling in the hearth—which was odd for summertime. But as we stumbled into the room, chilly air swept over me. I shivered, which only made me laugh.

"Oh, it's freezing in here!"

Rafael frowned, his mouth close enough to my ear that his warm breath moved the tiny hairs at my ear, tickling my skin. "She's part winter, this one," he said, nodding at Everence.

I glanced up at the blond woman, who shrugged and pointed toward a low sofa.

Rafael's hand cupped the back of my neck, and before I knew what was happening, he tilted my entire body backward, onto the couch. For the briefest moment, I stared into his dark eyes, almost hoping to see that flash of amber I'd seen in Puerta.

He coughed and stood but kept his eyes on me. "After dinner, she must have found some fruit."

"Yes, an orange! It was delicious. And a little tree-woman who said I wasn't going to change and that someone else was going to get this house."

Rafael and Everence exchanged a glance, then she knelt beside me and took my hand, her expression pinched with concern.

"I stabbed him with iron," he added. At a small disapproving *hmph* from his cousin, he turned away and added in a whisper, "And I stole the whistle."

"And how long do you think Fabian will sit idly by? He knows now, beyond the shadow of a doubt. Or he will, once his crows bring him the news of what you did tonight."

Rafael crossed his arms and turned toward the fire.

A tingling sensation began at my fingertips and quickly turned to the cold burn of ice on my palm. Then my head cleared and my smile vanished. I sat up quickly, head spinning.

"There now, don't get up yet." Everence held a hand to my knee before rocking back on her ankles and rising. I nearly missed the significant look she tossed at Rafael, but I glanced up to see her turning quickly away. "Thank you," I said breathlessly. My shoulders shook from the cold.

He grumbled his own thanks, but she waved away his gratitude and crossed her arms, throwing her eyes my way twice before Rafael sighed and sat down in one of the two large leather armchairs facing me.

"Um," I said, "You might not want to lean back. You have blood on your clothes."

Rafael leaned back slowly against the leather, his knees wide and his arms draped lazily to each side. The only sign of his unease were his drumming fingertips.

"Fruit erases all protective charms," Everence said apologetically as she took a seat beside me on the couch. "It's best for humans to avoid it."

"What did he do to me?"

She looked at Rafael to answer, but he stared at the fire. "He put a spell on you to make you follow him."

"Oh...okay." I could have been made to do anything. That was utterly terrifying. My shoulders hunched over and I wrung my hands.

"You and I must travel to my brother's court," Rafael snapped, drawing my gaze to his.

"Why?"

He stared at me for several long seconds, and I was certain he'd dodge my question. "Because my brother wishes to take you away from me."

I leaned forward, elbows on my knees. "Why?" I pressed.

"Because he desires that I remain forever unloved."

150

Those words knocked the air from my lungs like I'd just fallen off a bucking horse. I breathed out once more, "Why?"

Rafael's jaw tightened. He lifted one ankle and rested it on his knee. "Enough questions. Throughout the next week, you must do as I say, no matter how strange it may sound to you, or my brother will make you his slave." His face angled away, toward the flickering flames. "And you do not want to know what he does to his mortal slaves."

Encouraged by the answers he'd given, I tried one more question. "Am I your slave?"

He jerked forward so quickly I flinched. But he only leaned his elbows on his knees and held me with an iron stare. "You are my *wife*."

"So you did not bespell me, like he did?"

His jaw worked, but he remained silent, his dark eyes roving all over my face. Everence, meanwhile, stood with arms crossed near the hearth.

"Bringing you here was a mistake," he admitted and leaned back, one hand stroking his chin.

Inside my chest, a hole opened up. Like every other man who'd come before, Rafael regretted ever looking my way. The ache spread from my chest outward, until it pushed away all other sensations and left me hollow. I stared at my hands and rubbed idly at the skin on my knuckles.

"I see no way to avoid our invitation," he threaded his hands behind his head and stared at the wall, casually, as if he hadn't just split my heart open. "Which means you must convince my brother that you hate me."

"Wait, what?"

"If he thinks there's a chance you do *not* hate me, he will torture you. In front of me." His jaw flexed, as if he'd said more than he'd meant to.

Everence stepped forward, eyes on me as she spoke to Rafael. "Talia will prove to everyone that she despises you for ripping her from her world." She turned her eyes to me. "By doing so, you will ensure your own safety."

My husband breathed so loudly, like a stallion after a race, that I had a hard time keeping my eyes on Everence. As she and Rafael awaited my response, my mind flashed back over the past week—was that really all it had been?

Rafael had saved me—from Ortiz, from poverty, from my nightmares, and tonight from an enchantment that addled my mind. In the market, he'd offered me a deal, and I'd taken it. I'd never paused to consider *why* he wanted to save me. Why, indeed?

Sinsorias apparently knew. Hector knew. Everence knew. I alone was in the dark. And yet, it was somehow in my hands to save myself from slavery to a powerful fae sovereign, if I could but prove that I hated Rafael.

There was more to this than they were telling me. The creature in the kitchens knew more than I did. I was having a hard time recalling exactly what the dryad had said, now that my mind was again my own, but there was a secret here to be uncovered.

"All right," I said, voice low but growing louder as I continued. "I will convince them that I hate you." And in the process, I would, so help me sun and stars, discover his reason for marrying me.

Sunlight woke me, and I was fairly certain a bee was trying to extract pollen from my hair. I swatted at the tiny creature, still perplexed at why someone would build a bedroom that doubled as a beehive. Today, there were definitely more bees. I sat up and stared at the honeycomb wall. Overnight, the active part of the hive had doubled, at least.

A butterfly flitted in and landed on the rose-petal blanket. The edges of the petals were softer, less brown than they had been yesterday.

Flinging the covers off my body, I glanced at my reflection in the round mirror over a painted dresser. Last night Everence had drawn a bath for me in her rooms, after dismissing Rafael, and had proceeded to pamper me with every luxurious-smelling thing imaginable, including the nightgown I'd borrowed and worn back to my room. It smelled of lavender and was softer than melted butter.

Everence had talked of her magic, of her love for the cold, of how one can grow accustomed to living in a new world. She'd carefully avoided talking of Rafael, of Sinsorias, and of the looming invitation to the Sun Palace. After my bath, she'd given me a white lily, explaining that I was to keep it with me at all times. Its fragrance would not only hide my mortal scent from Fabian's spies, but its magic would also act as a shield for spells.

I donned a second set of riding clothes Rafael had left in my room and headed for the library. It was empty. Javier never started training before ten o'clock, which gave me exactly one hour. I'd slept later than I'd hoped.

Almost as soon as my head tipped sideways to read titles, I realized they were all in a foreign language. I slid my hand along the row of books, looking for something I could read. Then I was running down the length of the balcony. I tugged out one book at random and opened the pages. I couldn't read a single word.

I snapped the book shut. So tightly squeezed were the

titles that I couldn't see where I'd drawn the book out. They were all varying shades of browns or deep blues, and I worried that Rafael would notice if a single title were out of place. I glanced at the spine for the author's name, then placed it beside a book on Ancient Wars of the Fae.

Wait. I read the title again. The letters made no sense to me. How had I thought it was about warfare?

Backing up from the long shelves, I decided to hunt for answers in a different place.

The sun shone brightly on the white lily petals. They sparkled faintly and wobbled in the gentle breeze. There were white ones and red ones and deep purple ones. This part of the garden was the only part not overrun with weeds. The lily patch tucked up against the stone walls of the estate, in the corner where a rounded tower room jutted out from the main wall.

"You're harder to find when you wear that thing," Sinsorias' cold voice chilled my skin.

I stood slowly and turned. In the sunlight, his skin looked sallow. My eyes darted across the garden, hoping to glimpse Rafael, but he was nowhere in sight.

He tossed an apple in his palm. "Care for some fruit?" No wound remained, but his eyes appeared sunken.

My lips pressed tightly together and I gathered the fabric of my skirt, ready to grab my dagger. "Your spells won't work on me today."

He rolled the apple in his hand. "As long as you have that flower, you're right. But if it were to fall out, you'd be as vulnerable as a trapped mouse." His teeth were blindingly white. In a heartbeat, before I even registered that he'd moved, he loomed over me, snatching for the flower.

I screamed and ducked, scooping up my hem and yanking out my dagger. I spun away in a crouch, blade lifted. The flower hung on.

"Ah, fast little mouse." He eyed the tip of my dagger. "Steel, yes?" He exhaled. "Mortal dagger."

I tilted the blade a little in my hand, brow raised.

"Less iron, you see. Far more practical for your world, but less effective here."

Heartbeat scrambling, I scanned once more for Rafael. It was day. I'd never seen him once during the daylight hours. He wasn't going to save me this time.

He left the apple on the ground where he'd dropped it and paced with hands behind his back. "Your husband's little stunt last night will cost you. No one steals an item that belongs to the Sun Sovereign." He waited for me to speak, studying me with narrow eyes.

Recalling Rafael's words last night, I swallowed and tried to steady my voice. "He's no husband to me."

Sinsorias snorted. "Is that so? Last night you clung to him like a leech."

"You ensorcelled me. I had no idea what I was doing."

"Ah, but before that."

Cheeks heating, I realized I was doing a poor job convincing this man that I hated Rafael. I'd need to get better before meeting the Sun Sovereign. "He told me he doesn't want me."

That part was true, anyway. And fae couldn't lie.

The man's head tilted. "Did he now? He said those very words?"

"Something to that effect."

"Ah, but the wording is key." He lifted a finger. "He wants you to think he doesn't care for you because, my dear, he cares so very much."

My jaw fell open.

Then I shook my head. This man had tricked me, spelled me, and nearly taken me captive. I couldn't trust him. Stars, Rafael's snap bargain hadn't been all that different, but I'd at least agreed to it while in my right mind.

"Leave me alone."

He nodded politely. "I shall happily wait until the dips arrive."

"Dips?"

His smile widened maliciously. "The king's dogs. They really like mortals. The crows sent word to the palace, and I expect them to arrive within the week."

Dagger lifted, I bent to grab another lily.

"If you pick one of those, you must pay the price."

"I don't trust anything you say." My fingers closed around a stem.

"Well, it's your blood."

My hand loosened. "What?"

"Picking an enchanted flower always leads to a geas. Don't you know that?"

"A geas? Like a spell?" Plenty of stories had them. They never ended well for the people trapped by them. The man couldn't lie outright, so I stood and left the flower in the ground. I tucked the loose one back into my hair.

"I'm expected in the stables," I announced, stepping quickly away from the courtier.

Even when he was out of sight, I kept my dagger in hand as I made my way to the stables. Javier was brushing a mare and told me to track down Tinieblas, who'd been out to pasture since dawn.

"And be careful," he warned. "There's evil on the wind. Everyone's restless today."

24

RAFAEL

Talia marched with quick steps, eyes constantly darting about. Javi had done exactly as I bid in sending Talia out here, but still I couldn't keep my heavy bear breaths in control as I angled toward her in the tall grass.

Javi once been a little gray mouse, an awful curse even worse than mine. But he'd completed the requirements to break the enchantment—took him almost the entirety of four hundred years—and had regained his freedom. When we'd met at a horse auction, the decision to come work for me had been both one of pity, a curse bearer alone knows the burden I carry, and one of interest. I'd told him I could teach him the way of animal magic.

His voice was not yet authoritative over the animals, as mine was, but he could order the horses about well enough. They liked him, and it worked well for me to not have to pour so much of my diminished magic into handling them.

My efforts lay with the cursed guests I sheltered on my estate. From the knoll in the back pasture, I cast a glance at the large building to my right. I'd expended too much magic last night searching for Talia. What little remained had been barely enough to reinstate the enchantments that blanketed Starfell.

Not far ahead, Talia held the halter with tight fingers and with a hand over her eyes to shield the bright sun, scanned the wide, sloping pasture.

If she could sense my magic at all yet, she might try calling him, and he would, of course, come directly. But as yet, she had no idea that a fae's vows were designed to tie magics together.

I pawed my way forward, sticking to the tallest grasses and the shade of the occasional tree, always out of her periphery. Fae didn't marry humans because it tied us to their mortal weakness, an abomination to most of my kind. My kind married mortals to acquire their immunity to iron, but these were never the sole marriage of a high fae. A mortal bride was more like a concubine, a mistress even, though vows were technically exchanged to bind the magics together. In all our records, only a handful of immortals had ever truly married humans for love, and they were the laughingstock of our own histories.

There were, however, powers mortals possessed that fae did not. Like the power to see past weakness.

Talia spun around, looking for Tinieblas, and I flattened myself against the earth. My snout inhaled the rich scent of warm dirt and grass. It was because mortals were so fragile and fleeting that they could love that which was also broken and dying. My curse would never be lifted by the love of one of my kind.

How odd, that a thing as small and delicate as a blade of

grass, here today and gone tomorrow, had the very power I needed.

Sunlight danced off her hair and warmed her skin with a fine rosy blush. Glamours made women lovely, but they were masks, and Talia needed no mask to be lovely. She had a small bump in her nose that gave her a more authoritative look. She held her eyes tight, always scrutinizing and assessing her surroundings. She was not one to be trifled with. I doubted many mortal men had wanted to approach her, given her hard expression, but that made her all the more exemplary in my mind. I imagined Talia Balcázar didn't toss around flirtatious eyes meant only to tease. If she looked at a man with longing, it was real and unmasked.

Curse the stars, I wanted her to look at me that way.

I snorted and the grasses rustled.

She glanced my direction, eyes narrow and ears alert. Sun above, had she already inherited my fae hearing? It would happen eventually, but the full manifestation of magic in a mortal usually took a while, at least when measuring in their years.

After a moment, she kept walking.

A few steps later, I sensed it—the presence of another animal in the field. Large. Hungry.

Eyes sharp, ears alert, I tensed and scanned the field. One of my beasts had escaped his confines and was searching. Slinking faster now, I sniffed the wind, the ground, the grass.

Where was he?

Stars, Talia was still far away and completely oblivious that she was being hunted. Did she even have a knife on her? I started running, loping at full speed toward her.

There. On the wind, subtle as the smell of a steel blade, was the scent of dragon.

Sun forsake me. The *dragon* had gotten loose.

The wingless creature, once a fearsome beast had been cursed, and cursed again, twisted from a true dragon to that of a slithering monstrosity. He moved like liquid wax, burning his path with the fire in his belly that could never again produce true flames.

I charged, finally spotting the place the grasses rustled.

Friend or not, I would kill him if he touched her.

Talia! Curse this useless tongue!

Gathering all the magic I could, I screamed into the dragon's mind. *Leave her! Return at once.*

The dragon slowed, hissed, and watched her flee. The anger rolling off his scales soured in my nostrils. His diamond-shaped head jerked toward her, and the ground rent beneath me as my claws ripped up dirt and grass. I roared.

The dragon shrank back, then curled around and slithered back toward the massive barn that housed the cursed creatures.

Talia wheeled, dropping into a terrified crouch. Her eyes scanned, locked on me, and she blanched with fear. She must not have seen the dragon in the tall grass. If only she knew I was not the threat.

She breathed quickly, shallowly, but her eyes remained fixed on me from a short distance across the field. I waited for her to scream. Instead, as soon as my eyes locked with hers, she gasped.

Her voice shook as she called out. "Wait...are you...?"

Great sun above, she knew it was me. I stood to my full height, not that I could pretend to be a man in this furry flesh, but I hated to have to remain on my paws as she studied me with those piercing eyes. I came out here as

Hector suggested, to make her fear me—for her sake, she
needed to.

But as I stood there, great bear breaths heaving in and out,
I hungered for her gaze, for her to see my cursed flesh and
not flinch in fear.

She stepped back as I rose, her eyes widening. Was that a
smile growing on her lips?

First and Last, forgive me.

For in that small smile, I tasted my own freedom, and
with that taste I knew nothing else—nothing—save the intoxicating desire to drink in her approval.

25

TALIA

A massive grayish-brown bear stood before me. The bear breathed loudly as he returned my gaze, giving me a chance to study its beastly form. His sides were massive; his arms thick and his paws the size of dinner plates.

When he'd turned toward me a moment ago, I froze, pinned under both fear and wonder. I wasn't afraid of him, not the way I'd been afraid of the Wild Hunters, but his size and his nearness and the memory of the way he'd moved and growled sent little waves of panic down my exposed skin. He was utterly terrifying and also hauntingly beautiful, the way a dagger could be both lovely and frightening.

Staring into familiar brown eyes, realization dawned, like a map spread out to a wayward soul.

The bear's claws matched the scratch marks in the library. Sinsorias had assumed Rafael lived in a *cave*. He disappeared during the day, and when he'd roared last night, it had sounded entirely like the throaty growl this bear emitted as it charged across the field.

I stared long and hard, from the enormous hind legs to the way the fur clumped around his chest, to the snout and the claws and the...eyes. They were Rafael's without a doubt.

He was an animal.

I'd married *a bear*.

Why had he charged at me? My eyes followed the direction the bear had been looking when I spotted him. The larger, second barn stood in the distance. Rather than trees for walls and branches for a ceiling, this one was made of brick. From this angle, I noted it had no windows at all. A cage of sorts. A shudder rippled down my spine.

"Hello," I said, voice small and shaky. I bit my lip.

My skin tingled all over, the way it did when I used to watch my father's horses race—all jittery anticipation and bottled nerves. I'd wanted to know where Rafael went during the day, and now I knew.

"Can you understand me?" I asked, feeling a little foolish talking to a bear. Just how *bear* was he during the day? Not bear enough to attack me, surely.

The bear dropped to all fours.

"I'm not sure if that was a yes or no," I snapped.

The bear stood again and moved toward me. I remained perfectly still, the way I did when allowing a new horse to size me up—though a lumbering bear was nothing like a tall stallion. My instincts told me to run, at least, but my mind told me this beast was the handsome man who'd reached for me when I'd stumbled and who had instinctively yanked me back from Sinsorias.

The bear sniffed up and down my frame with its massive nose.

I scoffed and stepped away. "Excuse me!" I crossed my arms.

Its snout traveled up from my feet and, to my surprise, gently bumped my elbow, loosening my folded arms. I twisted away from his dry nose.

As my body instinctively jerked away from him, Rafael's golden-brown eyes peered up at me, almost forlorn. A stab of pity pricked my chest. He was used to this, to being reviled.

Before I could will myself to stand still, he emitted a strange bearish grunt and ambled a few steps away, where he proceeded to flop unceremoniously onto the ground and roll onto his back, rather like a dog. I half-laughed as he rolled back and forth a few times, scratching his back along the ground. Then he flipped over, stood, and shook his entire body, hair and dirt flying from him.

"Gross," I spat as fur flew toward me. "Now how will the horse come to me?"

The bear—Rafael—tensed and stood on his hind legs once more. I stumbled back, my heart pounding against my breastbone. Then he slammed down to all fours and walked between me and the back pasture, blocking my way. This was his way of telling me I wouldn't be collecting any horses today.

"All right," I said, hands up. "But I doubt if Javier will be pleased I refused his orders."

As I started back toward the barn, the bear walked alongside me, but not close enough to touch. He was giving me space, which I appreciated.

Every so often, the bear cast another glance at me. Rafael was in there somewhere, I had to keep reminding myself, willing my racing heartbeat to stop just shy of sheer panic.

As soon as we entered the paddock behind the barn, the horses cantering along the far fence, the one closest to the back field, whinnied and slowed, as if calmed by the bear's presence. I cast them a nervous glance.

The noise drew the attention of Javier, Hector, and Sinsorias, who stood in the smallest paddock adjacent to the barn. As their eyes discovered us, I nearly tripped at the force in all three gazes. The weight of intense scrutiny felt like these three fae were doctors with scalpels, fileting me and observing everything I hoped to keep hidden inside. A sudden urge to steady myself overwhelmed me, and I placed a hand on Rafael's hide, my hand sinking into his fur.

The bear froze. All three men watching us pinched their brows as one.

I'd done something wrong. Glancing at my hand, I wondered if there was some taboo against touching a fae in his shifted form. My hand slithered back to my side.

Hector raced forward, fingers on his dagger hilt. Javier tilted his head and crossed his arms, his expression entirely inscrutable. Sinsorias, on the other hand, grinned with exceptional delight, like he'd just witnessed me eating another orange.

Rafael walked past Hector and bumped him with his furry hide, nearly toppling him over. When he'd recovered, Hector eyed Rafael's retreating form and said, "Lucky for you, he can't seem to leave you alone." Hector flashed me a smile, as if we were sharing some dark secret.

Oddly enough, my heart fluttered at his words. But the man whose affections were in question was currently a *bear*. I'd talked to a tree-woman in the kitchens, and I'd seen winged horses pulling a giant flower. Wolves the size of horses existed in this world, as did homes with built-in beehives. Rafael was a shifter. It was not what I'd hoped for in a spouse. But I supposed there could be worse things.

Hands propped on his hips, Sinsorias cleared his throat, drawing everyone's eye but Rafael's. "Well, now. We have here a most interesting thing. Despite all reason, it appears she does not fear you, Romero." He turned to speak to Rafael, who continued to amble back toward the main house. "I set that hideous wingless dragon loose, knowing you'd go after her."

Rafael froze. A wingless dragon...lived here? In my mind, I saw that other barn, the one the bear had watched after racing across the field toward me.

"I wanted her to see you as you are, but I know now that was not enough to instill in her the proper distaste for your kind." Sinsorias was nearly shouting now at Rafael's retreating form. "Your brother has entrusted me with a single task, and I will not fail. Already the hounds make haste."

The enormous bear whipped his large head around, eyes leveled at Sinsorias. In that moment, the bear was fully monstrous.

Sinsorias flinched, tucking his arms at his chest. Hector stepped forward to stand beside me, his hand still poised over his dagger.

All eyes hung on Rafael, waiting to see what he would do. The fae courtier poured out scents of curdled fear. The bear had been my protector, but in that moment I too sensed he was dangerous, lethal even.

The bear took several steps toward Sinsorias. The sunlight bore down on us from directly overhead, and sweat rolled down my back. In a rather strange motion, Sinsorias lifted a hand straight up, as if to grasp the sun itself.

Rafael snorted and kept walking. The courtier, whose suit today was a bright blue the color of a peacock's chest, staggered backward, one arm upraised, the other hurrying to pull the bone whistle out from under his jacket.

Another snort from Rafael blew the dust into little swirls near his enormous, clawed paws. Rafael was a step away from Sinsorias when the skinny man sliced his hand down toward the earth. Sparks flew from his palm and sizzled against Rafael's face and the thick fur at his neck. He roared and lifted to his hind legs. I recoiled, certain he was about to rip off the man's head.

"Do you know why he married you?"

The courtier's question hung in the hot air. Rafael's paws remained still at his sides. Then he crashed back to the ground, blowing his bear breaths into Sinsorias' face. They held each other's stares a long moment, all the while my mind raced.

What was this enormous secret they were all keeping from me?

"If you don't tell her, I will," came the man's sticky voice. He cracked a wicked grin at Rafael. "But it will hurt all the more coming from you, so I leave that pleasure to you." He bowed slightly, his hair so close to Rafael's snout that he was tempting the bear to sink his teeth in. When he'd risen to his full height, he said, "By the time we depart, she will know."

26

TALIA

I followed him to the house, but he was much faster in his bear form, and I lost sight of him in the overgrown garden.

"Wait," I said for the third time. He clearly didn't want to speak to me, but sun forsake me if I wasn't going to track him down and learn this truth that had grown so large it hung over me like a storm cloud.

I tried the library first. The dining halls were both empty. I wandered down hallways I hadn't yet discovered. Everywhere I checked came up empty. Eventually, I followed sounds of a heavenly voice singing and discovered Everence in a room entirely enclosed with glass windows. She walked with a book in hand, singing to herself.

When she saw me, she smiled.

At my sideways glance at the book, she held it up so I could read the title, *Hymns of Winter*. The book was elaborately decorated with pale blue lines. "I miss the cold. Sometimes, in this eternal summer, I sing the songs of my mother's homeland and I feel the flakes of snow on my face. Here."

She handed me the book. I flipped to a random page and quickly realized I couldn't read a single word. I shrugged and handed it back.

"Try again. The words should come to you." She crossed her arms and nodded at me.

Perplexed at how I might read a language I didn't know, I peered down at another random page. The symbols were meaningless, and my mind began forcing the Avencian pronunciation as best I could onto the strange words. But as I moved to the second line, my mental voice slipped into an accent I didn't recognize, and a single word fell into place in my head. *Agrotha.*

"Blizzard."

Everence let out a tiny yelp of delight and clapped her hands. "Yes!"

"How did I know that?"

She slid a hand under the book and stepped around to stand beside me. One of her fingers traced down the lines and landed on another word. *Ymil*—Sing—*san rethmarka*—to the maker—*ta cora*—of all.

I gaped at her.

"How can I read that?"

She smiled a knowing smile. "Because he can."

"Who—*oh.*"

A fae's wedding vows, it seemed, bound two people together in ways promises never could. My increased sense of smell...was that from him too?

I stepped away from the book, fueled by an increased desire to find Rafael. "What else will I take from him to make my own?" His skill with a blade, his ability to read other languages, his magic—whatever that entailed? I cringed. "What will he take of mine and make his own?"

Everence offered a closed-lip smile. "Only time will tell. With all marriages, the bonds are made stronger with love."

"Where is Rafael?" I asked.

Her smile fell away. "Right now? I sensed him leaving the property a little while ago."

"He left me, with Sinsorias still here?"

"He doesn't have the whistle anymore, and you have a lily. You are safe."

I rubbed the outside of my arms. "He found me in the garden and tried to take the flower."

Everence bristled. "I will pay him a little visit. He will not do that again." She placed a comforting hand on my shoulder.

"Sinsorias said he would tell me the truth before we depart, if Rafael does not."

The hand on my shoulder twitched slightly before falling away. Instead of skirting the topic, the pretty blond fae pressed the book to her chest and said, "Then let me tell you where to find him at sundown."

The stair Everence had led me to descended to the level of the kitchens, then, just as she'd said, there was a small wooden door that looked like nothing more than a broom closet. I tried the knob and discovered, as she'd described, a narrow stair made of stone twisting steeply down out of sight.

With a slow breath, I tried to calm my racing heartbeat as I stepped onto this hidden stair and shut the door behind me. A light set into the stone wall flickered to life, casting dancing shadows on the walls. This was my husband I was sneaking up on, after all, not a total stranger, though I knew little more about him than I did the sellers hawking their wares in

Puerta. I'd waited until the sun had disappeared below the horizon, as Everence had instructed.

The stair curled around, then emptied into a wider cavern, not huge but not cramped either. The ceiling and walls had been hewn from black rock that sparkled in the light from several lanterns fixed to the walls. This was the cave Sinsorias had predicted.

My heartrate soared as I crossed the cold space. Moisture hung in the air, but I couldn't find a source anywhere. Then, as the tunnel curved, I heard the distinct sound of water slapping stones. An underground waterfall lay somewhere up ahead.

The water hit the stones in irregular bursts. The tunnel was longer than I'd expected, the sounds of the water amplified by the enclosed space. Then, the noise of the water evened out, as if something had been blocking its fall and was now out of the way.

I rounded a corner and yelped in surprise.

Rafael, clad only in loose-fitting trousers, stood with arms upraised, shirt poised over his head. He stiffened so violently at my arrival that every visible muscle in his torso hardened. The shirt fell quickly down, covering what my eyes couldn't now forget.

His hair was slick and dripping, and he slung his head back and forth in a very animal-like way to shake out the excess water.

"What are you doing here?" His voice was soft and curious.

I tried to swallow but couldn't. "Everence...told me..."

He huffed. "Of course she did. She failed to mention that I bathe every night after sunset, did she?"

My cheeks burned so hot I thought they might melt off

my face. Yes, she'd pointedly omitted this part. I would think twice about her innocent, sweet smile next time.

So entirely caught off guard was I by Rafael's half-dressed state that I nearly forgot why I'd wandered down here. But as he bent to collect a pair of shoes from the cave floor, I blinked hard and gathered my senses.

But every single thing I'd planned to say had evaporated from my mind. I was a bumbling idiot, void of all rational thought.

"The shift," I began, utterly at a loss as to what to say. "Can you explain it to me?"

He arched his brows. "Do you not find it abhorrent?"

The way he stood there, barefoot, holding a pair of shining shoes fit for a dancefloor made words almost impossible to conjure. "You were a bear a moment ago. Now you're...this. I'm curious how it all works."

He grunted. "You find my curse amusing, do you?" With that, he brushed past me and lifted a hand toward the stairs.

I snapped my jaw shut and whirled around.

Curse?

In that one word, my entire understanding of the man before me shifted. I'd assumed his fae powers were what turned him to a bear in the day, though I had no idea why a man would do such a thing. But if his transformation wasn't a *choice*, that changed everything.

For a long moment, I stared at him. His arm tired and fell slowly to his waist. He did not break my stare. In his eyes was a raging tempest, a storm so muddled I could no more comprehend what he was thinking than I could call magical sparks down from the sky.

Finally, I blinked and hurried past him toward the stairs.

As I rose up the steps, I couldn't stop myself from turning

to glance at him over my shoulder every few steps. His deep brown eyes met mine, and at first, they were shuttered, closed off, impenetrable. Then, by the third time I looked back, his expression had shifted, and in his eyes was a spark of curiosity, then desire. Questions spun in my mind, and I was more determined than ever to uncover his truths.

2 7

RAFAEL

As we reached the small door at top of the stair, Talia paused, one hand on the knob. Then she spun, once more, and fixed those large brown eyes on me, almost level with my own as she stood one step higher. In those eyes was the same blazing determination I'd seen in Puerta when she'd been hunting down the thief.

Her hand reached down and touched mine.

"Tell me about the curse." She spat the words so fast that I imagined she'd bottled them up with each step we'd taken and was afraid she'd lose her chance to speak once we walked through that door.

Stars, the warmth of her tiny hand on mine poured into me its own kind of magic. No woman had voluntarily touched me after learning I was cursed.

Here was a woman I could love. A woman whose beauty was the unadorned simplicity of a wildflower, whose tenacity rivaled the best summer storm, and whose compassion tore my black heart in two.

Tilting forward, I bent my forehead to hers, inhaling the

honey scent embedded in her clothes. Every part of me, animal and otherwise, craved what she was, what she offered.

Her breath escaped her lungs in a crisp *oh* sound that left me equally breathless. Cool fingers quickly found my neck, curling around and preventing my escape—for that was what I should do. Leave. Back away. Fight this.

Instead, I moved my head down to the crook at her neck, resting my mouth against the soft, warm skin above her collarbone.

There was nothing good left in me. Stars, how I wanted her to fall in love with me, if only to feel this passion requited for a single moment.

For that was all it could be, a single moment. Her life would end within hours of her taking my curse, whenever the sun rose and her body changed.

Curse my brother for this.

And curse my own soul for wanting to destroy her in exchange for a single moment.

My fingers reached up and slid beneath her hair, memorizing the way it felt, the way she didn't pull away but melted at my touch. One moment. One single moment. I couldn't pull away.

Into my ear, she whispered, "You can tell me. Please tell me."

At that, my senses returned. I lifted my head and stared at the door behind her. The real world waited there, cold and unfeeling. Her hand around my neck tensed.

"I can't," I whispered.

"Why not?"

Indeed, why not? If I told her why I'd married her, it would certainly be the cure she needed, the antidote to ever loving me. Selfish beast that I was, I couldn't do it. "Because you would see me as I am." Black. Murderous. Unredeemable.

Fingertips traced along my hairline, brushing long, damp strands away from my face. "Whatever it is, it can be forgiven."

I backed away, taking a half step down. "No." Because deep down, I still wanted to do this, to love her. To have her love returned. I pulled her hand away gently. "One cannot forgive a future act."

Rejection burned in those eyes and I lost a little more of my dignity when I pressed a kiss to her palm. Her brows lifted, confused.

"It is for you that I must not do this."

"But you..."

Married me hung in the air, unspoken.

I offered the briefest nod. Yes, I'd married her. Chosen her as my sacrifice. I'd never known how badly one could hate a choice made after the fact. "Trust me," I said, reaching past her to open the door that would take us away from this torturously tempting narrow stairwell. She needed to see that I was despicable, and if I couldn't admit to her the truth that would change her mind, I could show her. "Come, let's take a ride. I want to show you the village."

She cocked her head sideways at me. "If you're taking me into town, I'm not wearing this."

As she turned and marched out ahead of me, I knew that I had never felt so alive and yet so close to destruction. I would fade into madness, and she would live, if I had to burn the entire Sun Court to ensure her safety.

∾

In the barn, I opened Lily's stall.

"Let me ride him," Talia said, pointing to Espera. She wore a slim red dress that made it difficult to remember I needed to keep my distance.

I should let her ride my fire stallion—it was the least I could do for her tonight.

When I nodded, she clapped and entered his stall. Shaking my head, I saddled Lily and repeated to myself the reasons I was taking her to town.

By the time we rode into Moredo, the nearest fae village to Starfell, the moon was high and the residents were in the full swing of their nightly revelry. Moredo housed none of the great families of the Sun Court, and as such, fae with less power could find a place of superiority here. It was a town of little importance among the fae, which kept haughty fae like my brother and his favorites far away.

As we made our way among the pedestrians and slow-moving carts, a hush fell over every creature we passed. Heads turned. Women clapped hands to their mouths or clutched men's shoulders. A few fae children pointed and laughed, ugly cackling little sounds.

"Why are they doing that?" Talia whispered from atop Espera.

"Because they hate me."

Talia frowned at them. A kindness. But as we progressed through the canopied streets strung with magical lights that bottled sunlight and poured it back to us from tiny globes, her frown turned to a frozen, almost petrified expression.

Good.

"I don't come to town often. And the times I have, I've... left a bit of a mess. They hate me because I'm the reason this town is not favored by the high fae. I'm the reason the Wild

Hunt lurks in these woods, the reason the High Prince's crows plague this place, the reason none of the blessings of the Sun Court fall on Moredo."

Her face snapped toward me. "What?"

I blinked. "Are you even listening?"

She looked up and around before answering, a fearful expression on her face. "I heard you. But this place. There is magic everywhere, isn't there?"

"I hadn't thought of it that way, but yes." I nodded. "The lights were created with magic, diffusing the sun's light even when it doesn't shine. Many of the buildings have been constructed with rudimentary magic, not the magic of the high fae." I pointed to a hollowed-out tree. "Pixies live there."

Talia's lips curled into a cautious smile. "It looks like a tall cake laced with glowing icing."

The windows and balconies stacked closely on top of one another that she was right. I'd never considered that before.

"The brownies keep more humble abodes," I continued, pointing out the dirt shaped into single- or double-roomed domes that clustered here and there around the base of the largest trees. "The dryads sleep in the branches of the trees they tend." The dryads lived in the biggest trees, whose trunks were wider than two carriages lined up end to end.

I'd never really taken the time to compare fae villages with mortal ones. Mortals lived in dead houses, stone or lumber, while the fae dwelled in living homes, trees or fresh earth or even rushing water for the alojas. Only the high fae constructed homes that employed stone or wood.

Her fear dissolved into wonder as we walked the horses through town, talking of things I hadn't taken the time to notice in centuries. Her awe infected me as we dismounted and led our horses through the narrower streets that wound between large oaks and chestnuts and enormous cedars toward the center of Moredo. To see this for the first time would be a bit of a shock, and I found myself as entranced with her face as she took it all in as she was with the magic of the fae.

In the center of town, much like in mortal cities, there was a central open area, round instead of square, surrounding a natural spring that had been magicked to bubble up like twin dragons rising from the depths. Booths had been set up here by the industrious brownie selling vegetables or the artistic aloja, in her woman form, selling watercolors. Music drifted through the open space as a pair of wood nymphs drew bows across human-made cellos. The deep tones resonated through my blood, easing some of my tension. Human instruments were a wonder among fae, even though they employed dead wood. The community seemed to welcome the dead wood because of the way it brought life to the forest through the music it produced. An impromptu dancefloor took up one section of the greenspace, and all manner of creatures danced under the starlight and suspended orbs.

One dryad selling tiny plants in little pots tossed me a pointed glare. One would think after purchasing several of his seedlings over the years that he would finally cast off that judgmental eye.

Without glancing over my shoulder, I said, "They're following us."

"Who?" Talia asked, whipping her head around. "The Wild Hunt?"

"Don't speak that name here," I said under my breath. "I meant the trees."

Talia looked behind us again.

"Those two things that look a bit like walking trees. Those

are dryads. They have a particular hatred for my kind." I held up a hand. "Bear claws have done significant damage to their beloved trees. Many times. They have a right to watch me closely."

The more I could make her see of my darkness, the more I was protecting her, though each admission stung. "I have a tendency to fly into a rage during the day. Whatever is closest usually gets destroyed."

Talia nodded quickly, not meeting my eye. This was working, and it felt like swords thrust into my side. We left the horses to drink from the stream that fed the fountain. The fae gave us a wide berth, which suited me just fine. Every time I sensed a stare, I returned their gaze with hard eyes.

"They are so rude," Talia said, voice loud enough to be heard by an aloja with a rather nasty expression on her face.

Her question forced out a quick cough. She was kind, and that kindness made me smile. "Fae look at only one thing, and that is power. Here, where there are no high fae to make these lesser fae feel their own weakness, they pour out judgment on those they see as weaker. In my cursed state, I am beneath them. And even in this form, I can only perform the most rudimentary of magics, compared to the power I was born to."

The dimple between her brows deepened as her concern seemed to grow rather than diminish with these words. Seeing me as a bear hadn't scared her off. Learning how much I was hated wasn't working either.

"But why can't you do more magic while you're in this form?" There was a slight tremor in her voice that reminded me humans *did* fear magic.

A low grunt rattled in my throat. "The court I am a part of draws our magic from the sunlight. As I am incapable of building up my magic while in my cursed form, I am left mostly powerless, even at night."

"Oh."

She stepped a little closer, the warmth of her shoulder so near to mine a reminder that I needed to show her something that would push her away rather than draw her in.

"Tell me about your cur—about becoming a—well, tell me how it all happened, if you would." She fumbled over her words.

Stars, she was a curious one. "Talia, I brought you here to show you...to help you see that I am...not to be trusted."

She stopped walking and planted her hands on her hips. "Well, you failed. Because all I see is a man hated for what he is, and if it's true you have no choice in the matter, I find all of *them* despicable for casting you off simply for a lack of power."

The music reached a crescendo, and the vibrations of those strings lifted my spirits and fanned the flames in my blood. Talia turned to look at the dancers. Among them, two pairs of young fae danced, the women's long, caramel-colored hair swishing back and forth as they moved through the steps of a tango. The lesser fae danced like fireflies, looping and twirling all about with no precise steps.

"You want to listen?" I asked, following Talia's gaze.

She smiled and shook her head slightly. "No, I want to dance." She nodded at the two couples whirling in a fast-paced tango. Then, with a smile curling her lips, she said, "I require a dance."

Before I could reject this absurd notion, she tugged my hand and led me forward. I should warn her again now. The burst of adrenaline in my heart overpowered my misgivings and I followed. A beast following his own lamb to slaughter.

As she faced me, her eyes widened and she set her hand on mine. Her cheeks flushed and her breaths came in shallow bursts. Curse me, my hand slipped onto her waist.

As we waited for the music to begin again, she glanced at the other high fae. They scowled at us, and Talia scowled right back, then shot me a grin that made me laugh out loud.

The cellos cut their first deep notes and I thrust forward into the first step of a tango.

Talia nearly stumbled, but she caught on quickly as I led, recognizing most of the steps and feeling her way through the ones she didn't.

Soon she'd found the rhythm and was flinging her tiny little body into the dance in an entirely mesmerizing way. There was still a noted hesitation in her movements, doubt in her eyes, but she hid them well with her grand and fully committed spins. A desperation that I couldn't quite understand fueled her.

I dipped her and my chest ached as I pulled her back up, holding her close for longer than the dance required.

Her breaths were fast now, her eyes alive and bright, as she whirled back toward me for the final move of the dance.

Her leg hooked mine and together we angled slowly toward the ground. It was only the prescription of the tango —the other couples were doing the same ending move—but for me it was as if the world had constricted and there was nothing but Talia and her leg wrapped around my own. Her mouth was close, her breath fast on my face.

I'd brought her here to show her how hated I was, and instead, I'd done *this*. My mouth drifted closer to hers, entirely without caution for what it would mean. The look in her eyes, of hunger and acceptance and curiosity and delight all rolled into one, shattered my self-control and stripped me to my rotten bones.

She closed the distance between us, pressing her lips to mine.

Sun above, what have I done?

The dance ended. Applause rang out. We stepped apart.

Only then did I notice Sinsorias standing nearby, arms crossed, twisted sneer on his glamoured face.

28

TALIA

My pulse thundered in my ears and I could scarcely draw a full breath as Rafael's hand slipped off my back. I didn't care that I was in a city made of treehouses and little dirt homes, of twinkling magical lights and sprouting dragon fountains, that creatures with limbs like branches and flowering hair walked the same space. I couldn't tear my eyes from my husband's face. And for a moment, he held my gaze, an amber light flickering in the depths of his eyes.

In that moment, I glimpsed what I'd scarcely believed possible. For all his words and evasions, there was desire in his eyes...for *me*.

Then, his attention snapped away to something over my shoulder and a crease formed between his brows.

Suddenly, the world crashed back down around me, and I noticed several dryads with folded arms and surly bark-covered faces. A pack of the littler ones, brownies I believe, pointed and fussed at us. An aloja lifted a whirling paintbrush and studied us with a tilted, liquidy face. She tapped her paintbrush a few more times on her canvas, which was a curved sheet of bark, and then stepped back, satisfied.

When she whirled the painting around, I was shocked to see it was of us. Of Rafael holding me in the final dip of the dance, the hem of my dress all exaggerated and flowing in a circle around us. Rafael was depicted not as a man, but as a bear.

The creatures nearby started throwing stones at the painting. The aloja snatched it up protectively.

Rafael's hand in mine tightened almost to a painful squeeze. I didn't want this perfect moment to dissolve, and I knew when I turned around, it would. Already, it was breaking apart as the strange creatures turned angry eyes on us.

I returned a firm squeeze on his hand. I was here with him, and I would stand by him and face this grumpy mob of magical folk. After all, I'd vowed to take his curses and his blessings, and if that meant taking the hatred they all felt for him, I'd do it. Stars, I'd take him living half the time as a bear, if it meant having him.

His lips against my forehead stole my shaky breath.

"I'm so sorry," he muttered.

Every pinch and pull of his lips against my skin, the heat of his breath and the closeness of his wide chest made it hard to concentrate on his words.

Sorry for what?

He stepped back and scowled at something behind me. Finally, I turned.

Sinsorias strode toward us, arms opening as if to embrace us both.

"You would defy your brother even now, I see." His lips were red, too red, and his pale face glowed with magic that exaggerated his cheekbones and chin. Even still, he did not look masculine at all, but more like a jester. "Thought you could succeed before our trip? Mortals are fast-moving things, fast to live and die, but falling in love in a single night is too much to ask. A single dance doesn't turn a woman's heart."

I glanced at the ground, a fierce blush proving him wrong. No, it wasn't a single dance that had fanned my affection. It was my determined, unyielding choice. I'd married this man, and every part of me wanted to find reasons to love him. He'd held me, chased after me, protected me, given me the job I love most in the world, and danced with me. A happy marriage could be forged after a fast and disastrous beginning.

The entire clearing had paused to watch us, their gazes weighing me down. Rafael's hand in mine reassured me, comforted me. Then his fingers twitched and loosened. He wouldn't meet my eyes, and my dangling hand suddenly felt exposed and foolish. I was left standing alone, unmoored, beside him.

Sinsorias propped his elbow up with one hand and examined me with an arrogant tilt of his head. "She wants to love you, I can see that."

I wanted to punch him, that's what I wanted.

Rafael twitched. "Stop talking."

"And, oh, how you encourage it," the other man blazed on. The courtier was having fun, but his words were clearly poisonous to Rafael, who squirmed and shifted, the muscles in his neck and jaw flexing.

I wrapped one hand tentatively around Rafael's arm. He jerked away. My heart flared with pain.

Sinsorias laughed, his eyes bulging with false pity. "Stop

the charade, Romero. You cannot deny you still want to kill her."

My lungs froze inside my ribs, and I couldn't breathe.

"*Silence*, slave," hissed Rafael.

Ignoring him, the sunken-eyed Sinsorias stepped toward me, into my space, his glowing threads and skeletal face sending shivers of disgust down my arms. "Did you know, little mortal, that he brought you here for one purpose, to pour his misery and pain upon you until you break?"

I choked on my next breath. The world was shrinking around me, crushing and smothering.

"You should feel honored. He chose *you* as his perfect lamb, the one to take away his curse."

I stepped away from Sinsorias, with his wicked smile flashing and his purple suit sparkling. Tree-like bodies blocked my escape. Rafael stared at me, but I couldn't look at him. Instead, I blinked at the creatures closing in around us. Their faces were unfamiliar, but their anger was as plain as the moon above.

"Cursed beast," one snarled.

"Weak," another spat.

"Magicless," hissed a dryad with moss growing down his neck.

A squat brownie with a beard shouted, "The sun's forsaken him."

My eyes finally cut to Rafael. His brother, the Sun Sovereign, was the one who'd cursed Rafael. Sun forsaken, indeed.

Memories I couldn't shake tumbled over the accusations, muddling my brain. His hand on my back, his leg beneath my own, his face so close.

"Ah, ah," tsked Sinsorias. "Flee, and you won't get far. The hounds draw nigh."

A branch-like hand pushed me back toward the man I'd married. He'd made me promise, in my wedding vows, to take his curses and his blessings.

Stars, he *had* married me so I'd take his curse. My head began to shake back and forth. Words rose and died in my clogged throat. I wanted to fall to the ground, and I nearly did, but Zara's face popped into my mind, and I straightened my spine. I thought of all the men she'd snubbed since she came of age, all the lovesick bachelors she'd so easily offered a cold shoulder. Lifting my chin, I fixed indifferent eyes on Rafael, urging myself to hate him.

My arms and legs ached. Betrayal burned deep within my chest, raced in my veins, and echoed in my ears.

Rafael stepped toward me, his eyes desperate and fierce.

"Do not touch me," I said through tight lips. But his touch was all I could remember.

All of his affection, every time he'd saved me—it was all fake, all part of his plan.

I closed my eyes, unable to stand the agonized look on his handsome face. I couldn't pin down an actual lie he'd told me, but everything about him was a lie, like a mask—I'd never seen the real Rafael until tonight.

Sinsorias clapped and my eyes popped open. "Now, shall we? The Sun Sovereign is still expecting you two at his coronation ball, and it is not wise to anger the man who holds the power of the sun."

Rafael stepped into Sinsorias' face. "You don't have your whistle anymore. You cannot force us to go with you."

I scoffed at the word *us*. He'd destroyed whatever there might have been of *us*. In fact, he'd never intended for there to be a relationship. Only me, falling in love alone, simply to fall to my death.

The courtier curled his lip. "Be that as it may, thief, we should leave before the hounds arrive. You don't want *them* to bring your bride to the king. There wouldn't be much left."

Blankly, I followed Sinsorias to where the horses stood at the edge of the clearing. I mounted without anyone's help, and sat staring dumbly at the bobbing globes of light.

Sinsorias had ridden a white horse with a flashy purple saddle blanket. He trotted off, triumphant, in front of us. Rafael sat silent in his saddle beside me. As we rode back through the strange little fae village, my eyes glassed over and I barely saw the cute windows shining from the dirt mound homes or the gently swaying lights in the rooms way up in the massive trees. My mind wandered, and my anger deepened.

I gripped the reins so tightly my hands ached. Papa had married me off to a devil. He would break if he ever learned the truth.

A whispered voice from behind my right shoulder startled me.

"I vowed to protect you."

My head whipped around and I glared at Rafael.

His mouth never moved, but I heard his voice. *I did choose you to die. In the market in Puerta, I saw you only as my freedom from this curse.*

I grimaced and my head was spinning from his unspoken voice in my mind.

But from the moment I spoke the human vows to you, I knew I could never give you this curse.

My face couldn't frown deeply enough to match the confusion whirling in my thoughts. I shook my head and leaned forward, eager to put Rafael and this madness behind me. "Run, Espera," I muttered to the horse. "Light the world on fire."

The horse responded.

He lunged into a full gallop so quickly I nearly sailed off the back but for my tight grip on the reins. I tucked into a racing stance, the night wind pushing back the fear and rage heating my entire body. Sinsorias yelled, but there was no stopping this horse.

Below me, little pops of light stole my attention from the road ahead. His hooves glowed orange like hot coals, and the ground exploded with sparks, then flames, with each hoofbeat.

Crazed laughter spilled from my lips. I looked up at the stars and relished the thrilling freedom of this race. A snag of fear warned me that the hounds Sinsorias spoke of might appear, or that he might toss out a spell to throw me from the horse. But I charged on, not caring about the consequences.

Espera's gallop was the smoothest I'd ever felt. My traitorous mind pictured Rafael in that cave below his mansion, shirtless and vulnerable. I imagined his face against my neck, when he'd said I'd see the blackness of his soul when I learned the truth.

Black wasn't a dark enough color to describe it.

But he had warned me, hadn't he? Last night in the library. Then again when he and Everence had insisted I pretend to hate him. Little good he'd done protecting me from his hand against my back as we danced, his eyes after we'd kissed, his strong arms as he'd carried me through those awful gates into this strange world.

The fires exploding beneath me mirrored my own heart.

Hot, angry tears spilled down my cheeks as I rode Espera away from the little village. My entire body ached.

Rafael's voice again tried to speak into my mind, but I shouted as loud as I could, to no one but myself, "Your words mean nothing!"

Rafael had saved me only so I could live long enough to take his curse. I hated him, and I hated that I hated him. It was unfair. Marriage was supposed to be full of love, not deceit and death.

Maybe it was panic or madness or fury, but I drove onward, taking the road past the estate and thundering into the thick forest. We raced past fallen logs with curtained windows, spotted, tree-sized mushrooms with ladders up to the top. Tiny creatures yelped and dove out of the way. Running into the wilds of the fae lands wasn't smart, but staying meant death.

I gritted my teeth as Espera's hooves skittered to a stop and ceased sparking flames. "What is it, boy?"

Something heavy crashed in the woods. The skin on my arms prickled with fear.

"Talia, wait!"

My blood boiled at the sound of his distant voice. How dare he come after me?

A massive, scaled face surged toward me, fangs opening toward my throat. I twisted away so fast I crashed from the saddle. A red snake as big around as a fattened pig slumped to the ground beside Espera, whose hooves thrashed at the beast. It recovered for a second strike.

My hand fumbled so violently with my hem that I screamed in anger, but I finally grasped my dagger and drew it out. I yelled again, this time a battle cry, as I lifted my blade.

The sound disappeared under a loud hiss and the muddle of approaching voices as a second beast, a man with a bull's head, crawled right over the writhing snake and lunged for me.

The next second his hands were around my throat, squeezing hard, his awful ringed snout pressed against my left temple. Bull breaths snorted into my ear. He shoved me backward and lifted me to my toes. Lights danced in my vision, and I knew my last sight would be this nightmarish visage.

I spat, but most of it fell on my chin.

The monster squeezed and my throat burned. My vision tunneled. I couldn't breathe.

Then he tossed me to the ground so hard I dropped my dagger. Choking and wheezing, I clutched at my throat. The horrid beast rolled me to my back with his foot. Then his knee pinned my arm to the dirt. His black eyes gleamed with bloodlust. He grabbed my other and yanked it up before I could regrasp my blade. My lungs burned. I rocked my hips and kicked my legs, but my body was too weak.

He took my knife and stabbed the snake once, swift and deadly. The enormous snake flicked and twitched as it died. Panic drew more choked coughs from my lips. Then metal pierced my side, under my lifted arm. He slowly drew the point downward, bumping over two ribs and tearing my flesh apart.

I couldn't scream. A rasping sound hissed from my mouth as tears fogged my vision. I closed my eyes and was lost in the pain.

Then the knife was out and there was only agony.

Strange sounds floated around me, but I couldn't make sense of them. Blood slicked my arm and back and warmed my clothes. Each breath expanded the wound and each cough ripped me in half.

Death wasn't like walking into a white room or a pale fog or wandering into a deep forest, like the stories suggested. It was agony and terror and I fought it with every fiber of my being.

I opened my eyes, blinking against the tears. My mouth inhaled a bit of dirt, and the taste and grit pulled my mind ever so slightly away from the pain.

Blades clashed.

Blurry shapes lunged at each other.

I blinked again.

Rafael swung a blood-stained sword at the bull-man. The clashing sound was the blade hitting the beast's horns. Rafael moved so fast his hands were hard to track. Hector was whirling his hands in the air and Everence stood perfectly still, singing.

The snake lay still on the ground, unmoving. My dagger, coated in my own blood, lay beside me, within reach.

A moan of mingled relief and despair crept out of my aching lungs as my fingers scraped across the dirt toward the blade. I was nearly under their feet, the dust flying in clouds around me. I tried to crawl away, but the strain pushed more blood from the wound in my side.

Rafael attacked like no man I'd ever seen. A passion of rage blazed in his movements. He pressed the bull-man backward, away from me, back into the shadowy forest.

Then the beast dropped to his hands and charged. His horns knocked Rafael sideways, but Rafael grabbed ahold, bringing the beast's face around.

The creature's bare feet were close to me. In fact, he was standing in a puddle of my blood.

The bull-man stepped backward, struggling against Rafael's strength. As his other foot lifted, my eyes widened. It was coming down on my face unless I moved. With a last burst of adrenaline, I wrapped one hand around the beast's uplifted ankle and rolled. My side ripped apart and smeared into the dirt as the creature dropped with all his weight on top of me.

But when he didn't move to get off of me, even as my vision blurred and the world faded into darkness, I knew I'd held the dagger true. Rafael descended on him, stabbing he beast from above.

Warm blood washed over my hand holding the knife as I drifted into unconsciousness.

29

TALIA

My side throbbed. My head felt like an overfilled waterskin.

I tried to open my eyes—but they didn't obey. I tried again, and finally my eyelids pried apart, revealing a hazy, shadowed space. My vision cleared only briefly, but I recognized Rafael's dark hair and broad shoulders. Hector and Sinsorias stood nearby. My eyesight blurred again and my eyes drifted shut. I strained to listen to the men's voices.

"...longer can we afford to rest?" asked Hector.

"She is too weak to ride," said Rafael.

"The coronation is in five days."

The bed I was in tipped gently as a heavy weight settled beside me. I was too tired to open my eyes.

"If you are not present, you know what he will do."

A cool item touched my burning side and worked tenderly along my skin. Instantly the pain holding me back from rest slipped away, and with it, my awareness.

~

When I woke again, the walls glowed golden from sunlight, and an inconsistent breeze fluttered over me. I heard bees. Blue sky glowed happily outside my bedroom.

I tensed my muscles to sit up but could not. Pain flared at my side. Instead, I glanced around my room at the beehive wall and found there, beside the bed, curled up on the rug, a large bear.

His side heaved in a slow, steady rhythm. Under one massive paw was a book, as if he'd been reading when the sun came up and he hadn't moved since. He appeared utterly harmless in sleep.

I rolled, and the movement brought immense pain. I let out a sharp gasp, then clamped my mouth shut.

The bear lifted his massive head. His eyes were level with mine as he stood beside the bed.

His fast breaths pushed against the hairs at my temple. In his gold-flecked, human eyes shone both panic and pity.

He'd saved me, again. But was it only to keep me whole, a spotless lamb ready for the altar?

For a moment, he returned my stare. The hairs on my arm lifted. This beastly form was what he wanted to press on me. Then, as if sensing my fear and confusion, the bear turned his long snout away and ambled out the open wall into the garden.

I followed him with my eyes. After a moment, Everence stepped through the door and offered me water.

But as I drank, I couldn't pry my eyes away from the bear still watching me from the sunlight outside. I'd thought he'd *wanted* me. I'd been so entirely, grotesquely wrong.

"You should not have fled," came Everence's sweet, soft voice beside me.

Chastisement was not what I'd expected from her, given I'd almost died. I narrowed my eyes at her and tried to speak. My throat was hoarse, but eventually I called up my voice.

"What were those things?"

A pause preceded her answer. "They came from the second barn. The doors burst open and all the enchantments holding them broke at once."

I shivered. "Why?"

Everence stared down at me with sharp eyes and pinched lips a moment before answering. "Something caused Rafael's spells to falter."

The way she watched me with narrow eyes, she assumed this was somehow my fault.

"Why...why does he keep monsters locked up?" I asked, trying to erase that accusatory look on her face.

"Monster is relative."

I glowered at the blond fae. Her hair was down and flowing, luminescent with magic.

"To a rabbit, a hawk is a monster. To a hunter, a hawk is a friend." Everence didn't smile, rather her eyes pinched at the sides with deep concern. "The creatures in that barn are monsters to all but one."

"Who?"

"Rafael."

I rolled my eyes. "I suppose it only makes sense for monsters to be friends."

She scoffed, as if I'd cursed. "Rafael saved those men and women. They too, like him, have been cursed to appear as they now do. But unlike his curse, theirs have no times of reprieve, no hours when their forms can return to how they were born." She held a hand to my cheek the way my mother used to when I had a fever. "Those beasts all carry a curse, and they have failed to meet the requirements to break the enchantments. Most of them have gone mad, while others have resigned themselves to the darkest of fates—a life without hope."

I rolled my face away to stare at the sunlit garden once more. I could no longer see the bear. So, he kept a safehouse for the damned. Still, that didn't exonerate Rafael. He wanted me to die so he could live without his curse. He was every bit the monsters I'd seen in that barn.

"He has helped two others break their curses. His desire is to help the rest, but his magic is limited, as is his time," she continued.

"He needed a bride to take his curse so he could have more time."

Everence bit her lip. "Yes."

I thought she was a friend to mortals, and here she was telling me I was selected to die like it was no more significant than the chance of coming rain.

"Rafael's curse can only be broken by true love," she said. "Marriage alone won't suffice. You are safe if you do not fall for him."

If. As if I could love him now. The memory of my foolish kiss pressed against my every nerve. I returned her hard stare, unsure why she was angry in this moment. She was a beautiful immortal, a creature so lovely even Zara wouldn't compare next to her. She would make mortal men bow down, and she had magic to twist the world to her whims. It made sense that she would look down on me, but I couldn't figure why she would be mad that I didn't want to pine after the man who desired my death.

"The beasts smelled you, and they came after you, breaking their bonds to get to you."

"They need me to take their curses, too?"

She slid narrow eyes at me. "No. Only Rafael's works that way. His is the only curse I've seen in my four hundred years that takes a curse and gives it to another. His brother was clever, planning carefully how Rafael would forever be alone and hated—because if he ever found someone to love him, fae or mortal, it would simultaneously rip that person from him. If a fae, that person would hate him for pushing his weakness on her, and if a mortal, your body won't survive the change." Her voice came out pinched.

Awful curse or not, it didn't change the fact that *I* had been chosen as his lamb of sacrifice. His curse bearer.

"You want him to be healed," I said as Everence leaned back in the chair beside my bed.

"Yes," she admitted. "It's why I've stayed at Starfell."

I blinked at her. This woman wanted me to die too. I was surrounded by enemies. Beautiful, terrible enemies.

"Talia," she said, leaning forward to place her hands neatly on the bed beside me, "he has only until his brother ascends the throne to break his curse, for the enchantment was only ever breakable while his brother was a prince. Once Fabian attains the crown, and the power it brings with it, the curse will be permanent. Fabian has been trying take the crown for a long time, and only recently did he succeed in killing their father."

A scoff burst from my mouth. "I thought fae couldn't die."

"Oh, we can. Just not by natural means." She sighed and held out a cup of water to me. "The crown of a fae sovereign must lie fallow for one moon cycle, then it can be taken up by the successor. That month ends soon. Rafael is out of time."

"You think I will fall in love with a man who wants me dead?"

Her eyes pressed shut. "No. Of course not. We must all let that hope go, as he has."

"He what?"

She nodded. "He wants you to live, knowing now that he must carry his curse forever."

I snorted, unconvinced.

"Whatever you believe," she continued, "we all must travel to the Sun Palace for the coronation. Fabian has required it, and we cannot refuse without drawing down more curses on all our heads." She boldly placed a hand on my shoulder. "Talia, you must convince that entire court that you hate Rafael Romero."

Squirming under her touch, I twisted away. "Easy."

"Good," she said with a firm nod. "Then the journey ahead should also be easy." She stood and clasped her hands. "We leave tonight."

RAFAEL

My cold hands on her bare skin startled her awake. When her eyes opened, she yelped and twisted away.

I stood up, my hands never leaving her side.

"Try not to move," I grunted.

She froze, her eyes wide, her skin flaring warmer as my palms brushed gently across her ribs. She snapped her gaze down and flinched as she saw the jagged wound under her arm.

Over a pair of riding pants, she wore a large white shirt, one of mine, that I had cut up the side seam to better access the wound. There was magic to heal her, but I did not possess it, though she was mine to protect. I hated knowing she was in pain I could not dismiss. I tucked the loose shirt under her back. Her eyes narrowed, a short breath pushed from her parted lips.

Trying to ignore how much this noise increased my heartrate, I tapped lightly along the wound, dabbing a greenish ointment into it with the softest pressure. Everence was a gifted healer, and her poultice was already working wonders.

"I told you not to touch me," she muttered, her voice still rough from the near strangling she endured.

I hadn't gotten to her fast enough. By granting her wish to ride the fastest horse in the world, I'd put her in danger. She'd fled from me like a hare from a hungry wolf, and I couldn't blame her one bit. She'd almost died because my horse couldn't keep up.

To her harsh words, I only nodded and kept dabbing the poultice into her healing wound. The magic was strong, but the poultice wasn't working as fast as I'd hoped.

"I do not want you to be in pain," I admitted, though it sounded foolish and couldn't possibly atone for my sins.

Talia scoffed quietly. Words were difficult given how much of her body was openly displayed and the places my hands now touched. Carefully, I ensured the torn shirt did not reveal more than was strictly necessary to treat the wound. But my mind...I had to shut off its creative tendencies. She was not mine. Not now. Not ever.

Admitting my wrongs wasn't going to help, nor was any attempt to change her opinion of me. The only small relief came from the fact that now she knew the true extent of my wickedness. I no longer wore any masks or kept any secrets. My soul was entirely laid bare before her—and it was agonizing and freeing all at once.

My lips curled. "Now you see me as I am." I inhaled quickly and removed my hand from her side. The wound was treated. My work was done.

With deft hands, I pulled the torn shirt back across her and let it fall over the sticky green substance. I stood straight, tilting my head to examine her. She was the loveliest thing in all the lands I'd ever visited. Broken and sore, hoarse and angry. Her hair was wild across the pillow, and her eyes still held a glassy sheen, and yet her beauty struck me speechless. The weakness in her flesh wasn't something to disdain or disparage. Instead, the way she carried her life in the blood under her skin, the threat of losing it should her skin break or her organs fail, brought a vitality to her that fae lacked. She was flame and oxygen, fire and fuel. She consumed life and breathed it out all at the same, with every glance and every decision.

Her hasty choice had nearly killed her, running into the jaws of those creatures who hungered for her flesh, but in the end, she'd felled the monster with her own blade.

"You are brave, Talia Balcázar."

She turned her head away, the coldness of the gesture a knife to my heart.

"Your blade, when it entered the monster, disintegrated. Cursed flesh often destroys any weapon that isn't made of iron. Anyway, I left you one of mine as a replacement." I inclined my head toward the sheathed dagger on the bedside table.

Her eyes widened. The jeweled hilt sparkled in the glow from the candles. I'd seen the way she'd looked at the magical lights in Moredo, and I'd assumed she might prefer the familiarity of candles in her own rooms. They cast a warm glow on her cheeks.

As I moved toward the door, I said, "You are now among the honored few who've killed a minotaur in close combat."

"You stabbed it too, I saw you."

"Yes, but I wasn't able to use my iron blade on him until you tripped him and wounded him." Her brows lifted, but it was quite clear she wasn't going to speak to me, perhaps ever, unless I angered her.

With a bow, I left the room and nearly bowled directly into Everence, who waited, arms akimbo, in the hall.

My cousin assessed me with narrow eyes as I quietly shut Talia's bedroom door. The overpowering scent of honey diminished slightly as the door clicked shut.

I stepped aside so that Everence could enter. My brother would see Talia's indifference and be satisfied, which was something to celebrate, despite the emptiness in my cold, dark heart that would forever remain. As I brushed past my cousin, I nearly stumbled into the wall. Hands in my hair, I stared down the empty corridor, trying to find words to voice what had just occurred to me.

"I—" For several seconds, I stood there, mouth open, silent.

Everence waited quietly behind me.

My curse. For the first time in all my existing memories, I was *glad* I bore my curse. But these words could no more leave my tongue than a language I did not know.

My cousin took a step toward me, but I did not turn to face her. I couldn't face anyone just now.

"I think I understand," she said, voice carrying a little louder than I'd expected from her. "You are both pleased and crushed that she despises you."

I nodded, thankful she could find words when I could not.

"You see how valuable she is, and you are pleased to bear the weight of your curse now, if it means keeping her whole."

My eyes closed as I nodded once more. Talia's face filled my mind. I couldn't say this strange new truth aloud. I had hated my curse every day of my existence, with every drop of blood in my body and every breath I'd taken.

I shook my head in disbelief. "How can one be thankful for the thing I hate most?"

When she spoke next, I could hear the smile shaping her words. "Because for the first time, your eyes are not on yourself."

That stung. But she was right. I'd only ever cared about my own healing, and I'd decided that the world existed to purge me of my pains.

"I love her, Everence." The words fell from my lips as easily as drops of rain from a storm cloud. She was brave, confident, fearless—things I'd aspired to my entire life. Her beauty was amplified by the fact that it was real and unadorned. She saw a path ahead and marched down it with determination, even when that path took her into danger. She was a better person than I was, stronger in every way, and she deserved to live.

My cousin stepped around me, finally forcing me to look at her. She nodded, as if she'd known for a while what I'd only just discovered. Her smile, however, faltered. "And now you can never have her."

I scowled. "You wished for her to die too."

"No, I never wished that." She glanced over my shoulder at Talia's bedroom door. "I wished for something much greater from her."

"Greater than taking my curse upon herself, sucking the evil I was chosen to bear into her own veins?" I crushed my palms against my eyes.

Everence gently lowered my hands, holding them carefully in her own. A few brief notes of her music magic flowed over me, through me, and I exhaled in relief despite my whirling thoughts.

"I was hoping for this." She wiped a tear from her cheek.

"That when you looked into the face of the one who took away your curse, you would finally find what you have always longed for. Love. And I knew that love would change you, cousin. From the beast you were to the man I see now."

At the word beast, I tensed. "But she didn't take my curse —thank the First and Last."

"It wasn't the curse you needed to leave behind, cousin."

My pulse drummed in my ears. It wasn't my flesh that needed to change, it was the beast I had become, the cruel, unfeeling creature with a heart black enough to kill my own savior. It was the terrible and beautiful truth.

"But as it turns out," Everence added, "you fell in love and she did not, the best of all circumstances, and also the worst, because it keeps her whole while keeping you forever unhappy."

I'd thought my heart empty because it ached. Rather, it was, for the first time, full.

With two angry hands, I smeared away my own tears. I'd never known the depth of my brokenness until this day, and yet I was now whole—she'd taken my emptiness and filled it.

"I will keep her safe all the days of her life," I said through gritted teeth. "I will follow her into the mortal realms, and as long as I am able, as my mind disintegrates into nothing, I will defend her from every foe, every danger, every unworthy man who dares lay a hand on her."

Everence smiled, but it was tainted with worry. "The fallow crown falls to your brother in five days. There is but one way she can be saved from him. For despite what you think, he will not allow her to return home, not now."

My hand braced against the wall and my face fell. "He'll make me watch her die." I fisted my hand. "Sun above, I have to stop him."

Even as she nodded, a new sound reached my ears and I whirled on the spot.

Talia's bedroom door stood wide open. Leaning against the doorway, unkempt and dressed in my own ripped shirt, was my wife.

31

TALIA

He'd said he loved me.

I braced myself against the doorframe with my uninjured side and stared at Rafael. My pulse pounded so loudly he could surely hear it. Everence stood behind him, but I barely noted her presence.

For a long moment, no one moved. His chest expanded in rapid breaths, and his cheek bore the faint line of a tear stain. He was *crying*?

The way he looked at me made standing difficult. Or perhaps that was the throb in my side from a lingering knife wound. His fingers had touched my bare skin below my arm. The gentle way he'd administered the ointment had sent shivers down my whole body.

And he *loved* me.

I blinked hard, breaking his gaze. Could this be a well-performed skit to muddle my emotions? To manipulate me into falling for him?

Because it wouldn't work.

I pinned him with a skeptical glare. "Talking about me?"

His throat bobbed. He said nothing.

Everence slipped around him, her magical glow a welcome distraction from Rafael's stricken face. She lifted her hands toward me, ushering me into the room.

"Come, we must get you dressed for the journey."

She placed a guiding hand on my back and pushed softly so that I would turn around, but my eyes lingered on Rafael. He'd deceived me once already. I couldn't let his handsome face draw me in again.

As Everence reached back to shut the door, I caught sight of Rafael leaning sideways so he could see me before I disappeared.

When his face vanished from view, I slumped into the chair that had been scooted beside my bed. Bees hummed merrily to and from their hive. In mere days, the hive had blossomed with activity, as thousands more tiny creatures zoomed about. A few jars of clear, golden honey sat along the shelves, placed there while I was absent.

Everence spied me looking at the beehive. "It's come alive again," she said with a knowing smile. Then she carefully dropped to her knees beside me and lifted my arm. I grunted and tried to pull my arm back, but she hissed at my objections and lifted the shirt aside to examine the wound. After she'd clicked her tongue twice, I rolled my eyes.

"Something wrong?"

He loved me.

Focus. He was a murderer.

She stood, propped one hand on her hip, and tapped her nose with the other. "It should have healed by now. Mortal flesh mends as easily as it breaks." Her head tilted. "But the blade *did* have dragon blood on it when it pierced your side."

"Dragon blood? That snake didn't have any wings. Or legs."

"Yes, a twice-cursed beast, that one. It used to have both wings and legs."

I cringed.

"The poor thing never really did have much of a chance at restoration." Her face fell. "Rafael had never given up hope for her, though."

Her? "That thing was a woman?"

"Use to be." The blueish glow around her golden-white hair flickered momentarily as she stared at me with a pinched brow. Soon, she started bustling around the room, extracting items from the armoire, the bath chamber, and a squat trunk against the far wall.

She stacked them all up on the unmade bed. Dresses, bathing cloths, combs, tiny bottles and little wooden boxes.

As she laid out one particularly stunning gown, silver as moonlight and studded with tiny, sparkling beads, she caught my eye. "The longer a fae remains in his or her cursed form, the less they retain their original mind. That one had been alive nearly seven hundred years in her dragon form, then another five hundred and sixty in that awful body you saw. There wasn't much of her left in there. Only rage."

Everence paused a moment, hands on either side of the elegant dress, then pivoted and strode around the bed to take something from the table beside me. It was the jeweled dagger Rafael had mentioned as a replacement for the one I'd brought with me—Zara's dagger.

My eyes followed it and remained fixed on it as she placed it on the bed too. Emeralds glittered on the golden hilt. "I don't want that."

She ignored me and kept packing.

His cheek against my neck. Stop that. His words in my ear. I shook my head, as if I could dislodge the sticky memories. *You have no idea what you chose.* I huffed loudly, wishing Everence had a spell to make me forget every moment with Rafael.

"Does dragon blood make people sore?" I asked, tucking my knees up against my chest. The wound throbbed, but it no longer stung and burned. My muscles, however, ached from neck to toes.

Everence watched me as she came back around the bed with a fresh set of undergarments laid over her arms. "Sore?"

"My whole body hurts."

She dropped the clothes in her arms. "And your joints?"

I nodded, staring at the clothes on the floor. "Yes. They ache."

She bent down to collect the undergarments and set them hastily on the bed. "You are too weak to ride, but we cannot delay any longer. The hounds were spotted outside Moredo, which means they will be here soon, and the enchantments we placed around the estate will only hold so long. If we do not depart tonight, the hounds will... Never mind. If we make our way toward the Sun Palace, with Sinsoarias, the hounds should leave us alone. Sinsorias has offered for you to ride in his carriage, but Rafael would prefer that you ride with me."

A disgusted sound slipped from my lips. "I don't care what he prefers."

I could feel his arm holding me as he dipped me in the dance.

Blinking, I shoved away that ghost sensation and stared at the dagger. "But I will ride with you. Sinsorias gives me the creeps."

She chuckled and nodded. "Very good. We must ride through the day as well as the night. Then we can rest for one day and proceed into the Palacio del Sol."

I snapped my head up. "Wait, where?"

"The Palacio del Sol is where Rafael's brother lives."

"I...that was the name of my father's best horse." The horse that unwittingly threw me into this life. I'd dressed as the fabled wife of the sun that night, in my red, ruffled dress that I'd had to slice with the dagger that no longer existed. "You call him the Sun Sovereign. Does he have a wife? Our people have tales of a woman married to the sun who turns into a red macaw to fly around the world while her husband rules the day."

Everence's eyes widened and the garment in her arm nearly dropped to the floor as her arms loosened. "No. He has seventeen wives."

"Oh."

I made a disgusted face and bit my lip.

"He is the foulest of men, hungry for power more than the rest, and nearly every fae desires strength and power. He married each one of them to absorb their power, and he purged every bit of his own weakness by funneling it into them."

"Ick. And women keep marrying him?"

"Yes. It is an honor to marry a sovereign, or his heir, so they take his weaknesses, but they also all share his strengths. However, he has them all in such mentally altered states that they barely know their power, thus he gets to keep all the power for himself. Mostly. The occasional disaster has occurred when one of the wives wakes up from her magic-induced stupor and terrorizes the place in her confusion."

"He sounds awful."

She offered tight lips and a brief nod. "You have no idea."

I held my knees tightly to my chest. I could read a language I didn't know because of Rafael. I could smell things only an animal could smell. Javier had warned me that I might have the power to speak to the creatures in the second barn. "Did I set those monsters loose?"

Everence paused from folding the clothes. "It is possible that you have acquired enough of Rafael's magic to have said something to set them loose."

A knock at the door preceded the arrival of the female dryad I'd spoken with in the kitchen. She offered me a mossy smile and an angular curtsey before hurrying to take the undergarments from Everence.

"Good day." Her eyes snagged on the golden dagger and widened. "Oh, he gave you that, did he?" Her smile faltered and she gave the iron dagger a wide berth as she grabbed the rest of the items on the bed and threw them into a trunk.

Everence and the dryad helped dress me, careful to slow down when I winced, and soon I was wearing a clean, fresh-smelling day dress and simple slippers that suggested I would be doing no walking at all. When I was fully clothed, I sat down with a yawn and rubbed my elbows.

The dryad tilted her long face at me. "She's changing, isn't she?"

I snapped my gaze up at the creature. "Changing?"

32

RAFAEL

From behind the open windows in my bedroom, I stared out at the stars, frowning at the sound of a pack of dips howling and raging at the enchanted border of the estate. Hector stood beside me, arms crossed, legs wide.

"If that noise doesn't stop, I'm going to lose my mind," he said.

"It's Talia they want. Sinsorias will have to call them off. My magic can't stop an entire pack of hellhounds, protect Talia from Fabian, and keep the enchantments secure on the estate."

"The estate will manage," Hector said in a half-consoling, half-condescending way that only brothers can manage. "Javi knows what to do with the horses, and the beasts will be fine with the added enchantments."

"They broke their bonds."

"No, *she* broke them."

I ran a hand down my face. I needed a shave. "We don't know that."

He rolled his eyes. "You can deny that she loves you, but she *is* gaining your power already."

I grabbed his shirt collar. "If she loves me, she will die."

He pursed his lips, unphased. "Your fault, not mine."

My hand loosened and he stepped from my grasp. My shoulders fell and I leaned against the window frame. Explaining to Hector how badly I wanted Talia to forgive me was pointless. She *shouldn't* forgive me.

Shaking my head, I turned and stomped into the bathroom, where a willow wraith slept against the stone wall, her many arms stretched out, her thin head drooping to her chest.

"Get out," I barked at the wraith, waving a hand.

The creature lifted her ugly head slowly and peeled her feather-thin limbs off the wall one by one, until they hung in little gray, tentacular lines that wriggled like worms. Her feet, strange suctioned things, made little wet popping sounds as the creature made her way toward a window.

"Another one?" Hector asked over my shoulder. He grimaced at the translucent wraith as it fingered its way over the windowsill, all spiderweb movements and wet sucking sounds.

The thought of the waterfall below the house brought memories of Talia's warm skin against my cheek.

"She looked at me with curiosity rather than hatred and disgust, and it made me lose control." Now, I could never touch her again.

"I think you're gaining some of her human qualities, brother. Pull yourself together."

Hector half-turned away as I bathed and yelled at me over the rushing water pouring from a stone lily in the wall.

"You realize that if she *does* fall for you, that you'll get your magic back."

The water racing down my back chased away the scent of bear that clung to me. "She hates me."

Hector turned fully toward me. "But does she? Think about it. What if she already loved you, before that prude told her of the curse? You said she *kissed* you. You might already have more magic."

I raked water from my face and tried to ignore the way his words suggested Talia's own downfall wasn't yet avoided. "She's too smart to fall for a murderer."

Hector rolled his eyes. "Just try silencing those stupid hounds. Do it, Raf."

"Silence!" I screamed. When I opened my eyes, Hector was smiling dumbly at me.

The hounds had ceased their barking.

His hand fell on my shoulder. "It's coming back." Tears welled in his blue eyes—I'd only seen my brother cry two other times in our lives.

With a shout, I clapped a hand on his shoulder and shook him. Then just as quickly, my enthusiasm died. "But that means…"

He charged after me into my bedroom. "Wait, stop. It means—"

I whirled on him. "It means she's already leeching the curse from me."

"It means she loves you."

That was the worst news I could have heard. And yet my heart swelled. Clawing at my wet hair, I screamed. "I have to make her stop! Before the change."

Hector grabbed me and shook me. "Listen to me! Let this happen."

I knocked his hands away and stormed from the room.

The brightest stars already peeked out as I walked out the seldom-used front doors to the weed-infested front drive. I averted my eyes from the gaudy monstrosity of a carriage that reminded me of my twin brother's opulence and spotted Talia and Everence chatting softly beside the row of saddled horses. My breath caught at the mere sight of her.

Stars, keep it together.

The two women glanced up, Everence's eyes brightening like the dawn even as Talia's darkened with a warning. I bowed.

"Good evening."

Sinsorias, in a garish red suit with lapels wider than his shoulders, waltzed up. He wore his smug grin like it was required and toyed with one dangling earring.

"I called off your dogs," I said flatly.

He pursed his lips. "I wondered what happened to them." He cut his eyes to Talia. "Hmm, so you were *able* to silence them? I see." He wrung his hands at his chest and took a step away from me.

The fear creeping in to his voice brought a smile to my face.

Talia stiffened noticeably and turned her attention to the magnificent black horse before her. Hector, ignoring Sinsorias, sauntered by and hopped in the saddle of his bay mare. Lily was saddled and ready for me. When I moved toward her, she tossed her head and pawed the ground.

"Easy, girl." I patted her neck. She sensed something was wrong.

"Shall we?" asked Sinsorias, his tone a mixture of arrogance and trepidation. With a pointed glance from me to Talia, he lifted one hand and looked her up and down. I gritted my teeth and repressed the urge to punch his nose.

Talia lifted her chin.

Sinsorias leaned close to her face. "You cannot pretend to hate him, dear girl. So don't waste your efforts." He turned and marched toward his carriage.

"I do hate him," she seethed, eyes locking with mine.

A chilling distrust flashed in her expression. *Well and good.* But it clawed at my heart all the same. She angled her body away from me as I walked past.

Pausing before the black horse, I said, "This one is for you, when you are strong enough to ride."

The horse's sleek coat shone in the warm firelight. Its mane was combed and long, and it had the little tufts at its feet that marked it as a Vessian, one of Avencia's most notable breeds. A little reminder of her home. Now that she knew the truth, there was no danger in giving her gifts. No danger in doting upon my bride—she would never love me. No matter what Hector believed.

To my utmost delight, she admired the horse with wide-mouthed wonder. She let the horse sniff her hand. He must have been expecting a treat, or he smelled her last meal, because he batted his lips playfully at her palm in a way that made her giggle. The sound was like a balm to my blistered soul.

"What's his name?" she asked in clipped tones, not taking her eyes off of him.

"Phantom."

From his saddle nearby, Hector called out. "He bought

him for you. Slipped away in the night and came back with that horse."

I shot a warning glance at Hector. Talia jumped, as if startled I still stood beside her.

"It suits him," she said.

At her approval, my heart leaped like a deer. She slid her hand back to the saddle and paused, glancing about awkwardly.

"You're not strong enough to ride alone." I cleared my throat. "Not yet."

She grabbed her elbows, holding herself as if still in pain. "Well, I'm not riding with you, that's for certain." She glanced at the grand carriage, but a disgusted shudder said she wouldn't be riding with Sinsorias either.

"Does it hurt still, the wound?" Instinctively, I reached for her, then, at her gasp, shoved my hands behind my back.

She loosened her arms. "No." Her brow puckered a little and she bit her lip. "The wound doesn't hurt much at all."

Everence leaped into the saddle of a dapple-gray horse and whispered something to Hector. I only caught one word: *convincing.*

Hector called out, "Who's going to take care of that pack of hounds as we go by?" He lifted a hand to the carriage. "I'm not putting my money on him."

"I'll ride with Everence," Talia announced.

Everence shook her head. "Not a horse person, remember? I'm a terrible rider. It's all I can do to stay in the saddle when we have to hurry, much less outrun a pack of hellhounds. I'm sorry."

Talia's face blanched.

"Ride with me," I muttered so only she could hear.

She shook her head.

"I'm not asking you to forgive me. Only ride with me."

When Sinsorias' carriage lurched forward, the dogs again began their slavering howls. Down the long drive, their black figures could be seen frantically leaping at the enchanted gates.

I clicked my tongue and Lily trotted forward. I quickly knelt and waited for Talia to accept a leg up. For a heartbeat, she only stared at my hands. Then, she *hmphed* and lifted her foot.

Her dress snagged as she threw her leg over the saddle, but with quick hands I dislodged the fabric from the back of the saddle. Her eyes briefly locked with mine, and the passion I'd felt as we'd danced flared in my chest.

Sun forsake me, this was going to be a long trip.

33

TALIA

The hounds threw themselves at the gates, barking madly. Sparks flew as their black bodies collided with the magical barrier. Their eyes glowed red and their lips dripped with saliva. They were twice the size of the biggest dogs I'd ever seen. My body curled into itself as fear took over. But as I pressed harder into Rafael's chest, firm against my back, I recoiled slightly.

"If your brother sent them to chase us to the palace, will they hurt us when they see we're headed that way?"

Rafael breathed hotly against my ear. "If my brother sent them, there is no telling what they've been ordered to do."

"Can you silence them again?" The sound of their snarling was raising my blood pressure.

He twisted his hands in Lily's mane and whispered, "Don't listen to them."

At his words, the dogs' barking muffled and at once I breathed with relief.

Everence cantered up beside us. "I will sing them to sleep."

Her words were still sharp. "I will tell Hector to enchant the horses to keep them safe."

"I will do this," Rafael called over the sound of the hooves, pressing his horse faster.

Everence started to object, but Hector thundered past her, grinning.

As soon as we neared the end of the drive, the ornate iron gates burst apart, sparks flying as we sailed through the enchantments. The horrifying dogs flew outward, blasted by some unseen force. Rafael's chest heaved. His knuckles were white on the reins. The animals tumbled over each other and charged us, their mouths moving but my ears barely registering their sounds.

Rafael lifted a hand and sliced it downward through the air. "Enough!"

Every hound stopped, hunkered down, and tucked its tail between its legs, red eyes downcast. Faint whimpering sounds reached my ears, and I stared over my shoulder in amazement as the black hounds all cowered and ran.

Hector whooped victoriously. Everence, on the other hand, stared in open-mouthed shock at Rafael as she hunched in the saddle beside us. She really did look uncomfortable on a horse. I nestled a little deeper against Rafael, hating the way my heart hurt at his nearness, hating the way I felt safe in the arms of my would-be murderer.

I jolted awake, and my head slammed back against Rafael's jaw.

He let out a little grunt but said nothing. The scenery had

changed from forest to flatlands and the eastern horizon blazed with pale golden light. The road curved and there were no longer gigantic trees like the ones in Moredo, but an open expanse framed by mountains in the distance to the left and the flat line of the sea far away to the right, out the opposite window. Color exploded everywhere. Red poured down from one hillside in clumps like a mudslide. Purple bubbles rose and popped in strange little pools that dotted one low area off to the right.

The enormous flower carriage was nowhere in sight.

"Where's Sinsorias?"

Rafael lifted a finger off the reins and pointed straight up. I craned my neck and saw, floating in the sky a little way ahead, a carriage pulled by six winged horses. Oh. Right.

"We call this area Las Tierras Pintadas, the painted lands."

Rafael's voice startled me. It was soft and, annoyingly, reassuring. I groaned slightly as I tried to stretch my arms. My joints were stiff and achy. My head throbbed with a dull pain.

"Do you need to rest?"

"I was just asleep. I'm fine. Just...uncomfortable."

He shifted. "We can stop. It is nearing dawn."

He whistled, and Everence pulled her dapple-gray horse around. Hector's bay mare trotted up beside us. "We'll stop here."

"Why? I'm fine. I can keep riding."

Everence shook her head. "Not for you. For him. For the change."

Rafael *hmphed*, and my body went rigid as he leaned forward, swung one leg over, and dismounted Lily. Then he reached for me, but I snorted in offense. I hopped to the ground without his help. My feet throbbed with pain at the harsh landing, and I lost my balance.

Rafael stuck out a hand to steady me. "You're hurting."

"I'm fine." Everything ached, but he didn't need to know that.

He and Everence exchanged a glance. Hector whistled contentedly to himself as he walked his horse toward a creek that ran alongside the road.

To our right, lemon-yellow mushrooms the size of breakfast tables circled a trio of lumpy, brown dirt mounds. Everence drew a blanket from her saddlebags and spread it out for us to sit on. She beckoned me over, unwrapping a loaf of bread and a handful of walnuts. Her words I'd overheard outside my room, that she'd never wanted me to die, but to change Rafael, echoed in my head.

Chewing on a walnut, I studied him as he squatted and checked the horses' silver shoes. *Had* I changed him?

He'd sounded genuine in the hall, but I couldn't let myself trust him. Falling for him would kill me, after all. Easy to avoid. Simple.

He looked up and caught me staring. I turned quickly away, stuffing bread in my mouth.

"It's unfair," I said to Everence, watching a fox scamper across the plains.

Without asking for clarification, she nodded. "Yes, it is."

For several minutes, we sat there, eating a meager breakfast as the horses rested. Then she sat up a little straighter and nodded at someone behind me.

"The sun rises," she said.

I glanced behind me. Rafael paced away from us, stripping off his surcoat, then his waistcoat, and finally his shirt.

"Look away," Everence begged, touching my arm.

But try as I might, I could not tear my eyes from Rafael.

All at once, his limbs shot out in seizure-like jerks and his chin jutted upward. An awful gurgled moan rasped from his lips as he fell to the ground. I froze in place, unable to look away.

His muscles spasmed violently. His cheeks hollowed, his chest became a skeletal specter, and his body stretched. His skin rippled like the surface of a pond. My stomach heaved, and I clapped a hand over my mouth. His limbs stretched, bones cracking, and then, lying in his place, was a massive bear. In a breath, he stood. He twisted his head back and forth, shaking the skin on his wide shoulders, flinging fur in the bright sunlight.

Rafael turned his brown eyes upon me. My mouth opened and closed several times before I finally clamped it shut.

Everence was beside me, her quiet presence a small comfort as I stood. For a long moment, I stared at Rafael. Wanting freedom from a curse wasn't wrong, but paying for it with someone else's blood *was*. I rubbed at my chest, where a sharp pain darted from between my lungs and sliced upward, toward my neck and outward toward my arms.

"Ouch," I hissed.

"What's wrong?"

I shook my head. I'd been stepped on by a horse, thrown from a saddle countless times, and kicked in the shins with an iron-shod hoof. I wasn't going to complain about sore muscles and aching joints.

Rafael broke my stare and wandered off, loping out of sight behind a cluster of red-topped mushrooms that looked like card tables. The long, powerful strides of his bear body reminded me how very unlovable he was. *Stars, that's exactly what his brother wanted me to think.*

I'd wanted to love him. From the moment I'd married him, I'd set my mind to loving him, no matter how long it took or how many obstacles I might have to overcome. But I'd never imagined that he'd married me simply to dispose of me the way the ancients sliced the throats of bulls and goats to appease their god.

I hadn't realized my hand was rubbing my throat until Everence stepped around me, brows lifted.

Her smile brightened. "May I look at your wound?"

I lifted my arm and sighed. Everence placed a palm against my dress, directly over the wound, and closed her eyes. It was awkward, holding my arm up as she hovered so close, eyes closed and melodic voice humming softly, but my muscles relaxed, and a wave of energy flushed out through my extremities.

Her eyes fluttered open. "You are still weak, but the wound has fully closed." She stepped back. "Your muscles must be holding on to the exhaustion that accompanies severe injury in mortals. I didn't expect that. Your body, for some reason, is resisting my magic." She tapped her nose with a finger. "I sense more pain in you than you are admitting."

My lips pinched. "Perhaps."

"Sit. Rest. We will ride again soon."

When I turned to scan the surrounding area, she added, "He will follow. You are strong enough to ride, I think, now that the hounds have left us alone."

We sat on the blanket again. The sun rose over the colorful landscape, and I felt like I was sitting in a bizarre painting. A mouse scampered past us and sniffed at the bread. I flicked him a little piece. He took it and darted away.

"Tell me of the Sun Palace. I know nothing about this world, about the king we're going to meet."

Everence snorted a little. "He's only a prince. And the only reason he will take the crown is because he murdered his own father."

"And no one cares that he did that?"

"No." She shrugged, offering no further explanation.

"Then tell me of the courts."

Everence picked a clover and twirled it in her finger. "The four main fae courts have separate areas of dominion, separate sources of power. The sun for summer, moon for autumn, stars for spring, and darkness for winter. The First and Last granted us the right to manipulate the light and the dark, though little remains as it once did, when the courts were first established."

Rafael had used the term First and Last in the hallway. I'd never heard it, and yet they'd both used it like the name of a deity. I opened my mouth to ask about it, but Everence's expression darkened and she continued.

"There is a fifth court, however. The Shadow Court." She frowned and pressed her hands firmly into her lap, as if smothering some unpleasant memory. "A subset of nobles under the Night Sovereign wanted to gain power on their own, apart from their king, so they created an entire scheme of marriage bonds that would amplify their magic and satisfy their ambitions. When they were strong enough, they took the power of darkness with them and created a counterfeit court, one where darkness was never permanent, but was doubly potent with its magic of deception. They were rejected by every other fae court, so they took their power where it was strongest, the mortal lands. The fae in Rivenmark do our best to ignore their existence."

My people worshiped the sun, but according to the fae, one of their courts controlled the power of the sun. I was about to travel to the palace of the sun, a place I'd thought humans only reached in death. If the stories of Rafael's brother were true, he was no deity.

Everence talked on, explaining that her strongest magics were a combination of song and ice, of spirit and elixir. All fae gained magic through marriage, and children contained an unpredictable mixture of their parents' magics.

It all sounded a bit like horse breeding. Champions begot champions, and the like. Rafael had married me not for my power, but as a means of casting off his greatest weakness upon a vessel crafted for a quick death.

The sun grew hot quickly, and Hector approached, holding out a flask.

"What's in that?"

He chuckled. "Water."

I chugged a long sip and handed it to Everence.

To my surprise, Hector sat down beside me and crossed his ankles. His long, blond hair was knotted on top of his head, and he stared down at his linked fingers as he rested his elbows on his knees.

"I want you to understand something," he said quickly. "I hoped you would be the one to save my brother. Yes, that means I wanted you to die. Yes, it means I care more for my brother's life than your own. I admit that." He finally looked at me. "Rafael deserves to be free. He is a good man, and I would cut off my own arm if it meant he could taste life without a curse. As it stands, I see he will never be healed. Time is over for that hope." His eyes darted over the land-scape. "You and Rafael are about to walk into a maelstrom at that palace. Step carefully, or you'll end up cursed or dead or enslaved. For Rafael's sake, I do not want that to happen. He's bade me protect you, if he cannot. If they...if anything happens to him, I will get you out."

So, Rafael still wanted me safe, even if he was dead.

That wasn't just a ruse to get me to love him, was it? I swallowed. Fae were tricksters, and I couldn't afford any more tricks. I offered a small nod, unsure what to say.

Hector stood. "The dagger he gave you has iron at its center. The hilt is harmless to a fae, but the unsheathed blade will silence our magic, and a stab can kill us. If you are ever in danger, use it." He walked back toward the horses and began checking all the buckles on his tack.

I glanced at the jeweled hilt sticking out of the saddle bag on Phantom. Rafael had given me a weapon that could kill him.

Soon, we were on the road again, and I was riding atop my new horse, pleasantly alone in the saddle. My eyes kept darting back to the golden dagger. Of all the things Rafael could have gifted me to seek forgiveness after what I'd learned of him, he'd chosen a weapon capable of ending his immortal life.

My lips parted in a quiet gasp. "He does love me," I breathed quietly to myself.

I scanned the plains, searching for the massive bear. A small distance from the road, he plodded along. His enormous head lifted and he noticed me.

I heard his voice in my mind as clearly as if he sat beside me.

I told you some things were unforgiveable.

The road wore on, and my body ached more acutely with each passing hour. We stopped only so that I could sleep. Fortunately, the magic of my companions made setting up a luxurious bed inside an elaborate tent as easy as a few spoken words. The second day of travel passed slower than the first. The only entertainment was the occasional chat with Everence and the endlessly bizarre landscape. Stacks of rocks so high I couldn't see the tops. Moving rainbows that twisted horizontally along the ground. Mushrooms large enough that homes had been built on top of them. Marshes made of purple liquid. I'd seen deer with antlers so large they nearly dragged the ground at his sides. Hawks as large as draft horses with riders buckled on their backs.

We couldn't enter the Sun Palace while Rafael was a bear, so we would have to enter at night, and we had only one more day to cover the distance before we'd miss the coronation ball entirely.

On the second night of travel, moonlit vineyards rolled by, and a glistening river wound its way alongside the road. Sinsorias remained high in the sky above, watching us. Making sure we remained on course. Rafael rode on Lily at the head of our little caravan.

"What's that?" I asked, squinting up at the starry sky, where a dark shape wove among the thin clouds.

Everence followed my gaze and stopped humming. "That is a shadow lord."

My throat constricted and I couldn't ask for clarification. Instead, I gaped at the figure approaching. He rode a winged creature, black as night, that dove and flew nearly flat against the ground, moving fast. With one massive beat of its wings, the thing—a dragon—lifted up and over us.

Everence reached for me. "Get off the horse!"

I obeyed. She beckoned me toward the long rows of grape vines nearest the road. Heartbeat racing, I huddled under the overhanging vines beside her.

"They hate the summer court, and any with the power of the sun. Tormentors. Pests. They usually don't bother Rafael, as he has so little power now. But the fac that he is brother to the Sun Sovereign must be reason enough to attack."

The dragon swooped over Rafael's white horse and lifted Lily in its claws. I whimpered as I watched the horse kick. Rafael crawled up the dragon's leg, knocking the rider to the ground. They fell hard. I cringed. But then they were wrestling and my fists were tapping nervously on my upraised knees.

My muscles tensed and I thought of the dagger in my saddle bag. "The dagger!"

Everence's hand on my shoulder made me jump. "Stay here."

The dragon's rider sliced at Rafael with a knife that glinted in the moonlight. He was fast, but not as fast as Rafael. Hector was there, lunging at the shadowy figure. He was hard to see, almost as if he was part of the night, the darkest of shadows from head to foot. A second dark figure leaped, seemingly out of the first—where there had been one man, now there were two.

Hector and Rafael now each fought a separate foe, though the two shadowy men moved with such mirrored movements that it was like watching the same man fight in two different places. My brain couldn't process what it was seeing.

Rafael howled as he took a hit. I flinched. Hector was pushing the other figure back, but I noted that Rafael had put his back to us. He was protecting us—or rather me. Everence hissed at me to stay put and darted forward, little ribbons of what might have been ice crystals carving through the air before her. The predawn sky had lightened, making the scene below easier to discern.

The shadow figures were now outnumbered. Within seconds, they were driven back, and, to my horror, the two shadow men merged once more into one man. I rubbed my eyes and looked again. The foe was already on his dragon and climbing into the sky. Rafael slumped to his knees.

I choked on my next breath and stumbled out from the shadows of the grape vines. Rafael was now lying entirely on his side, his knees curled up, small moans issuing from his lips.

"Help him!"

Everence and Hector stood by, the one with her arms neatly pressed to her sides, the other bent over panting, blade still in hand.

"Step back, Talia," Hector warned.

"He's bleeding!"

"Get back!"

The first bright shard of sunlight broke over the horizon, and at that moment, Rafael's body lurched.

When his body finished its grotesque morphing, I dropped to my knees beside his furry hide. He didn't hop up instantly this time, but lay still, his side moving up and down quickly.

"Is he still injured?"

A cool hand slipped around my arm. "Yes," Everence said, "but in this form, there is little my healing magic can do. Cursed flesh rejects magic—it's part of the ugliness of the curse. I will have to wait until he is a man once more. They timed their attack well."

My eyes widened and I placed a hand over my own healing wound. She'd said my body was resisting her healing.

But that meant...

The eyes of a man watched me from the body of a bear.

His nostrils expanded and contracted as he breathed labored, loud breaths. He was in pain, but there was nothing to be done. He'd suffered more than I could ever imagine, bearing this curse for three hundred years without reprieve. His only hope had been in finding someone willing to take his curse, willing to love him enough to bear all his pain.

My hand moved from my side to my lips and I spun away. I couldn't endure his piercing stare. In my body, in my *heart*, lay the key to his healing.

Watching his body change had terrified me. A tearless sob shook my body. I wanted him to be healed, but I couldn't be the one to do it, for now I understood that the change would surely destroy me.

I met Everence's watchful eye. Her expression indicated she knew what I was thinking, but she said nothing.

"Does your love not suffice?" I whispered, voice strained with tears I was holding back.

She offered the smallest shake of her head.

My bones hurt so badly they burned. Squeezing my eyes shut against the pain, I focused again on Rafael. When I'd kissed him, this pain had begun. Barely noticeable at the time, but now undeniable.

"What's happening to me?"

Hector, Everence, and Rafael stared at me, and the weight of their gazes nearly brought me to my knees.

"I'm changing, aren't I?" Hands shaking, I cupped the sides of my face and stared at the sunlight filtering through scrubby pines. The pain doubled, and I coughed in agony. "How long do I have?"

Knowing I was about to die brought a strange, panicked clarity to my mind. There was nothing but this space, these people. My mind emptied of everything else.

Hector squatted beside Rafael and checked his wound. Then to me, he said, "The change will likely be gradual. And as agonizing as possible. Fabian didn't want this to be easy."

Terrified, tearless sobs shook my chest. Everence wrapped an arm around my shoulders and squeezed, and it seemed as if I might burst apart if she let go.

"As long as you deny what's happening," Hector continued, "the change will be drawn out."

"Hush," hissed Everence. "She doesn't need to hear that." She pressed closer against me. "We can't know when the change will be complete. Only you know your own heart."

A disbelieving laugh burst out between dry sobs, and I met Rafael's gaze. "You succeeded, then. Are you happy?"

Everence drew in a sharp breath and Rafael turned his great head away. In the bright morning sun, this colorful world suddenly felt entirely fake and irreverent. Everything here was manipulated, even nature.

Needing to think of something else, I said, "In the hallway, I heard you say Fabian will try to kill me."

She dropped her chin to her chest. "Yes. He will sense Rafael's feelings for you, and he will aim to increase his brother's suffering by torturing the woman he loves."

"Oh. Lovely." I jerked my shoulders free of her grasp and stormed toward Rafael. "I trusted you. How could you say you wanted to protect me, while all the while you only needed my blood to set you free?" Everence and Hector called out to me, but I wasn't listening. I wouldn't hear their protests. Rafael backed up as I blazed forward. "How could you hold me and want me dead? How could you kiss me and know it would kill me?" I fell to the ground, fingers sliding into the dirt.

Warm breaths blew against my fallen braid. Every hair on

my arms lifted and chills spidered down my spine. Slowly, I looked up into Rafael's bear face. His eyes glowed amber, brighter than I'd ever seen.

"Come, we cannot linger," Hector beckoned. "We're still a day's ride from the palace, and while the hounds are keeping their distance, they track us still."

34

RAFAEL

Talia rode on the horse I'd bought for her. She'd climbed in the saddle without a word, and despite the fact that she'd witnessed the attack by the dragon rider, she kept her head high and her shoulders back, unafraid, as we proceeded toward the town that hugged the outside of my brother's castle. Simply her presence beside me alleviated the pain burning in my side.

At a bend in the road, the Sun Palace came into view, and Talia's lips parted.

The buildings that abutted the Palacio del Sol—a city in its own right—glittered like sun-struck snow and clung like icicles to the massive walls of the pale sandstone rising in the center, tall as a mountain. Light shone out from the walls and stood in a bright column that stretched clear up to the heavens. My brother always did have a flair for the absurd. Even from the womb, when he'd come out hanging on to my ankle so that we'd both be the firstborn. The hatred had begun then, but it would end soon.

Sinsorias' ridiculous flower carriage soared over our

heads toward the palace. Finally, he was leaving us.

From his saddle, Hector looked down at me. "Remind me why we are doing this? Fabian has almost infinitely more power than you, and an entire castle full of people who adore him for it."

I snorted and pawed the ground.

Hector let out a mirthless laugh. "I know. I'm not saying we should back."

The windows in the whitewashed stone buildings gave the town a skeletal feel, despite the many flowers and impressive fountains. This part of the town had been built by alojas, with walls that curved and flowed, and the roofs were domed like skulls rather than flat like boxes. Aloja architecture created a somewhat dizzying effect.

Everence walked in front of her horse, more at ease on the ground than in the saddle. She explained the architecture to Talia. "The alojas rose to prominence as architects ever since Fabian took one as a wife."

I snorted. I hadn't faced Fabian in nearly a century, and still it was too soon. All around, fountains sprang out of the walls, cascaded from the rooftops, and soared to the skies in all manner of shapes and forms. Glowing colored tiles shot rainbows of light into the arcing fountains.

For so much beauty, the place twisted my insides with dread.

We had traveled too slowly, my pace slower with my wound, and already the day drew to a close. The royal palace likely already teemed with guests, as the coronation ball was set to begin at one hour after the last light of day. The party would proceed until dawn, when the fallow month would officially expire and my father's former crown would fall to my brother.

Meandering through the tight streets of the lower city, I smelled the hounds for the first time that day. On the open road, the wind had been on our faces, hiding the scent of the dips from me. But the city walls stopped the breeze and trapped the scent of our pursuers.

Everence tapped Hector's leg, whispered something up to him, and then climbed back in her saddle. Hector stopped his horse, waited for Talia to catch up, then spoke to her in hushed tones. "If we didn't arrive by the time the ball starts, the prince will unleash his crows, the hags with black feather wings. They're the ones who craft all of his curses, and they never fail to find their prey."

And if we did arrive on time, and my brother detected my affection for Talia, he would disfigure her in front of me, so I could carry those memories into my dismal eternity.

From ahead, Hector grunted. "We're out of time."

"Is that an inn?" asked Talia, pointing at a building with a door that moved like a woman's mouth and sang about sweet dreams.

Everence chuckled. "No. That is a harpy's house." She turned all the way around in the saddle and lifted a brow at Hector.

Hector's jaw worked, but he said nothing to Everence's pointed stare. Instead, he cleared his throat and announced, "After the change, we will proceed to the palace."

Talia frowned. "We can't go straight there?" she asked.

"Best not to arrive when he's a bear," Hector said. "Rafael has almost no magic in this form. As a man, he can at least speak and wield a blade."

Talia's hand brushed the dagger she'd strapped at her waist. After the attack from the Shadow lords, I was glad to see her carrying a weapon. This place was full of danger.

The sun dropped below the rooftops. I loped forward, searching for a place to change. I wanted as few witnesses as possible. After another turn, I hurried across a wider avenue, hoping the lanes on the other side would be less crowded. Alojas in watery thin dresses and high fae in silken ballgowns streamed toward the palace. Duendes, with their gnarled faces and tiny eyes, sneered and pointed at us from upper story windows as we passed. Few of them would be present at my brother's coronation, confined to the houses they served. But they were apt at insults and tossed them out like leprechaun coins. The harpies wore next to nothing, but their charms didn't work on me in this form. I darted down a narrow alley, sniffing the wind for threats.

"We're out of time!" yelled Hector.

He didn't have to tell me.

I lunged at a gilded door set in a bulbous, whitewashed wall. It burst apart and I crashed to the floor inside a sparkling, vacant entryway. The other left the horses in the front courtyard, beside a bubbling fountain.

Inside the house, Talia ran her hand along the stone, looking up at carved wave frozen in place over her head. Tiny threads of light followed where her fingers brushed the wall. She jerked her hand back, then, with a breath of delight, she raked her hand again across the stone. More light flared.

My blood heated and I snuffled loudly, hating that I couldn't speak. She glanced back, eyes soft at the edges, as if she was about to smile. How could I show her that I hated myself for what I'd done? That I wasn't happy she'd fallen for me because she would suffer for it?

Before I could settle this dilemma, she moved on, fingers drawing lines of light on the wall. Boldly, I bumped her other hand with my muzzle.

She lifted it quickly away—repulsed, perhaps?—and stopped walking. Over her shoulder, she said, "Rafael, I don't want..."

My heart soared as she used my name, even when I was trapped in this body. But she never finished. She walked swiftly to catch up with the others, leaving me agonizing over what it was she didn't want.

Talia let out a small yelp. I hurried to her side, but I felt in my bones that the change was about to take place. In the foyer, an oval-shaped room with glittering blue floors, a willow wraith who had clearly spent the night soaking in water, skittered stickily from the room. I exhaled with relief.

"This way," Hector said, snapping his fingers to ignite a small flame over his right shoulder. "The house is empty."

"How does he know that?" asked Talia, still staring after the wraith.

"His magic is related to space and sound, similar to the way my magic is related to song," Everence offered, tugging Talia along. "That is only a willow wraith. Nothing more than a pest."

The hallway quickly darkened around us, as all the magical lights in the house fell dormant as a cursed creature passed. Hector's flame was now our only light. I hadn't been in the home of another high fae in a long time, but I hadn't forgotten the way they wore their prejudices like fine jewelry. Even their homes rejected the weak.

I paused in the hall, the pain in my side hot and throbbing. Talia paused and looked back at me.

"You can make it," she whispered.

If she believed I could, anything was possible.

But the day was over. I stumbled and crashed into the wall. The entire house rattled, and three faces turned toward me. My curse was festering, intensifying my pain as it drew near the moment it would become uncurable.

A small hand touched my furry shoulder, and the world condensed into that one, delicate, electrifying, point of contact.

"Get in here, and stop wallowing," Hector snapped, waving me onward. His tone, however, betrayed his fear.

He opened a door and strode into the first room off the hall. Light poured in from skylights that opened with his progress across the room. He lifted his arms out at his sides, and floor-to-ceiling windows burst open, letting in more light and a warm breeze. Talia stood right inside the door, gaping at the room as it came alive. It was a sitting room, complete with couches and a settee.

I flopped to the floor, enjoying the coolness of the marble as I felt the change pressing over my body. Talia leaned against the nearest wall and slid down, her hands pressed to her middle, eyes closed. My muscles tensed to move toward her, but at that moment, the sun vanished for the night, and for several seconds, I could neither see nor hear Talia. The world darkened, my vision blurred and spotted with purple and gold, and my bones shrank and snapped. The wound at my side smarted and flamed as it shifted with me, pouring out fresh blood.

Then, I was lying at Talia's feet. Tears hugged her eyes, and her breaths came quickly. She leaned forward and wrapped her arms around her knees. I tossed out all expectation, all hope, and reached for her hand.

Her warm fingers looped through my own and a thousand years of madness could never erase this feeling from my mind.

Everence hurried to my side and tugged at my jacket,

revealing the wound in my shoulder. "Let me see." She huffed at the sight of the dried blood on my clothes.

The acrid smell of fear rolled off Talia as I rolled onto my back, exposing the wound on my shoulder. Everence opened a vial. I barely noticed as the healing ointment stung my skin. My eyes remained fixed on Talia.

"I don't expect you to forgive me," I whispered, voice rough and ragged.

She shook her head. Tears dripped onto her arm. I smeared one away with my thumb.

"If I hadn't run to Puerta that night, I'd..." Her words cut off with a shake of her head.

Emboldened by her words, and the fact that she hadn't yet flinched back from my touch, I sat up, pulling her face toward mine as I did. Her body tensed and shallow breaths sucked in through her lips. I pressed my forehead to hers.

"If I had never met you, Talia, I would never have accepted that bearing a curse for ten thousand years would be better than living with the guilt of having harmed the one person in this world that I love."

She sniffed but didn't pull away. "I'm scared. My whole body hurts."

My other hand flew to Talia's face, and I tilted her head to look me in the eyes. "Where does it hurt?"

Panic touched her eyes. "Everywhere. My bones ache, and my muscles feel as if they will tear to pieces."

"Sun forsake me," I hissed, scooping her into a hug against my chest. "First and Last, not this. I'll live a thousand lives of pain and torment, but do not do this."

She loved me.

My wife, my bride, my sacrifice.

And now I wanted nothing in the world but to hold her

body together, to keep it from shifting, to reverse her love for me and keep her whole.

"Talia, try to stop," I begged. "You have to try to stop loving me."

She pressed her hands to my chest and shook me. "I can't, you idiot! I love you," she shouted. "I want to keep loving you. And if that means turning into a bear, and loving you only at night, I don't care, as long as you never let me go."

I planted a kiss on top of her head, tears spilling into her hair. "Why do you have to be so stubborn?"

Everence cleared her throat. I'd nearly forgotten she was present. "We must hurry. The coronation ball starts in less than an hour."

I pulled Talia to her feet and wrapped and arm around her. Everence snapped her fingers and a fresh suit emerged, woven with iridescent thread. I'd be at home in the palace of the Sun Sovereign.

"Now that it is night, the curse is active once again," I told Talia as I slid my arms into the new jacket a few minutes later. "The pain will likely increase until the moment the curse has completely transferred from my body to yours. When that happens, I will..."

But in truth I had no idea what I would do, when the moment of her death arrived.

Instead of finishing that sentence, I stepped forward and kissed her.

I took Talia's face in my hand, threading my fingers into her hair. She smiled and a small half-sob, half-laugh sputtered from her. I wrapped my arms tightly around her.

"I will hold you until the stars fall and the earth melts, if it would mean I could keep you safe." She crashed against me.

Over her head, I met Everence's cold stare. My shoulder

was already healing, her poultice working quickly. The curse was indeed fleeing my body. As if to prove my words, a spasm hit Talia and she moaned in pain.

I slammed a fist into the stone wall, cracking it and causing the whole room to shudder. Talia winced in pain as another round of muscle spasms rocked her small frame.

"Ev, help me. I can't lose her."

Everence stood beside us. "You'll be gaining strength now. Do you feel it." As I nodded, she continued, "Then you should also be able to call up more magic now. You're true magic. You can try to keep her alive with that."

Talia's fists curled around the fabric of my loose shirt. I smoothed away hairs from her face.

"I don't even know my true magic. It's been too long, and I never fully learned." I'd been twenty years old, still a child in fae years, when Fabian had cursed me. Fae often spent two hundred years learning about the magics they'd been born with, and then another thousand years perfecting it.

My cousin placed a hand on my shoulder. "You'll know enough."

Talia's eyes peeked open and she sat up. "There's a chance I can live through this?"

I tucked my face against her neck once more, the way I had in the stairwell. For a moment, hope surged like an inferno in my veins, and my body tingled with crackling energy.

Everence answered before I could. "He's the heir of the Sun Sovereign." Then to me, she added, "That crown belongs as much to you as it does to your brother. With the crown, you could save her."

35

TALIA

When he looked up at me, his eyes burned amber, bright and strong and terrifyingly beautiful. "I will get that crown."

I nodded, but I had no idea what lay ahead. Pain and bloodshed and the high possibility of one or both of us not surviving the night. Just then, Hector popped his head back in the room.

"Look lively now!" he said, rushing in. "Sinsorias reported to the palace, and our brother just loosed his dragons."

I raced from the room holding Rafael's hand. A single word replayed in my mind. *Love.* How could it be that I'd stumbled into a marriage to a breathtakingly handsome, wealthy horse trainer who also happened to love me? It was more than I'd dreamed possible.

The house seemed to wave and wobble around us as we fled, amplifying my dizziness. The magic of this place weighed on me. Or maybe that was the curse I was pulling into my body. A shooting pain in my leg tripped me and I went down.

Rafael's arms caught my shoulders before my body hit the tile. Faster than I'd ever seen a man move, he scooped me in his arms and carried me outside. Once we were beside the horses, he breathed deeply and set me down.

He squeezed my hand. "Ride with me."

Before I could protest, he grabbed my waist and lifted me onto Lily's saddle. A second later, he settled directly behind me. It was different this time, sitting on a horse with him, and when he leaned around for the reins, my heartrate tripled.

A spasm shot through my back and I knocked into him. One arm held me tightly across the middle, the other held the reins. I linked my fingers with his.

Love shouldn't have to hurt like this. It wasn't fair.

As we took off down the cobblestone road toward the massive, gleaming palace, I yelled over the sound of the hooves. "I'm happy I could set you free." I just wished I could be free with him.

As we raced past a tall pillar made of rocks, I noticed with a grimace of horror that the rocks were skulls. Tucked in among the beauty of this place were reminders of death. These fae were not all rainbow fields and sparkling walls.

The sound of massive beating wings stole a small yelp from my lips. Above us, the stars flickered as something large flew across the sky.

"Dragons!" Hector yelled from behind us.

We leaned into a gallop.

Around the next corner, the sprawling palace popped into view. The reddish stone walls rose high atop a lone hill surrounded by the white city. Though it was awe-inspiring in its grandeur, there was something sinister about its pale, windowless outer walls. The parapets caught the last of the fading sunlight, like tiny bloodstained teeth along an open jaw.

We thundered up the slope toward the palace as the bone-chilling sound of dogs barking pierced the night. The hounds burst around the edge of a building, their red eyes alight again with a thirst for blood.

Rafael whispered to his horse, and she put on more speed. She wasn't lighting the ground on fire with her hooves, but we moved so fast I could barely breathe from the thrill. Even the pain dimmed in comparison.

The solid stone wall of the palace rose before us.

"How do we—?"

My question died out as a tunnel appeared at the base of the enormous outer wall just as we charged through it.

The hooves made a riotous clatter in the tunnel. Behind us, snarls and animals hisses sent shivers down my spine, then we were exploding out into a broad courtyard.

In parallel lines leading through the center of the courtyard were tall, burning torches, lighting the way. Rafael tugged on the reins and Lily pranced to a stop. He spun the horse around, breath heaving, and we peered back at the tunnel's dark entrance. I couldn't see the other side.

Everence and Hector did not emerge, and the sounds of the dogs had disappeared. All I could hear was the small snapping fires of the torches, and the distant music of an orchestra. Above us, two great, winged shadows circled.

"Are you here for the ball?" a voice said behind us.

Rafael tugged the horse around again, and I stared down at a pointy-eared man with a bald head and an elaborate jeweled headpiece that draped over his forehead and down to his shoulders. He wore a red and gold robe that spilled out far behind him. He had only the tip of a beard at his chin, and was at once both startlingly pretty and terrifying. He reminded me of Sinsorias, but darker and his smile, somehow, more sinister.

"You cannot expect that the king will allow you entrance in *those* clothes." He clicked his tongue.

"He is not king yet."

"Ah." The man tapped his fingertips together. "So you are the brother. In that case, we've been expecting you. Follow me. Leave the horse." He spun around, his liquid movement unnerving as he slid down the courtyard's lit path toward a wide stairwell leading to a domed entrance.

My heart hammered so fast I worried my body might collapse from my racing pulse. Wafting scents of cinnamon and cloves eased my tension a little, but Rafael caught my eye and gave a small shake of his head.

"The air is bewitched to draw you in to my brother's whims, as is everything here. Be on your guard."

By the time we'd crossed the wide courtyard, my heartrate had slowed and my eyelids began to droop.

"Talia!"

Rafael grabbed my hand, turning toward me. His eyes burned with intensity as he studied me. "Stay alert." Then, stepping closer, he whispered in my ear. "Here."

My body flooded with a new vigor, a strength not my own. I bounced on my toes. The pain, for the moment, was gone.

"But you need your strength!" How could he take the crown from the most powerful fae in his court without every bit of his magic?

He looked me up and down while our guide tapped his foot in annoyance. "That should help ease the pain for now."

Rafael had said the change would be gradual, but what

exactly did that mean? Claws first, then fur? A snout perhaps? The thoughts sent gooseflesh down my arms.

The sound of music intensified. Violins, a cello, a horn of some sort, and voices sweet as an angelic host cascaded down the steps. I sucked in a captivated breath. The music was not like Avencian melodies, but there was a familiar rhythm underneath the humming violins.

We stepped onto a terrace so large the shiny tiled edges disappeared into the landscape to my left and right. Ahead of me was a dancefloor walled on each side by four long tables arrayed beneath the emerging stars. A veritable forest of greenery vined among the chairs and over the tables, and tiny little hovering lights mingled with the flowers and the branches and the moss, casting a blueish hue over the plates and crystal goblets.

Aside from the madly passionate musicians, who appeared lost in their melody, the terrace was empty.

The fae wearing the long tunic turned sharply to face us. "The celebration begins within the hour, with dancing, followed by the crowning ceremony. Whoever is left standing by dawn will be invited to sit and dine with their new sovereign."

"Left standing? Is there something I'm not aware of?"

Our guide coughed politely. "I take it you have never attended one of the Sun Sovereign's dances." His eyes slid ominously to Rafael as he flashed a mirthless grin. "Follow the deer."

"The what?" I asked.

The man whirled, tossing up an annoyed hand, and floated away across the terrace. I hadn't taken the time to fully appreciate the walls in this place. Every inch was carved stone. Delicate, intricate patterns of leaves and flowers covered every inch of visible wall. Even at night, the stone had a faint sparkle that gave the place an ethereal glow.

It was truly the most beautiful place I'd ever seen.

Every doorway cut into the pale stone was capped with dripping arches that made the dark spaces below look like spreading flower petals—or open mouths ringed with fangs.

Two deer trotted silently toward us, noses twitching and eyes sparkling.

"Oh, those deer."

Rafael stood close, his arm radiating heat. "They will want to separate us."

The deer bounded off toward the palace, sure enough, heading toward separate entrances.

I glanced back down the steps toward the courtyard she'd first entered. "What happened to Everence and your brother?"

"I presume the palace wall did not open to permit them entrance. Fabian wants me here without any allies." At my concerned look, he added, "The hounds will be no match for the pair of them. It was me the dogs wanted, anyway. And the dragons he'll want nearby. Stay close."

I wasn't sure how two deer could pose a threat, but I accepted his hand as it twined with mine and squeezed. The doe pranced on tiny hooves toward a wide archway, the stag toward an archway much farther down the terrace. "Don't leave me," I insisted.

"Never."

He walked with me through the archway, following the doe. Inside was another archway, and yet another. Stacked together, each one smaller than the last, creating the sensation that the palace was shrinking around us.

The deer skittered up a set of shallow steps tiled in bright colors that depicted a sun rising. Light shone in alcoves along the wall, but not from flames. More relaxing cinnamon smells, now mixed with a citrusy orange scent, permeated the air. I inhaled deeply.

This would be a fine place to live.

Rafael tightened his grip on my hand. "Don't let it twist your thoughts. My brother's magic is in every crevice of this place. I can feel it. How is your pain?"

I shrugged. What pain? This place was lovely, and I never wanted to leave.

Strong hands gripped my shoulders and Rafael's ember-bright eyes locked with mine. "Do not forget what we are about to face. And Talia, look."

He held up my hands and to my horror, my fingernails had turned to sharp points. I screamed. My fingers throbbed. As soon as I snapped out of the foggy thoughts induced by the strange magic here, my knees buckled and I yelped in pain.

I clung to Rafael, my mouth open in silent agony.

"Stars, the curse is moving faster than I thought." He supported me as we continued to follow the deer up the steps. "My magic should have lasted longer than two minutes. Hold on a little longer, *paloma*."

"Will I die?"

"Not if I get the crown."

I loved him. I loved my husband, the man who'd married me in order to kill me.

Sun above, how had I fallen for him?

His strong hand dug into my ribs as my weight sagged toward the floor.

But I knew how.

I'd fallen just a little the moment I'd seen him lounging in that opulent armchair in Puerta, his handsome, dangerous face and casual posture enough to stop my heart.

The veins in his arm stood out from the effort of holding me up.

I'd fallen just a little more the moment he'd fought off the Hunter to keep me safe.

He bent and scooped my legs into his arms and hurried up the rest of the steps.

I'd fallen when he'd pulled me into his arms as we rode through the hanging gate.

My breaths came raged and fast as we mounted the stairs.

I'd fallen still more when I'd learned he kept the world's most beautiful horses.

He walked down the hall after the deer, holding me tightly.

But when he'd raced me that night, a twinkle in his eye revealing a man I wanted to get to know, I'd taken a running leap. I'd chosen to love him at that moment. Finding him in his cave, shirtless and disgruntled and worried about unforgiveable sins, had only drawn me in. And dancing with him under the stars had nailed my coffin shut.

I spread out one fully clawed hand and stared a long moment. No, there was no going back now.

We followed the deer down a long hallway toward a beautiful oaken door carved with the same intricate geometric patterns that lined the walls.

The door swung open, but as Rafael attempted to help me into the room, he was knocked backward with such force he slammed into the opposite wall. I hit the ground, clunking my head against the doorframe.

When I glanced back at the deer, it was gone. A voice whispered in the hallway, *Only her.*

That was creepy.

Rafael darted to me, his hands finding my face. "I knew they would do this."

"You won't leave me?"

"I cannot enter that room. And if you are not dressed for the ball, they will..." He swallowed.

"What will they do?"

"If anyone offends the king, he has them dismembered in front of the guests. And he is very easily offendable."

Oh. I glanced back into the room. It was unoccupied, contained a large bed set into the floor and a standing bathtub large enough for three people. Water already fell from a hole in the ceiling and filled the tub. Delicious lavender notes scented the air. Across the bed lay a spectacular blue gown. A warm bath would feel amazing.

"Leave the door open," he said, hands on the doorframe. "I'll stay right here."

I swallowed. Pain coursed down my arms and legs.

"And do not get in the water," he added, eyes flicking toward the copper tub.

A whimper escaped my lips.

"Everything here will attempt to twist your mind. No bath."

It might have been my imagination, but I caught a whiff of disappointment in his tone and the scents rolling off him.

"I'll hurry."

He nodded again as I backed into the room. For a heartbeat, I stared at him, his disheveled hair, his crinkled shirt from where I'd knotted my hands in it, his exposed collarbone and the point in his throat. Ignoring the pain, I stepped forward and kissed him.

When his hands tried to reach around my face, he was

again blasted backward against the far wall, a startling end to the brief moment of bliss.

I bit my lips and turned to the dress, cheeks flaming as I realized what leaving the door open meant. I whirled back to face him. He was my *husband*, after all. Only we'd never…and this was such an odd circumstance.

When I tried to hide behind my hands, my claws poked into my forehead. "Ouch." I looked at my monstrous hands.

"I won't look, if that would make you more comfortable."

His eyes, however, told a different story.

I didn't respond, only moved deeper into the room. Breaths heaving, I began to remove my clothing. When I was down to my underthings, I nearly glanced over my shoulder but couldn't bring myself to see if he was watching or not.

Why shouldn't he?

I'd be disappointed if he *wasn't*. And yet, I'd be mortified if he was.

I kept Rafael's dagger strapped to my thigh, just in case any other fae or strange creatures appeared.

With shaking, clawed hands, I fumbled my way into the exquisite dress, trying not to groan as the pain danced nearer to the edge of what I could handle. The deep blue was richer than most fabrics I'd seen and was ruffled down the skirt. The style was, surprisingly, Avencian and would have been perfect to wear to the Festival. If Rafael didn't succeed in killing his brother, I'd soon shift into a bear and my mortal flesh wouldn't survive the change.

As I shimmied into the bodice, another spasm of pain shook my frame. I hit the bed on the way down, and my face was smothered against soft blankets as a full-body seizure locked my muscles into violent shakes.

36

RAFAEL

My wife hit the bed, and I charged at the door, ready this time for the force that would knock me back. I held my ground, gritting my teeth as I watched her body buck and writhe as her ugly, strangled sounds frayed my sanity.

"Talia!"

I gripped the doorframe and tore it from the wall. The ensuing crackle of energy told me I'd weakened the magic there. I headbutted the space where the enchantment held me back, and a shattering sound filled the hall. Little bolts of lightning snaked outward from the impact. With a final kick, the spell broke with a loud *pop*.

I raced into the room. Talia's body still thrashed, but her mouth was open and her eyes vacant.

No.

With one hand, I rolled her over, and with the other, I sent a wave of magic into her. I sensed my own strength waning as I did so, but I didn't care. I'd give her every bit of life in me.

As her eyes sharpened and her muscles relaxed, a woman

THE STARLIT PRINCE

in a billowy, white dress appeared in the hallway outside, followed quickly by six women with feathery, black wings. The crows had come.

"Step away from her," said the woman in white.

From her black hair that trailed the ground to the melodic nature of her voice, I guessed she was a harpy in her alluring form. Her garish beauty appalled me. I'd grown used to Talia's unglamoured loveliness.

The hags crept into the room like a pack of silverfish. The youngest had the dewy eyes of youth, and the oldest had the dead, white eyes of blindness. The oldest had to be nearing seven thousand years. No telling the curses she'd set in her wasted lifetime. Talia's dress slid off her shoulder, but I caught up the fabric and clutched her limp frame.

"He wouldn't come meet me himself?" I asked, readjusting Talia so that I cradled her across my arms. Her head lolled against my chest, and her muscles quivered. She might burst into the change any moment, or it could still take hours before it was complete.

The harpy tilted her narrow face at me. "He is busy preparing to acquire the most powerful item in all of Rivenmark. You should have stayed out of this room."

With a flick of her wrist, my arms shot outward and my body lurched backward. Talia crashed to the floor and let out a sharp yelp. Before I knew what had happened, I was flat against the wall, head jammed up against the ceiling, arms pinned straight out beside me.

I called on my magic, but nothing happened—I'd sent all my available strength into Talia. She rolled to her knees, then stood and faced the harpy and the pack of circling hags. In her hand was the jeweled dagger. Good girl.

"I will go willingly. Do not hurt him," she said, holding on to her dress.

"Talia, no."

She cut sharp eyes at me—how could I argue with the woman who said she was glad she'd set me free? She slipped the sleeves of her dress back up and stomped toward me. "At least let him secure my dress."

The harpy let out a shriek that was likely a laugh, and her magic released me. I landed on my feet and touched Talia's shoulders, my nose bumping against her sweet-smelling hair. My fingers fumbled as I secured the buttons and loops at the back of her dress. Her skin was warm against my icy cold fingers.

"Don't look too long at that woman's eyes. And don't listen to the music. Don't eat anything. Especially fruit." My fingers finished and I grasped her shoulders. "I love you."

The hags closed in, their wings folded and dragging the ground, their eyes hungry. The one with white irises reached for Talia, but I knocked her hand away. One of the middle-aged creatures grabbed my wrist and dragged me out from behind Talia.

My wrist seared at her touch and I groaned, backhanding her. She barely flinched. Another reached out for my legs, wrapping her arms around them.

Talia swung the blade, but the winged creatures evaded her. The youngest of the crows darted forward and jammed a raspberry in Talia's mouth, clamping her jaw shut. As Talia's eyes locked with mine, a black bag was dropped over my head.

37

TALIA

The first thing I wanted to do was to laugh. But I choked on the sound. I stared blankly as the strange bird-like woman dragged Rafael's body away. I was supposed to be doing something, but I couldn't remember what. My hands hurt.

"Come with me," said the lovely dark-haired fae. She beckoned me, and I followed. "Our king is most excited to meet you."

I was going to meet the king!

The winged women, who weren't nearly as lovely as my guide, scurried down the hall and out of sight. Rafael's feet slipped around the corner. I hoped he was going to get to meet the king too, though it was odd for him to be going the other way. And dragged.

"May I see your blade? You won't be needing that."

I handed it to the woman, admiring the way the light caught the emeralds in the hilt.

She accepted it with a smile, though for some reason, her smile made me uneasy. The dagger disappeared into the folds of her flowing dress. "You should wear this in your hair," she said, smiling, as she reached up to stick an orange bloom over my ear.

I touched it with gentle fingers. "Thank you." My smile faded and I glanced back over my shoulder where Rafael had just disappeared. "He wanted me dead," I said.

The woman nodded enthusiastically. "Yes, he did. But he will not harm you now. Come, the king waits."

She hurried me down a flight of stairs, out onto an enormous terrace that looked vaguely familiar. So polished were the tiles that I could see the stars reflected in the floor I now walked. A bell chimed nine times, and at the final chime, every visible door on the palace walls opened and out streamed courtiers, dressed in their finest. My jaw dropped as I watched them come.

A man in a golden suit with a pair of tiger's tails in place of regular tails marched out twirling a cane. His face was oddly contorted to look like a tiger's as well. I shivered. That was no mask. His skin crinkled as he flashed us a grin, the fur and stripes at odds with his human bone structure. One woman's dress was so wide she blasted part of the wall away to pass through the door, only to flick her wrist and reconstruct the wall once she'd passed through.

Cheeks glowed, hair sparkled, and every brow and ear and wrist dripped with jewels.

These people looked like circus performers, but the disguises were part of them, not easily taken off like a mask or a costume.

One woman looked me up and down, offered me a strange smile, then waltzed past toward the open space before the musicians, who each sawed frantically on a stringed instrument. My heartrate amplified with their tempo.

"She approves of your costume," said the woman beside me.

I glanced at my hands. They'd stretched and widened, and my fingers had awful claws hanging at the ends. I almost laughed, but for the grinding sensations in my joints. A wave of pain shot through me and with the pain came a burst of clarity.

The fae streaming all around me were not friendly. Their eyes leered at me. Their noses turned up. The woman beside me was no friend either. But even as I tensed to step away from her, I couldn't recall why I wanted to. She was so lovely and the people here looked to be having such a grand time.

"Why is no one saying anything?" I whispered.

"Because it offends our king for anyone to speak before blood is spilled. It isn't a party until there's blood."

I nodded, though I couldn't say why I agreed with her. It just sounded right, though the idea of bloodshed turned my stomach. The woman nearest me, an aloja, I guessed, had a dress made of an actual waterfall.

"You people kill each other for fun?"

The dark-haired woman clicked her tongue. "It isn't death you will see here tonight. It's much more fun."

When the courtiers stopped moving, I noticed they all stood in a large circle. I was part of that circle. I smiled at the wonder of it all, a little sad that my hands looked so strange and my back ached, but also unsure what to do about it.

Across the huge circle, a commotion started. Several courtiers stepped aside, and a pair of winged women dragged a man forward. He had a bag on his head and his legs appeared to be limp.

A spasm of pain rocked my body and I fell to my knees. Instantly, the woman beside me yanked me up, lifting something toward my mouth.

My vision cleared, and I swatted her hand away. "Rafael!"

His head shot up, but he didn't fight his captors.

Then, a column of light pierced the night and at once every fae hit their knees. Rafael crashed to the shining tile as his two captors knelt. He scrambled to his feet and jerked the black bag from his head. For a breath, we were the only two standing.

From the sky, a figure descended, dressed in white and holding a sword, point down.

"Ah, brother, is this how you greet me, after so much time?"

The voice was eerily like Rafael's. So was the face, but his hair was shorter. Rafael tucked into a sprint, eyes locked on me. My heart seized with a tangle of joy and fear.

"You run like a bear," teased the man in white. He wore a thin golden crown of twisting vines.

My body lurched and my feet lifted from the tile. I screamed and twitched as I rose higher and higher over the circle of courtiers. Rafael stopped and stared up at me. In his eyes glowed a blazing inferno.

"You don't think this will be simple, do you?" Fabian asked, twirling his hand in the air. As he did so, I spun, my skirts twisting around my legs.

Rafael straightened and finally looked down at his brother. In a loud voice, he called out, "I am Rafael del Sol, first born of the slain king, and rightful heir of the Sun Crown."

Collective gasps issued from the crowd now rising to their feet.

"I challenge my brother for the throne."

Silence fell but was quickly shattered by a deep, cackling laugh. Fabian laced his fingers at his stomach and grinned. "Oh, how quaint. A challenge. We haven't seen one of those in a while. It would be delightful to destroy you, brother, but it's my wish to see you live out your pathetic life in continual misery." He sighed dramatically, appearing less like Rafael the more he spoke. I wanted to spit on his shining, white suit. "I accept your challenge, on one condition." The crowd inhaled collectively. "I will fight you only if she," he pointed at me with his naked sword, "Receives an injury every time I do."

That was the stupidest rule I'd ever heard. Rafael clenched fists at his sides, but before he could speak, a slender, pale woman emerged from the crowd. A delighted shout burst from my lips. Everence shone in a blue-tinted glamour that made her look like she was standing in her own private snowstorm. Beside her stood Hector, hand on his sword hilt.

Fabian pointed at them. "How did they get in?" He twirled in a complete circle. "Who do I need to kill for this oversight?"

"You cannot deny his challenge in so cowardly a way," Everence said, to the courtier's horror. "Fight him, or don't, but you reveal your lack of honor, and your weakness, if you do not."

Fabian snorted and turned away from her. "This woman thinks me weak. *Weak.*" A chorus of disgusted remarks rose from the crowd. "I think I shall teach these three a lesson. What say you, shall we invite the mortal to our dance?" He lifted both hands in dramatic fashion. Cheers rose from the courtiers. "You know my rules. I toss out power like confections to those I like, and I strip it from those I hate. My lovely enchantresses—" he swept a hand at the winged women "—

are hungry to spill the curses we've concocted together this week. Let us try them on these traitors. Whoever traps them will be rewarded. Kill the moral."

He flicked his wrist, and the courtiers sprang forward.

But instead of drawing weapons, they paired off, as if about to dance. The magic holding me aloft dissipated and I crashed to the terrace.

The music began again, and Rafael was at my side, scooping me up.

"Are you all right?" he asked, concern pinching his brow.

He plucked the flower from my hair and tossed it aside. Clarity again dawned and I shook my head of the fuzzy confusion.

"We must dance." He lifted me and swung me around. I wobbled on unsteady feet, but his strength steadied me. "If you stop, if you miss a single step, they will hurt you." His fury bubbled under the surface.

"But I don't even know this dance."

"You need only follow my lead." He kept his eyes pinned to mine.

A grunt of pain stole my attention from Rafael. The couple next to us was no longer dancing, but the man was bent over, clutching a wound in his middle. His partner cackled with laughter, a dripping dagger in her hand.

Whistles of approval rang out from the crowd, and a few sparks crackled over the dancing pairs.

"Keep your eyes on me," muttered Rafael. "This game is designed to hurt." He moved my waist back, then tugged me gently forward. My claws made it hard to hold his hands, but he gripped hard enough that I barely had to hang on. "These dances are all about power. On nights like tonight, one can harm their enemies, gain new alliances, forge new bonds, and most of all, gain the favor of their sovereign for their ruth-lessness."

The stories had it all wrong. Fae weren't tricksters. They were monsters.

"That woman took my dagger. Do you even have a weapon?" I asked, throat tight.

Rafael didn't answer.

Every turn put me closer to someone who might lash out with a blade. I wanted to curl into Rafael's arms and stay there. One woman fell to the ground, and the couples danced over her. She screamed, but no one listened.

"Can't you help her?" I begged.

He maneuvered us toward the fallen, writhing woman, but just then, a man toppled over, clutching at a wound that made me gag. When I looked, I saw blood everywhere.

A woman jabbed at me with a dagger. I only saw the attack because her skin was sparkling. I spun into Rafael, avoiding the blade.

"They want you to miss a step," he hissed. "They can only hurt you when you do."

The woman's eyes lit with an eerie white glow. I'd just given her permission to stab me. Rafael kicked out, sending her dagger flying.

Figures from all directions descended upon us, one even fell from the sky. It had wings.

I lifted a hand to block whatever swung at me, and to my and surprise, someone yelped. My claws had pierced flesh. I slashed again with my long, horrendous bear claws.

Then like lightning inside my body, pain needled outward from my heart to my every extremity. I crumpled forward into Rafael's arms. This was it, my body was going to rip at the seams and pour my life onto this polished dancefloor.

His nose brushed against my cheek. "I've got you."

My skin lit like a match. At the same time, a hollow cavern opened up inside me. I would die from this change and return to the dust. He would live on for centuries, free from his curse, but without the one he loved. Perhaps, in time, he could love again.

Fae around us lunged for us, weapons drawn. I'd missed many steps now.

But each attacker blasted backward, clutching their hands as blisters rose on their skin.

"I've got you," he said again. "Don't worry about them."

I threaded my hand into his hair. "Don't choose to love something that will last only a moment. It's like loving a flower you've already picked."

The pain intensified and I closed my eyes against it. Bright spots danced across my closed eyes.

He wrapped his arm tightly around me, pressing me close. "Yes," he breathed, bending down to brush his nose along my neck. "You are my lily. And as long as you take breath, I'll love you." His lips grazed my jaw, then my forehead. "And when your petals fall off and you wilt, I will love you still." Now his mouth hovered before mine. "And a hundred years after I last touch you, I'll remember your smile and the way your lips felt against mine."

He pressed a gentle yet desperate kiss against my mouth. All protests melted away and I grabbed his head with both hands.

I was on fire.

My body kicked and jerked, and suddenly the pain stole my breath and I choked, collapsing to the ground and bringing Rafael down with me.

I wanted to love him for longer than a single day.

Then my body convulsed so violently my face smacked the stones.

Every muscle quivered, and my back arched. I gritted my teeth and a groan howled from my lips. Rafael pressed his body down on top of mine, and with a whispered word, strength flowed into me once more. For one blazing instant, I took a deep breath, then my throat ripped apart and my bones disconnected and I was lost to the pain.

RAFAEL

My heart battered my chest as the change took her. A blade cut through the air toward Talia's head. With a growl, I shoved my hand over her twitching frame, not even certain my magic would work. The sword bounced off my palm, and the attacker, in his glittering red suit, stumbled backward. Behind my shoulder, a woman in a silver gown dove at my wife. I dropped to a knee, spun, and grabbed her sword before it was in Talia's throat. My fingers closed around the blade and yanked. This time, blood seeped out through my fist.

The woman toppled forward, onto Talia. With a shriek of disgust, the woman released her sword and thrust herself backward.

I stood and locked blades with a winged man. I blocked. Cut. Blocked again. If I took even a single step away, the next attacker would be upon her.

Talia's body bucked and writhed. Each limb elongated, her muscles stretching thin across bone. Choking, gurgling sounds erupted from her limp mouth. The change was taking too long, and the pain itself would be enough to knock her unconscious.

"Enjoying the show?" called Fabian. "The change is fascinating to watch in slow motion. I can make it last all night. Each breaking bone, each ripping muscle. So. Very. Slow."

I roared in rage. My borrowed sword sent two more attackers staggering backward.

Hot blood raced through my veins, feeding me with energy I'd never known. My magic was returning. Talia's limbs knocked against the marble tile, and her brown skin had gone blue at the joints. Her neck was striped with black veins.

"Stop!" My guttural yell drowned out all other sounds.

For a moment, everything paused, save Talia's awful writhing.

Fabian locked eyes with me across the sea of bloodthirsty courtiers. His muscles tensed and he leaped into the air. I swept my arm in a circle and an inferno encircled Talia and I. Pure white light radiated all around us. Angry faces and upraised swords flickered in and out of view on the other side of the flames, but for a moment, no attacks could reach us.

Her chest expanded, each rib visible as her disintegrating dress faded into fur, and her body went still. It was over.

My wife, my love, was dead.

39

TALIA

The pain ceased, and I was floating in a strange sea. My eyes blinked open.

I wasn't floating, but my body felt entirely different. I couldn't understand why my skin felt so strange pressed against this shining floor. White light surrounded me. Angry shouts rang in my ears.

"Ev, take her!" Rafael yelled.

Everence bent down and shoved a hand under my back. The first man who swung a knife at Rafael received a punch in the jaw that sent him sprawling backward into two other charging, murderous nobles. Hector was at his side in a heartbeat, the two brothers against dozens of fae.

Rafael stuck his sword into a man's stomach. The man held the sword as he fell away, and Rafael was weaponless again. I couldn't move. Couldn't call out.

My body felt like it was made of lead. Everence was humming softly, scooting me backward. I could hear *every-thing*. Light glinted off tiny shards of ice on the air. All around, breaths hissed between clenched teeth. Clothing whispered, and shoes scuffed. The flutter of Rafael's hair and the tensing of his muscles drew my attention.

Rafael ripped a sword from a woman who swung it directly at his neck. Holding the blade with his bare hand, he spun and smashed the face of the tiger-striped fae sneaking up with a dagger. He flipped the sword and held the point out toward the next set of eager attackers. They hesitated a moment, then charged as one. He leaped into the air and blasted them all to the ground with a burst of magic.

They grunted and moaned, but all three stayed pinned to the terrace.

Rafael whirled that sword faster than my eyes could track, fending off attacks from three sides. Hector fought beside him, a blur of motion.

But still, they were terribly outnumbered.

Pressing my hands to the ground, I moved to stand, but it felt strange.

Instead of hands and feet, there were paws. And fur.

A roar tore from my open mouth, and the way the noise rattled inside my head satisfied the rage I now felt. All the fae on the terrace turned to face me.

Rafael spun, his eyes wide. "Talia!"

Like a dam reaching down into my bloodstream, I shut off the flood of terror that wanted to take over and focused on a single fighter. If he hadn't been glamoured to have wolf ears and fangs, or if he hadn't been growling as he attacked my husband, I might have thought it harder to stuff my claws in his shoulder. As it was, it happened easily. His howl of pain, however, curdled my blood.

To choose someone, to give oneself entirely to another, was to accept their battles and their dreams, their deepest fears and their sharpest qualities.

You will not take him from me now, I grumbled in my mind. Words fought against my long tongue, stirring even more anger in my chest. The ability to speak stolen from me, I lifted onto my hind legs, enjoying the familiarity of standing but also sensing the strangeness of balance in this new form. I crashed forward.

When the first attacker leaped, I roared and swatted with a paw. It was so much bigger and reached so much farther and faster than my human hand.

He slammed into one of the adjacent dining tables and fell to the ground, groaning. He did not rise.

For a moment, I couldn't draw breath, surprised by my power, but also worried I'd killed the man. I'd killed that hag, but she hadn't seemed human. These fae, with their bloodlust and glamours hardly seemed like men and women either. Still, I didn't want to have to kill.

The presence of the next attacker stalking toward me snapped my focus back to survival. I jumped, shocked at how far I flew with a single leap. I sprang fully over Rafael, only to turn back and scramble awkwardly on my paws to defend him.

The attacker spun to face me, her braided silver hair whipping out like a hundred snakes. Her eyes blazed with magic and rage.

Silver streaks of light shot at me, stinging as they buried into my furry hide. I grunted and snapped my jaws. Everything felt strange. My mouth was enormous. My awareness of my limbs had become so confusing, as my hands were more like feet now, but I still wanted to use them like hands.

The fae woman leaped and flipped in the air, soaring over me.

I crashed to all fours and turned, nearly tripping as it took each of my paws instead of just two feet.

My head spun as a sparking arrow pierced my side.

"Big bear claws aren't as helpful as you thought," the woman jeered, trying to lure me away from Rafael's fallen body. "I can see it in your eyes—the change is going to turn you mad." She knocked another crackling arrow. Tiny white lightning bolts sizzled around the sharp point. "And madness doesn't disappear. You'll be as mad as Prince Valor by morning." She chuckled at this and aimed at me.

This time, I ducked and felt the arrow nick one ear. It stung and tiny prickles raced down my face and neck. My muscles grew sluggish.

The woman watched me with eager eyes as she aimed another arrow.

No. It couldn't end this way. To reach her, I needed to move away from Rafael, but to my left, a shining figure in a white suit crept forward, glinting dagger in hand. I could not fend off this woman and the Sun Sovereign.

"Rafael!" The sound came out not as a word but as a ground-shaking roar.

Rafael's hand twitched.

An arrow sank into my shoulder. My next roar was high-pitched and full of pain. At this sound, Rafael rolled toward me, and for a single breath, we locked eyes. There was more power, more light, in those eyes than in the sun itself, and I couldn't look directly at him.

As his brother descended upon him, night vanished and light burned so brightly around the two men, that I had to look away.

Then I jumped, a little more aware of how far I would

travel in one leap. My sluggish muscles responded, even if a little slowly.

The woman blinked and fired an arrow without aiming. It stuck in my outstretched paw. As I landed on my attacker, the woman's own arrow stuck perfectly into her neck, just shy of her collarbone.

I had only meant to pin her to the ground.

Now the arrow was sticking up through my paw and down into the screaming woman's neck.

I knew better than to rip the arrow out like that, but being pinned to a fae warrior with strange electrical magic was not something I wanted to savor.

Before I could free my paw, the fae let out a feral snarl and yanked the arrow from her own neck. I recoiled from the outpouring of blood.

The woman tried to raise her hand to the wound, the crackling magic now skittering over her palm. But the hand collapsed across her chest, the white lines of magic dying out in fits and bursts as the fae took her last breath.

Shaking, I sat up, feeling enormous and entirely foreign in my own body. I really would go mad by the time I changed back into a human—whenever that would be. How had Rafael endured being a bear for so long?

Rafael!

When I looked back to him, my heart flipped over in my chest.

Fabian circled Rafael, twin swords flashing. The air around the two brothers swirled with streams of light. Rafael batted away each thrust.

As Fabian lifted his arm to swing again, a dart of pure, white light shot from the end of his sword. To my horror,

Rafael stuck his hand out, and the shard of light cut through him. Blood splattered his face.

Fabian cackled with laughter.

Then Rafael lunged, and the shard of light shot forward into Fabian's chest. For a heartbeat, the blindingly bright weapon connected the two brothers. Dark red blood spilled from the both.

"The crown was never yours," Rafael spat through gritted teeth.

He lifted his arm, and Fabian, still stabbed through with the shard of light, rose with the movement, until he hung directly over Rafael's head. With a shrug, Fabian's body slid down onto the beam of light, and he went limp. Right arm raised to the sky, holding up the limp, lifeless body of the wicked former sovereign, Rafael spun in a slow circle, stopping when he found me. The spear of light pierced through the dead prince's body, shining high into the starry sky. Blood ran down Rafael's arm, tracing the lines of his veins and the groove of his elbow.

Everyone still standing watched as Rafael dropped Fabian to the terrace floor. A sickening *flump* filled the quiet night. The bright shard of light vanished and darkness veiled the grim scene.

A single bell chimed.

Only then did it occur to me that there were no other attackers. The fight was over.

40

RAFAEL

I turned until I spotted her, ignoring the carnage all around me. When she met my eyes, her bear ears twitched, and she looked quickly away, as if in pain. I lurched toward her, stepping over Fabian's body. Whatever pained her, I would remove it from this world. The energy blazing in my veins heightened every sense to an over-whelming degree. Blood stained her shoulder and soaked into her fur. The smell of her iron-rich blood and potent fear filled my nose, but as I stepped over fallen courtiers and those scrambling to get away from me, I also caught the scent of her bear form.

It stopped me in my tracks. My wife, my bride, had become what I had so long loathed, what I had desired to leave behind, even at the cost of another's life. She'd taken my curse upon herself. And lived.

A hush settled over the terrace, even among those moaning on the ground. To my right, Hector looked up from yanking his sword out of a fallen fae. I nodded at him, and he returned the gesture.

When I reached Talia, I dropped the dagger and knelt before my wife. She didn't meet my eyes. Without a word, I touched her furry cheek, and with my healing magic, she fell forward.

By the time she crashed into me, she was a woman again. This time, the change had happened in a single breath.

Gently, I moved her limp arms, her powerless shoulders, her drooping neck. I pulled her up with me as I stood, grasping her chin with one hand and tilting her face toward me.

"Look at me," I urged, voice low.

When she did, she blinked back tears. "Your eyes. They're so bright," she whispered.

Calling on the energy of the sun, I pushed more strength into her. Though it was night, I could access the sun as if it was hanging directly above my head, like darkness had no hold on me whatsoever. I'd never felt so free in my entire life.

With a deep breath, I searched out still more energy, the source at my fingertips endless and unfathomable. I could get lost in this power. But I focused instead on Talia's face as her own energy returned and she took her own weight. I would not drown in this power as my brother had. Though my chains had fallen away, and my power was restored, even now I detected a whiff of decay inside me, a gear beginning a slow grind to an inevitable halt, still yet centuries away.

"How did I survive that?" she whispered.

I planted a kiss on Talia's forehead. "We become like what we love," I whispered back to her. This was the way of the fae, and it had led to much bloodshed here tonight. "My love for you will make me like you, destined for the grave, as your love for me has lent to you a sliver of my long life. *I will take of yours and make it also mine.*" She breathed deeply as I held her, though she couldn't possibly know all that was transpiring, all that she'd vowed that day in Leor. I would help her understand. I had centuries to help her understand.

When she had the strength to stand again on her own, light shone under her skin, peeking out from every cut and wound, especially the gash on her shoulder. The skin closed over and the light faded. She sobbed with relief and touched the place the wounds had been.

"How...?"

With a finger, I lifted her chin. The world existed in that single point of contact. "You have my magic in your veins now."

Everence swept toward us, flanked by a dozen others who moved silently, heads half-bowed in reverence.

"The crown," she whispered. Her own hands were bloody, but she had no visible wounds. Then, in a stronger voice, she announced, "The crown will now fall to a new sovereign."

At her words, a crown of gossamer, silvery-white metal like twisting vines appeared in her hands.

The entire terrace inhaled in awe. The fae who hadn't entered the fight leaned forward, eyes bulging, as if they might fall down, sick with envy.

At their hungry faces, Everence clicked her tongue and held the crown close. The well-dressed, bloodstained fae tensed and stepped back, altogether like a pack of wolves salivating over a meal.

I smiled at Talia, then looked at my cousin. "I do not want to rule this court." My voice boomed out across the open, starlit space. A breeze cooled my sweat-dampened hair.

The fae exchanged eager glances. They wanted the crown. I readied my magic, ready for any fool deluded enough to fight me now.

"But I alone have the power to wield it. Whoever takes this crown without the power of the sun itself will die, as Fabian did."

The greedy-eyed crowd fell back.

One woman in a gown made entirely of feathers stepped forward. "You can't claim to know how to control that power yet. You only just stripped it from him." She pointed at my dead brother.

Everence shook her head, but I answered.

"I was born his twin, the first heir to the former Sun Sovereign." Several faces nodded, others looked at each other, aghast. "The power of the sun runs in my veins, I stole nothing from him."

The crowd stilled.

"As I do not wish to rule you wicked people, I alone can choose my successor." Without hesitation, I turned toward Everence, who still clutched the softly glowing crown. I lifted a hand toward her. "My cousin, Everence Bristleberry, of the House of Ice and the House of Sun, do you wish to wear the crown of the Sun Sovereign and rule these wretched souls?"

Everence stared at me with an inscrutable expression. Her mouth was tight, her eyes only a fraction wider than usual. Every eye turned to her.

She glanced down at the crown in her hands.

"You have the power of the sun in your veins, as I do," I continued, "but you also have compassion, a power none here knows, except, perhaps, my wife."

I opened my arm to Talia, inviting her to stand beside me. With quick hands, she wiped away the tears that had slipped down her cheeks, and stepped into my embrace. I put her back against my chest and wrapped my arms around her. She rested her chin on my forearm.

C. F. E. BLACK

Everence's stoic expression eased and she smiled warmly at us. Her hands lifted the crown. "I will," she said. "I will rule these people and these lands with honor and power, strength and dignity."

I'd always known she was fit for a throne. She was the one fae I knew who didn't crave power like the rest—even Hector always wanted more, even if he couched it as a means of helping me. She alone was fit to wield the true power of the sun and rule the summer lands, though it meant she would forever be away from her beloved winter.

With a nod, I loosened my arms from around Talia and nodded. "As only you can, cousin. By my blessing, accept the power of the Sun Sovereign." I reached out a hand and placed it on her shoulder. Light shone under my hand.

Everence lifted the crown to her head and settled it on her silver-white hair.

I stepped around Talia and dropped to one knee, every other courtier present mirroring my movements. Talia knelt in reverence beside me.

Everence dipped her head at me and then at my wife and moved toward one of the long tables, humming as she went. Her tunic sparkled, though it was still night, and her hair glistened, clean and free of any tangles from the recent fight. In fact, as I glanced around, no sign remained of the recent slaughter, as if it had never happened. No blood, no bodies. No death. It had all vanished, even Fabian.

The blood from my hands had vanished, and my shirt no longer held a single red stain.

As every fae waited for Everence to take her seat at the center of the longest table, Talia whispered to me, "What now?"

I swiped around with my hand until I found hers, sliding my fingers between hers. "Let's go home."

She squeezed my hand hard.

Everence lifted her arms to her guests, inviting us to sit and dine with her. Her first move as a queen was to bless her enemies. She would make a fine sovereign. Slowly, and with repeated bows along the way, the courtiers around us moved toward the elaborate tables. I wasn't in a hurry to move from this spot.

I turned Talia's face back toward mine. "I am entirely your own, for all the days you live." Her eyes sparked like two small fires. I hated to douse those flames, but I felt this needed to be said. The first time I'd said my vows, I'd been focused entirely on myself, on what I would gain. My eyes cut to the stones where Fabian's dead body had lain, only moments ago. I was no different, really. Driven by a curse, or driven by greed, we'd both been consumed with a desire to help only ourselves.

My forehead tipped down to meet Talia's. "I will take on your victories and your losses, your blessings and your curses," I whispered, ashamed of the man I'd been when I'd spoken them only weeks before. We were the only ones not moving toward the tables, but no one rushed us.

"I'm sorry, Talia. I should have never—"

She pressed a kiss to my lips.

"I'm not sorry. You kept me alive. You healed me. If I hadn't taken your curse, you never could have stopped Fabian. It was *meant* to happen this way."

I cleared my throat and smoothed her hair out of her face. "It was too much to ask of anyone, and yet you did it willingly. You surpass all expectation, Talia Romero Balcázar."

At the use of her name, her brow pinched. "Earlier, you used a different name."

I nodded. "Rafael del Sol is my true name. I am the heir of the House of Sun."

For a moment, she looked up at me with wide, fearful eyes. Then, to my surprise, she chuckled. "That means I really am the wife of the sun."

"That you are," I said, a broad, mischievous smile spreading across my face. "I can give you wings, if you like."

"Really?"

"Really."

"Maybe in a thousand years, when I get bored of these feet," she said with a nervous laugh.

I tucked my nose at the crook of her neck and kissed the skin there. "Whatever you want, my *paloma*."

She exhaled, and I wished we didn't have to dine just now.

"I guessed the legends had it wrong," she said. "It wasn't a red macaw that wed the sun, but a plain little dove, the one he'd meant to sacrifice."

My face snapped up to stare into her eyes. "I suppose altars have a way of showing us what we love most."

She laughed as I crouched down and lifted her off the ground.

41

TALIA

The first warm glow of dawn lit the horizon as Rafael and I rode toward Starfell. From atop Phantom, the world looked less foreign, despite the enormous tree houses and twinkling, magical lights that bobbed along the road ahead of and behind us.

As the house came into view, I smiled at the incredible sight, and a wave of emotion swept over me. This was *home*. I'd not thought so until this moment.

I glanced at Rafael as the sun broke over the horizon. His eyes were pressed shut, his mouth in a tight line, as if struggling against three centuries' worth of anticipation.

His eyes were red when he looked at me. He laughed through his tears and wiped them away with his riding glove. "You gave this to me," he said, his voice thick with emotion. "This will be my first day as a man in my own house."

My smile faltered. I'd only been a bear for a few minutes—though I'd never forget it as long as I lived. Enduring that mental and physical agony for hundreds of years would have turned my mind to mush and my will to dust. How he'd held on to his humanity, I had no idea. But now I had a thousand years to uncover all his secrets. He'd told me of the mixing of my mortality with his immortality. Fae vows really did make two people one.

Rafael cleared his throat and blinked a few times. His eyes sparkled with mischief, and my pulse thundered. He leaned forward. "See that knoll over there? There's a cave there, and it'll be entirely empty right now. Race you?"

I flashed a broad smile and, calling on the magic in my veins, whispered to my horse to win this race.

ALSO BY C. F. E. BLACK

Secrets of the Fae:

The Shadow Heir

Scepter and Crown series:

Shield of Shadow

Blade of Ash

Crown of Dust

Scepter of Fire

Other titles:

The Veritas Project

To read a free short story, sign up to be a reader VIP at

vip.cfeblack.com/join

If you enjoyed this book, please consider leaving a review. It helps more than you know.

ACKNOWLEDGMENTS

Guys, we did it! The Scepter and Crown series is finally complete. There's no way I could have written an entire series while parenting two small boys without lots of help.

First, to Will, for understanding how much this dream means to me. I couldn't do this writer thing without your support. And truthfully, you've taught me what it actually means to work hard and be efficient. So, thanks for being such a great example to follow!

To Dad, for being the best dev editor in the world. Now I know how your students feel when you shred their hard work and tell them how to improve. Don't worry, I can take it. My stories thank you, and my readers thank you.

To Mom, for being there when I needed a little more time or a little more gushing enthusiasm. Every writer needs these things in vast quantities.

To my two boys, for napping at the same time, and for getting me outside as much as possible. You two help me keep my work in perspective. I hope one day you appreciate that.

Also, Hannah. This book is as much for you and because

of you as it is any other single person. Your friendship and encouragement along the way have meant so much.

I wouldn't have made it this far without my street team. You people keep me going and bring a smile to my face. Like I said, every author needs heaps of encouragement, and you guys are the best.

To Sarah Wilson, Constance Lopez, and Anastasis Blythe, thank you for talking me down from my ledges, for helping with blurbs, for being my friend, for spilling your heart about art, and for being generally awesome. I'm so glad to have you as friends.

Thank you to my editor, Monica, and my amazing early readers (especially Jade and Constance). You all improved this story in countless ways.

For everyone who has made it this far in the series, thank you! I hope you have enjoyed this adventure as much as I have.

And thank you, Lord, for allowing me this incredible dream come true.

As always, soli Deo gloria.

ABOUT THE AUTHOR

C. F. E. Black loves to get swept away in books, both reading and writing them. Fantasy and science fiction have been her bread and butter since childhood, and she can't imagine life without her beloved fictional worlds. She lives in beautiful north Alabama with her superhero husband, sons, and fur-family. Connect with her and find free stories at www.cfeblack.com.

Printed in the USA
CPSIA information can be obtained
at www.ICGtesting.com
LVHW050816300823
756652LV00001B/3